MARKED SAFE

ROSEMARY J. FISHER

Riverview Press

info@riverview-press.com
www.riverview-press.com

Table of Contents

Also by Rosemary J. Fisher

So Many Secrets, So Many Lies

Books in the White Dove Series:
Under His Wings
Safely Abiding
Marked Safe
And coming soon:
Heaven's Waiting Room
Also look for
That's My Sister,
a children's book about sibling rivalry,
coming in early 2024.

DEDICATION

This book is dedicated to all the hardworking, faithful family farmers across the United States. They are the unsung heroes of our country. Whether raising crops or cattle, sheep, pigs or chickens – farmers and ranchers supply the food that feeds us all. Anyone working in agriculture deserves our gratitude. And when we sit at our tables laden with food, we seldom think about all the effort it takes and the sacrifices that have been made.

So Thank You!

A SPECIAL THANKS TO

-everyone who read *Under His Wings* and *Safely Abiding* and asked for more!
-my beta readers Jerri, Lila and Marilyn–your suggestions helped!
-my sister Betty for cover help on all the White Dove books
-friends Aimee and Linda for answering my random questions about farm or ranch life
-my husband John for, once again, encouraging me and never begrudging the time writing takes away from him.

ABOUT THE AUTHOR

Rosemary J. Fisher is mother of two, stepmother of two, grandmother of eight and is about to become a great grandma for the first time. In addition, she claims hundreds of children as her own – those she has taught and cared for during her forty-five year career in education.

Retirement has given Rosemary the time she needs to pursue her new passion – writing! If you would have asked her five years ago what she intended to do in retirement, reading and traveling would have been at the top of the list. But today, she does her traveling through books she reads and locations she creates for her novels. She builds her stories around scriptural principles of forgiveness, hope and trust in the Lord Jesus Christ.

In her free time, Rosemary enjoys singing, playing with her collies Regina and Brynn and reading. You might also find her walking the dogs on trails in the Columbia, Missouri, neighborhood where she and her husband John have lived since 2007.

Follow the author on Facebook at
Rosemary Gossell Fisher-Author
And her website
Riverview-Press.com

Chapter 1

SOME DAYS ARE LIKE THAT

Becky Smith stood at the kitchen sink washing baby bottles. With her hands wrist deep in hot sudsy water, she sighed and relaxed her shoulder muscles. It was good to have a moment's peace. Nicholas was asleep and Jenny was not due home from school for a while yet. If she was lucky, she'd have half an hour to herself.

The morning had been a blur of activity with one thing and another and Becky hadn't gotten to her devotions. Now here it was, middle of the afternoon, and she finally had a chance to sit at the table with her journal and her Bible. It always bothered her when her normal early morning routine was upset because she liked to start the day with a quiet time with the Lord. But things happen sometimes and today was a doozy.

Holly had awakened the whole house with frantic barking before sunrise. That was unusual. Holly seldom barked in the house at all. Knowing that something must be wrong, Coop had gotten out of bed to see what was going on. While he got dressed, Becky went to the baby's room to soothe Nicholas, who had been frightened by the barking. Jenny came padding into the room too, confused by all the activity this early in the morning.

Before long, the screen door slammed, signaling Coop's return. "I'm going to need you, Hon. One of the ewes is having trouble with her delivery. I already called Dana. She's on her way over to watch the kids. Put your warmest jacket on; it's chilly out this morning. Don't know why that ewe is having a baby in September, but she needs help. "

And that's how the morning started. By the time the twin lambs were delivered and declared small but healthy, Dana had given Nicholas his morning feeding and Jenny was dressed for school. But during breakfast, Becky had gotten a text from the school saying there was a problem with Jenny's bus and it was running late. Becky decided to take Jenny to school herself, which meant hurrying to get everything together. She dressed Nicholas, threw a couple of diapers into his diaper bag, ran a comb through her short brown hair, and put the breakfast dishes into the sink to soak. She made sure Jenny had brushed her teeth, packed her book bag and fed Holly.

Becky put Nicholas into his car seat carrier and he began to cry. He kicked his legs and struggled, all the while red-faced and angry. Becky asked Jenny to try to make the baby happy while she ran to the bedroom to find her shoes and her purse and keys. From the living room she heard a loud wailing. It was Jenny, protesting the smell coming from the lower regions of Nicholas's seat. Sure enough, he had messed his diaper and required a complete clothing change. When he was finally cleaned and put back into the carrier, Becky couldn't find her car keys. Jenny finally found them on the diaper changing table, where Nicholas had been using them as a teether.

Just as they were getting into the car, Coop had come up from the barn. Becky explained that she was taking Jenny to school, there was bacon cooked and bread in the toaster for toast, and he would have to make his own eggs because they were already late.

In typical Coop fashion, he had kissed her, told her to drive carefully, finished putting Nicholas's carrier into the back seat, tickled Jenny and gave her a morning blessing, and went into the house, slamming the screen door.

Becky smiled, remembering, as she sat at the table and opened her journal. Yes, it had been a crazy morning, but she had a lot to be thankful for. Every day she wrote four things she was grateful for. Topping the list today was Dana. What a blessing she had been for their family. Always ready to help any way she could. And such a good aunt! Yes, Dana was a gift. 'I hope she knows how much I appreciate her,' Becky thought.

Her gratitude list continued. Number two was baby bottles and Nicholas's acceptance of them! Becky had been exclusively breast feeding for three months, but had recently introduced bottles and was pleased that the little boy was doing so well with them. It sure was convenient to have some frozen breast milk on hand for times when Dana, Marla Jean or Coop needed to feed him.

That thought led to number three – Marla Jean. Becky was thankful for the relationship that had been formed between herself and her mother-in-law. She couldn't have asked for a more loving and helpful woman to be mentoring her in the ways of farm life. Whether gardening and canning, cooking and baking, or general help around the farm, Marla Jean was a wonderful example of Colossians 3:23. She was working for the Lord. Becky found the verse in her Bible and copied it into her journal. It was time to memorize that one.

Blessing number four was easy too. Hot water. Or availability of fresh water of any kind. Lately, Becky had been impressed with the importance of water and how crucial it was for life. No wonder Jesus referred to himself as living water. His water is essential for eternal life.

Her mind wandered to the remote villages in Nicaragua, where Dana was planning to go on a mission trip with her friend Tucker. Carrying water from the lake was a normal way of life for those people. It would be a real eye-opening experience for Dana. Lots of things there would be different, but Dana was sure excited about this opportunity to travel with Tucker's church group.

Dana's name was already on Becky's prayer list. She added Tucker's name today, as well as Tim Swift, the leader of the group going to Nicaragua. Then she wrote H2O, not knowing exactly why she would think to jot that down. Well, everybody needs water, so why not pray for it?

Becky settled her mind and began to pray. She started with praising God for the things on her gratitude list. Then she sat in silence for a moment, listening for the Holy Spirit's direction. She was lead to pray for safety, particularly of school children. There had been a news report last night about another school shooting, which tore at Becky's heart. She prayed for those families, the medical teams, the teachers and children in the school who were not injured but were affected none-the-less. She shuddered and asked the Lord to protect Jenny and her classmates, to keep them safe in this sometimes evil world.

Becky was deep into her study book when Holly suddenly rose from her spot near Becky's feet and stretched deeply. Becky looked at the clock on the kitchen wall and chuckled. "I do believe you know how to tell time!" she marveled as she rubbed Holly's head. "She'll be home soon." Holly went to the front door, nails clicking on the hardwood floor. She turned and looked at Becky with her head tilted as if she understood Becky's words, but she waited patiently. Becky marked the page where she had stopped and stacked all her things on the end of the table. She had hopes that tomorrow morning's devotion time would be more on schedule, but she breathed a soft prayer of thanks for the time that she had been able to squeeze in this afternoon.

Becky opened the door to let Holly out to wait for the school bus. The air was crisp and cool; good thing Jenny had worn a sweater this morning. Fall was coming early this year. Becky breathed deeply and closed her eyes. She let the autumn sun warm her face and smiled. It was good to be alive.

The baby monitor alerted her with a soft rustling sound. Nicholas was stirring in his crib. Becky poured a glass of milk for Jenny and sat out a plate of chocolate chip cookies. She just had enough time to wash her hands before Nicholas gave out a hearty wail to announce that he was hungry. "Hold on little man, Momma's coming." Holly began barking and running, spinning in circles as the bus came down the dirt road. It always made Becky laugh to see the collie carry on so. There was certainly a bond between Holly and her little girl.

Nicholas was changed and feeding hungrily when the screen door slammed and Jenny burst into the house. Her sweater was drooping off one shoulder, her hair was a mess, and there was yellow paint on her pant leg. She ran into her bedroom, dropped her backpack on the bed, and ran to Nicholas's room to plant a kiss on his head. "Oh mommy, I smell cookies! Thanks!" and she turned quickly to run back to the kitchen.

"Wait just a minute, Jenny. Slow down. Why are you running in the house? What's our rule about running?"

Jenny put on her brakes and turned around slowly in the doorway. "We walk like a lady in the house and we run like the wind outside!"

"Good girl!" Becky answered. "Now come tell me about your day. What in the world happened to your hair?"

Jenny reached up and felt each side of her head. One pony tail was intact, pretty much, but the hair on the other side was flying completely loose. "Oh, well, see, we had races on the playground at recess and I was almost winning but then I felt my hair come out and I didn't want to stop and look for the pony-tailer so I just kept going and I figured I'd look for it later but then after I won, and I finally beat Kendy for the first time and she always wins but this time I was really running like the wind like I do outside, not in the house, and anyway, I was so excited about winning that I forgot to go back and look for it." She finally stopped for air and sat down on the floor with a plop. Legs crossed, hands on her chin, she added, "And man, I'm pooped!" She looked around and saw the trash can near the diaper table. "And I can still smell Nicholas's poop from the morning explosion. Yuck!"

"Yes, I think you're right. I guess we need to take out the trash. Can you do that for me, before you wash your hands for snack?"

"Sure," Jenny said and hopped up to tie the trash bag.

"So, tell me, was this big race at the morning recess, or the afternoon recess?"

"Morning. And at lunch everybody was telling me congratulations!"

Becky smiled, imagining her daughter sitting at the lunch table, with her brown hair hanging in a flyaway mess as she soaked in the praise of her classmates. And then, the rest of the school day, basting in the glory of her win, with her hair a disheveled disaster! Oh what must the teachers think of this rambunctious little girl?

"But then, you know what?" Jenny headed out the door with the trash bag but stopped to finish her sentence. "I saw at lunch that Kendy was sitting by herself, and she looked kinda sad. Probably because she didn't win this time. So I gave her my cookie that was in my lunch bag. And that's why I'm starving now!" Jenny kept talking as she went down the hall. "Oh, and Mrs. Novak wrote a note to you. It's in my backpack."

Becky heard the screen door slam. 'When would the girl ever learn to close that door softly? Well, just look at her daddy. But if slamming doors and running feet were the girl's biggest faults, well, that wasn't so bad, really.

A note from the teacher though. I wonder what that's all about.'

Chapter 2

JOHN SPEAKS

Jenny poured water into the glasses sitting on the table. She poured slowly, being careful not to spill. She moved around the table, first Mommy, then herself, then Daddy. She stopped at the head of the table, where Daddy always sat. She put the pitcher down and looked at his plate.

Lying on the plate was the letter from Mrs. Novak. Jenny didn't know what it said because it was written in cursive. Something about the note made her nervous. Why would Mrs. Novak want to write a letter to her parents? Was she in trouble? Did she do something wrong?

Jenny thought back over the day. She couldn't remember doing anything wrong. Two of the boys in the class had to sit in the office during recess because they had been fighting, but nothing like that had happened to her. She thought she had followed the class rules to be safe, kind and responsible all day. This was puzzling.

Jenny sat quietly at her place, deep in thought as she waited for the rest of her family to come to the table. Becky put Nicholas into his high chair and adjusted the tray. She gave him a teething toy to chew on while he waited for his food.

Coop came into the kitchen and put his arms on Becky's shoulders. "Honey, this supper smells good. Lasagna is my favorite. You've outdone yourself this time."

Becky laughed and said, "Last night you said meatloaf was your favorite. The night before that, it was tuna casserole. Can you not make up your mind?"

"Well, truth is, I like pretty much whatever you cook. As long as you don't make liver!" He sat down at the head of the table and picked up the note from Mrs. Novak.

As he opened it and read it, he raised his eyebrows and looked up at Becky. Becky gave a nod and took her seat. Coop folded the paper and laid it beside his plate. "Let's pray," he said, and the family joined hands and bowed their heads. Even baby Nicholas was learning how to do this.

Jenny peeked out of her half closed eyes to look at both of her parents. Their eyes were closed and their faces looked normal. They didn't seem upset about the letter. Maybe it wasn't too bad.

"In Jesus' name we pray," Coop said and Jenny quickly squinched her eyes shut. "Amen," they said in unison. Becky prepared food for Nicholas and allowed him to feed himself. It was messy, but how else was he going to learn? He was already learning to poke at his food with a spoon. He hadn't been very successful yet, and he soon gave up and went back to picking up food with his whole fist. But he'd learn eventually.

Coop dipped a serving of lasagna for Jenny. Then he served Becky and himself while Jenny got her own salad. As Jenny passed the salad bowl to Coop, he looked at her and said, "So, I think we need to talk."

Jenny lowered her eyes. 'Oh oh, here it comes. I must be in trouble,' she thought. Out loud she said, "Okay Daddy."

"Well Jenny, I need you to look up at me," Coop instructed. "This is very important and I want to know you're paying attention."

The little girl slowly raised her head and was surprised to see her parents both smiling widely. Maybe this wasn't bad news after all.

"We got this letter from your teacher," Coop said, tapping the paper with his finger. "She told me what you did today. But I'd like to hear about it from you."

"What I did today?" Jenny asked. "I did normal stuff. Spelling and math and science. And reading, and recess. Oh, did she tell you I won the race? It was my first time."

"She did tell us about the race, but we want to talk about what happened after the race." Becky put some cooked carrots in front of Nicholas and watched him pick up a piece and pop it into his mouth. She smiled at him and turned back to Jenny. "Tell us about lunch time."

"Oh, well, Kendy was sitting alone and looked sad, and so I thought about why she was sad, and I just wanted to be nice to her because she lost the race, and I know how that feels so I gave her my cookie and I tried to do what John said. So that's all I did." Suddenly she thought of something and asked, "Did I get in trouble for sharing food?"

"No, no, Sweetie, you're not in trouble at all. You did a very kind thing, and Mrs. Novak wanted us to know about it. She said you were a good example about how to be a gracious winner." Coop took a forkful of his lasagna and chewed thoughtfully.

Becky seemed to read his mind and asked, "But what do you mean, Jenny? You said John told you to do something. John who? I don't think there's a John in your class."

Jenny wiped some tomato sauce off her face and smiled at her mom. "No, Mommy, not a real John. The Bible John."

Coop immediately understood. "I think you must mean the Bible verse you've been trying to memorize for Sunday school. We've been working on it while we do barn chores," he explained to Becky. He turned to Jenny and asked, "Should we say it together for Mommy and Nicholas?"

Jenny nodded and took a sip of water. She sat up straighter in her chair and looked at Coop. Together they recited 1 John 3:18. "Dear children, let us not love with words or speech but with actions and in truth" Jenny said it almost perfectly. She had been practicing!

Becky beamed at her daughter. "Not only do you know the verse, but you've been putting the words into practice. By sharing your cookie and being a friend, you were showing love to Kendy with your actions. That's much better than just knowing the words of the verse."

"Mommy's right," Coop added. "Knowing the scripture doesn't do much good, unless you use what you know and follow Jesus and do good things. There's a verse in Ephesians that says God has already prepared good things for us to do, so we should get busy doing them!"

"You mean, God already knew he wanted me to be nice to Kendy? He knew already that she would be sad, and it was my job to cheer her up?" Jenny sat back and sighed. "Wow! That's pretty cool!"

"It is," Becky said. "Just think of all the other good things God has planned for you to do. And if you don't do them, who will?"

"Whoa! I hope I haven't missed any. I better start listening real hard so he can tell me and I can do my jobs." Jenny forked the last bite of her salad into her mouth. Nicholas threw his sippy cup on the floor and Jenny jumped up to retrieve it. "I'll get it Mommy. That's my job."

Becky and Coop smiled at each other across the table. Their little girl was certainly developing into a child of Christ.

"The letter says that there is going to be a special program at school next Friday and they're going to give you a Citizen of the Month Award. We can invite your grandmas and Aunt Dana if she doesn't have class. And Daddy and I have decided that we'll all go out for pizza after the program, to celebrate. We are very proud of you, Jenny."

"Oh wow! Pizza! I can't wait! Thank you Mommy and Daddy!"

"It's just a little way we can say thank you to you! We are so happy that you are learning your verses and putting them into your life." Coop reached for her hand. "Keep listening to Jesus. He will always be with you."

Chapter 3
PIZZA PARTY

The waitress at the pizza parlor had pushed several tables together so the family could all sit in a group to celebrate Jenny's Citizen of the Month award. The conversation was lively, the pizza delicious, and the center of attention was glowing! Jenny placed the framed award certificate in the center of the table and stood proudly behind it while cameras flashed and everyone again offered their congratulations. Even their waitress and other employees came over to their table to join in the celebration.

Becky had been surprised when Jenny asked if she could invite somebody not in her family to have pizza with them. She expected Jenny would want to ask her best friend Hannah, and in fact, Coop had already called Hannah's parents, Greg and Nancy Martin, to invite them. But they had another commitment for that evening, and it turned out that wasn't who Jenny wanted to include anyway.

Kendy Barkdale's parents Tom and Tabitha were surprised when Becky called to invite them to the celebration. The family was new to the school this year, and apparently hadn't made a lot of friends. They seemed to appreciate the chance to meet other adults and get to know them.

Coop watched as Jenny and her new friend stretched strands of cheese from the pizza slices. Silly cheesy grins brought out bursts of girlish giggles. He looked up to see Becky and Tabitha also watching the girls. They shook their heads with laughter and turned back to their conversation.

Once again Coop was aware that Becky was good at making people feel comfortable. He had witnessed her friendly manner at Sunday school, when she warmly welcomed newcomers to the class they taught for married young adults. Becky just seemed to have a knack for showing interest in others and setting them at ease. It was a God given gift, Coop believed, and he took a moment to thank the Lord for his wife and her godly influence on people. He smiled when he realized that Becky was inviting Tabitha and Tom to come to church on Sunday. She even invited them to come out to the farm after the service for a fried chicken dinner.

Coop's mom and Becky's mom sat at the other end of the table. They had become fast friends, especially since the wedding. They were deep in conversation now and Coop listened in. As usual, the discussion centered around their beautiful grandchildren. They were laughing now as Marla Jean told Elizabeth about the shocked expression on Nicholas's face the first time he had rolled over from his tummy to his back. "He looked so surprised. His eyes got so big and it was like he was trying to figure out what had just happened! Then he looked at me and smiled his toothless grin! I think he was proud of himself!"

"Well, he is kind of young to be rolling over, isn't he? I'll bet it did surprise him! Maybe he's going to be ahead of the norm physically! A big strong boy!" Elizabeth paused and said with a sigh, "Oh, they grow up so fast! It seems like just yesterday Becky and her sister Joyce were playing outside on the swings, singing away. I can see it clear as day." She was quiet for a moment, letting the memories wash over her. "So long ago, but like yesterday."

"They do grow fast! That's why we must make the most of every day. I want to hang onto the memories as tight as I can. I'm not sure the young people know how important these days are. Before long, they will be the ones looking back and wondering where their babies went!"

Marla Jean Smith, though older than Elizabeth by a couple of years, seemed to be in better health. Coop was grateful for this, but aware that changes can happen quickly. His own father had passed away just two years after his cancer diagnosis. 'Our days are numbered,' Coop thought and a scripture verse popped into his mind. "My times are in your hands" Psalm 31:15. He silently prayed for his mother and for Elizabeth, knowing that their days on earth were drawing to a close. No one was guaranteed tomorrow, and only belief in God's perfect plan could bring them comfort. There would be difficult days ahead, days of change and adjustment. He prayed that they would all remember that God would never leave them or forsake them. And he determined to do his best to provide for his family through all the dark days they may face.

Coop's attention was brought back to Tom, who began telling a funny story about his job at the Atkins Hospital. He was an x-ray technician and met all sorts of characters throughout his day. Tom had a comedic way of telling stories and describing people. Before long the table was railing in hilarious laughter.

Their laughter was gathering attention from other diners, and many people were smiling. At a table across the room, Melissa Madison and Craig Cashman were enjoying their pizza with Craig's cousin JJ and his wife Bev. Melissa recognized some of the people at the rowdy table and got up to say hi. She walked towards Elizabeth with a smile and said, "Sounds like you people are sure having fun! It's nice to see you, Elizabeth."

"Hello Melissa! Imagine seeing you here." She turned toward Marla Jean and explained, "Melissa works at the hospital. We just had coffee together Tuesday as a matter of fact."

"You told me you were going out to celebrate Jenny's award. I didn't know you were coming here though." She looked at Jenny to congratulate her. "Way to go, Jenny! Citizen of the Month is a very important title! Good job!"

Jenny picked up her certificate from the table and said, "Here's my award. Want to hold it?"

"Sure do!" Melissa took the frame and read over the certificate. "Congratulations! You must be very proud of your daughter," she said, addressing Becky.

"Yes, she's a good girl. She's been trying to do what Jesus wants her to do. Being kind, helpful, caring for the feelings of others. She's learning to listen to Jesus and follow his example."

"That's great!" Melissa put the frame back on the table. "Well, I just wanted to say hi. I better get back to my own table. I know you recognize Craig. We're having pizza with his cousin JJ and JJ's wife Bev." She bent close to Becky and whispered softly, "I invited them to come to church, but so far I haven't gotten an answer. But I'm like Jenny; learning to listen to Jesus and follow his example. So I'll keep asking them, and I'll try to live my life so they see Jesus in me."

As Melissa walked away, Becky smiled to herself. What a change there had been in that woman's life! Just a few years ago, she had been a thief, a drug user, and a kidnapper. She had tried to extort money from Coop, she had endangered his life, and she had nearly damaged his reputation. Becky's relationship with Coop had almost been ruined by Melissa Madison, yet here today, because of forgiveness and the very grace of God, she was growing in Christ, witnessing and inviting and encouraging others to pray for salvation. Yes, a lot had changed, and it proved again that God loves the worst of sinners and can use them to lead others to him.

Craig Cashman had been faithfully attending church with Melissa for over a year. Becky believed it had started out as a way to get near Melissa, and she sometimes wondered if there was more going on there than just church attendance. But Coop reminded her that judgment was left to the Lord, and she prayed for forgiveness for her attitude. Then she watched as one Sunday Craig came to the altar for prayer and gave his heart to the Lord. David Cole, the leader of the young adult's Sunday school class, had taken Craig under his wing and been a mentor and teacher. Already Craig was finding ways to serve the church. He had joined a team of men who drove the bus to pick up people who couldn't drive and bring them to Sunday services. It was heartwarming to see Big Craig interacting with the elderly and sometimes frail passengers as he helped them on and off the church bus.

Yes, Becky marveled at all of the good things that had happened in the last few years. Her marriage, their baby, Jenny's spiritual growth and understanding, and watching God work through the lives of people she knew and cared for. Oh yes, God was good.

Even when things didn't go smoothly, even when there were difficulties and sorrows, even with the loss of her earlier pregnancy, Becky knew that God had never left her. She had felt alone and angry at first. Those were dark days, and she had struggled with depression. It took a while to get past the feeling that God was punishing her or had left her completely. And the funny thing was, it was Melissa Madison who had been the one to remind her that God would never leave her or forsake her.

Becky did come to the realization that God was not a god of vengeance. He had not gone away from her. He was still there, still loving her, and still offering her comfort. God was good, not just for all the good things he did, but because goodness was his very nature.

And now, their family had grown to include Nicholas. Becky was reminded to trust God, through whatever came their way. It wasn't her job to understand; that was probably beyond her human capabilities and a total waste of brain power. But she could trust God's plan. Leaning on him, giving up control and trusting. They were concepts Becky had been wrestling with for years. 'I'm not the woman I want to be, but I'm not the woman I used to be either,' Becky often thought. Spiritual growth could be slow, but she had a lifetime to work towards holy perfection.

The celebration party broke up and everyone headed out the door. Becky was holding Nicholas and juggling his diaper bag. Jenny carefully carried her award. Coop put his hand under Elizabeth's elbow and helped her out the door. She sometimes needed a little help with balance and was grateful for his assistance.

Tabitha, carrying a box of leftover pizza, stopped at the Smith's car to say goodbye. While Becky strapped Nicholas into his car seat, Tabitha said, "We can't come to your church this week, but we'll think about it. Thanks again for inviting us for pizza tonight."

"It was fun getting to know you," Becky said with a smile. "Enjoy the leftover pizza!"

The little girls said their goodbyes too, and Jenny took her seat in the back. Coop and Tom shook hands and the families parted ways.

Elizabeth and Marla Jean rode together, with Marla Jean driving. Elizabeth's car was at the farm. She'd drive home to Winslow before it got dark. Driving after dark was getting harder and harder for Elizabeth and she knew she needed cataract surgery. One more thing to deal with as she aged. She remembered what someone had told her once. 'Getting old is not for sissies. But it sure beats the alternative.'

Chapter 4

GROWING GARDENS, GROWING FRIENDSHIPS

Marla Jean wiped droplets of perspiration off her forehead and took a step back to admire her handiwork. Lined up on the kitchen counter stood row upon row of canned green beans. The kitchen was hot. Water from the canner steamed as it cooled on the stove. She went to the table and pulled out a chair as Becky poured two glasses of iced tea.

"Let's take a little break," Becky said. "We've been working hard."

Marla Jean took a long drink of the cold tea. "But look what we've accomplished," she said. "There's nothing like the taste of vegetables fresh picked and canned up. Especially in the middle of winter. We had a great crop of beans this year. I've never seen such a mess of green beans!"

"The potatoes did well this year too. Cucumbers are still producing. I've already put up a dozen quarts of carrots. There should be more about ready to pull soon. I planted them several weeks apart, so we wouldn't get them all at the same time." Becky clinked the ice cubes in her glass. "God has really blessed our garden this year."

A jar lid sealed with a *ping*, followed closely by a second and then a third. "One of my favorite sounds!" exclaimed Marla Jean. "That and baby giggles!"

"Speaking of babies, I haven't heard Nicholas wiggling. He's taking a nice long nap. He had a rough night, so I guess he's making up for lost sleep." Becky tucked a wisp of brown hair behind her ear and stifled a yawn. "I guess I could use a nap too."

Marla Jean looked at Becky with concern. "You know, they say mothers should nap when their babies nap. I could have done this canning myself. You should have been resting."

"Oh no you don't!" laughed Becky. Another lid sealed and Becky said, "You'd make me miss all this fun!" She looked at the clock and said, "It's almost time for Jenny to get home from school. Her new friend Kendy is coming home with her. I'll get this stuff cleaned up and still have time to get those brownies cut for their snack."

"You let me take care of that. Just go sit down and take a little rest till the girls get home. Now's your only chance. Go put your feet up."

Becky gave her mother-in-law a peck on the cheek. "You're the best," she said with a hug. "It'll just be a few minutes, but I'm sure I will feel better. Thanks!" She went to the living room and sat back on the sofa. It did feel good to get off her feet. She heard Holly's nails click on the hardwood floor as she crossed the kitchen and stood waiting at the back door. Marla Jean let the collie out to wait for the school bus and Becky closed her eyes.

Psalms 24:1 popped into her thoughts as she drifted off to sleep. "The earth is the Lord's, and everything in it, the world and all who live in it." Ten minutes later, the sounds of collie barking and little girl giggling brought the brief nap to a quick closure.

The screen door slammed and the noisy threesome scurried into the living room. "Kendy put her jacket and her backpack by the door, Mommy. So she has it when it's time to go home." She spun around and headed to the kitchen. "Mmm, I smell brownies!"

"Hold on, just a minute," Becky said. "Hello there Kendy. Welcome to our home. I'm glad you could come over today. We're going to have spaghetti for supper. I hope you like it."

Kendy smiled shyly and said, "Thank you, yes I do."

"Jenny, show Kendy where the bathroom is, and you girls wash your hands. Then Grammy has some brownies and milk for you.

Jenny took off down the hall but Kendy hesitated. "Can I call my mommy please?"

Becky bent to lower herself to Kendy's level. "Are you worried about your mommy?"

Kendy nodded with her head down to hide the tears that were starting to fill her eyes. "When is she coming home?"

"I talked to your daddy on the phone just a little while ago. He is at the hospital with your mom right now. She has to stay there overnight, but he will come and get you after supper and take you home. Tomorrow, when he goes to get her you can go along.

"Is she okay? She was crying when the ambulance came."

"I'm sure that was scary, but the ambulance people took good care of her, and now she's at the hospital and the doctors there are helping her feel better. She should be able to come home tomorrow." Becky gave Kendy a comforting hug. "But for now, you don't need to worry. You can stay here and play with Jenny and have supper and then your dad will come and pretty soon your mommy will be home and everything will be back to normal." She looked Kendy directly in the eye and said, "We've been praying for her ever since your dad told me she was going to the hospital. Jesus is with her."

Kendy seemed relieved and looked at Jenny. With a wave of her hand, Jenny beckoned Kendy to follow. They went to the bathroom to wash up and soon light-hearted giggles could be heard once again. When they went into the kitchen for their snack, there was no indication of worry.

The canned green beans continued to ping and pop as they sealed. Each time there was a ping, the girls burst into fits of laughter. Soon the laughter turned to howls and snorts and hand slapping on the table. The joy was contagious and Marla Jean joined in with giggles of her own. Troubles were forgotten, at least for the time being.

A crackle of sound came through the baby monitor as Nicholas began to thrash around in his crib. Becky headed towards his bedroom but stopped short when she looked at Jenny. The little girl was laughing so hard, bubbles of milk were oozing out of her nostrils! Becky shook her head in amusement as Marla Jean handed Jenny a napkin. Seeing the milk bubbles make Kendy laugh even harder, which left Jenny gasping for breath.

'Ah, giggly girls!' thought Becky. She opened the door to Nicholas's bedroom and crinkled up her nose. "So you have a smelly present for me? How nice of you!" She scooped the baby up and carried him at arms length to the changing table. A complete wardrobe change was required. Before she was finished changing the bedding in his crib, the girls came in to see the baby.

Nicholas was lying on the floor looking up at a dangling butterfly attached on his activity mat. The girls sat on the floor near him and Jenny tapped the butterfly to make it move. He stared up in fascination.

"You girls can play with Nicholas while I go put these clothes in the washer. Jenny, you know the rules. You aren't allowed to pick him up. He stays on the floor until I get back."

"Yes, Mommy, I remember." Jenny replied.

Jenny plopped herself down on the floor, lying on her tummy, elbows on the floor, facing Nicholas. She rested her chin in her hands. Kendy took one look at the position and copied her friend. Becky found them that way when she returned. The girls were singing "Old McDonald Had a Farm" to the baby, and he seemed to be enjoying it immensely.

Marla Jean popped her head into the bedroom and announced, "I'm going to go on home now. The snack dishes are done and I got the kitchen cleaned up. I do believe every single jar of beans sealed. They are still a little too hot to move, so you should probably leave them on the counter another hour or two."

Jenny jumped up from the floor and hurried to the doorway. She gave her Grammy a big hug. "Thanks for the brownies, Grammy. They were yummy!"

"I'm glad you liked them!" Marla Jean turned towards Kendy and said, "It was nice to meet you, Kendy. I'm praying for your mommy to get all better and come home soon."

"She'll be home tomorrow," Kendy declared.

While the girls played in Jenny's room, Becky nursed Nicholas and then went about fixing supper. Spaghetti sauce was just beginning to simmer on the stove when she heard the motor of Coop's four-wheeler as he pulled up to the house. Holly took up a barking welcome as Coop crossed the yard. Becky smiled, thinking about how much that collie loved her people. Getting Holly was one of the best decisions they had ever made. She gave the sauce a quick stir, placed the lid on the pot, and turned to see Coop coming into the house. He was carrying something hidden behind his back.

Coop leaned forward to plant a kiss on Becky's cheek, all the while keeping the object hidden. "So, when's the last time you were out in the garden?" he asked teasingly.

"I picked the end of the beans this morning," Becky waved her arm with a flourish to display the canned beans on the counter. "And I picked a couple of cucumbers for tonight's salad."

"Well, I want to know how you missed this," Coop said. From behind his back, Coop pulled a zucchini. Not just a big zucchini – this one was huge. He hoisted it to his shoulder and held it like a baseball bat. "Batter up!" he teased, and took some practice swings.

"Oh, my goodness, wherever did you find that thing? It must have been hiding! I sure never saw it growing! That's the biggest zucchini I've ever seen."

The girls came into the kitchen to see what was going on and Jenny said, "Whoa! That thing is huge! Are we going to cook it?"

"No, probably not. But what we'll do is, we'll scoop all the seeds out and save them to plant next year. I think there will be plenty!" Coop put the zucchini down near the jars of beans. "See, God has provided us with enough canned beans for many meals this winter, and now he has also given us seeds for next year's crop of zucchini. God is good!"

"All the time," chorused Becky and Jenny while Kendy looked on.

"Well, you go get cleaned up. Supper is almost ready." Becky took plates from the cupboard and gave them to Jenny. "Set the table please. Kendy, can you do the forks and spoons?" The girls got to work while Becky dropped spaghetti noodles into the boiling water. "There's a salad in the refrigerator. Could you put it on the table, Jenny? And show Kendy where the dressings are. She can bring them to the table".

Coop came back into the kitchen. He had washed up and changed into a clean shirt. "Team work! That's how we get stuff done around here!" He lifted Nicholas out of the bouncy chair where he had been sitting quietly. "When are we going to put you to work, young man? I'm going to need some help in the fields next week. It's almost time to harvest the corn. Can I count on you?"

Nicholas patted his hands on Coop's face and Coop bent to nuzzle his neck. "Okay, maybe next year then. You just keep growing." Turning toward Kendy, Coop continued, "It's nice to have you here for supper. I'm sorry to hear that your mom is in the hospital. We've been praying for her all day."

"She's coming home tomorrow, Daddy says."

"That's great news." The family held hands, Jenny and Becky welcoming Kendy into their circle. Coop prayed "We thank you, Father, for all the blessings of this day. For doctors caring for Kendy's mom, for garden vegetables, even gigantic zucchini, for good crops and good weather and good food and good friends. We know that you give your children good gifts, and we thank you. Amen."

Just then, Coop's cell phone began to vibrate. He took it from his pocket and looked at the caller ID. "It's Tom. Better answer this, I think." He stood and walked from the table. It was a family rule that there were no phone calls during dinner, but this might be an emergency.

When he came back to the table, Coop announced, "Your daddy will be here in about an hour. He's leaving the hospital and coming right here to pick you up."

Supper dishes were going into the dishwasher when Tom Barkdale arrived. He was wearing the scrubs he had put on for work, but he hadn't actually worked his shift. Instead he had spent the day with his wife, first in the ER, then pre-op and recovery. Now that Tabitha was settled in a room, Tom realized how tired he was. Waiting and worrying could take a toll on even the strongest of men.

Now he watched with pleasure as his daughter assisted with supper cleanup. Kendy smiled up at him as she carefully placed all of the forks into the dishwasher basket. "Nice to see she's helping out. I can't thank you enough, Becky, for taking her in after school today. I was really in a bind when I found out Tabitha needed surgery."

"No problem, Tom. That's what friends are for. How did everything go?"

"The surgeon said we got there just in time. The appendix was about to rupture, which would have made everything more dangerous. But the surgery went well; there was no rupture so it was fairly easy. She should be able to come home tomorrow afternoon."

Becky put soap into the dishwasher, closed the door and dried her hands. "That's good. Will she have restrictions?"

"For a while, yes. No lifting, no strenuous exercise. And we have to watch for fever or signs of infection. But I think we'll be back to normal soon enough."

Becky pulled an aluminum baking pan from the freezer. She turned back one corner of the tin foil covering and nodded. "Here. I want you to take this lasagna home with you. That way you won't have to worry about meals for a couple of days."

Tom, appreciating the offer and grateful that he wouldn't have to do the cooking, said, "That's mighty nice of you, Becky."

"Take some brownies, too," Becky added as she filled a sandwich bag with chewy chocolaty brownies. "Chocolate always makes me feel better!"

Kendy spoke up, "Mommy loves brownies." She turned to her dad and added, "I ate some after school with Jenny. They are good, but I'll let mommy have all these."

On the way home, Tom asked his daughter, "Did you have a good time at the Smith's house?"

"Yes. They are nice," Kendy replied. "They have a dog named Holly. She waits for Jenny at the bus. She can do tricks." Kendy was quiet for a minute, then added, "They said a prayer at supper. They prayed about Mommy."

"That was nice," answered Tom. "They do seem like good people."

"Why don't we say prayers at our house?"

"I don't know, Honey. It's just not a habit we've gotten into. Grandpa and Grammy prayed at meals when I was a kid, but when I got older I just stopped." Tom was quiet for a moment as he remembered his parents. A lump formed in his throat as he thought about the last time he had seen them. They had been celebrating his graduation from college and he had felt like he was on top of the world. He already had a job lined up. He had a girlfriend who made him happy and they were planning a future together. Everything was going his way. The future looked wide open and bright. His parents were so proud of him.

That was before a drunk driver slammed into their car. His dad was killed instantly; his mom died two days later in the hospital. Tom's whole world changed in that moment.

Kendy brought him back to the present. "They thanked God for green beans and zucchini."

"They did, huh?" Tom remembered the last time he had prayed. He remembered the emptiness he felt when he got no answers. The anger he had suppressed for so long bubbled to the surface and he gripped the steering wheel tightly. He had never talked about this to anyone except Tabitha, and her only briefly. He certainly didn't want to let his anger overflow to his daughter. But likewise, he wasn't going to encourage her to pray to a God who didn't listen. Prayer was pointless. A waste of time. Didn't keep his mom alive, despite all the pleading and tears.

"I guess the Smith's believe that their God can hear their prayers. Some people do."

"We don't?" Kendy asked innocently.

"Well, when you get older, you can decide for yourself." Tom shook his head. "I just haven't ever thought praying made any difference."

"Maybe you should try again. Maybe God will listen to you next time."

That made Tom laugh out loud. "Maybe, who knows? Want to start with a prayer at suppertime? That couldn't hurt, I guess. Saying thank you for our food would be good."

"Okay. That's easy. I'm always thankful for food!" Kendy reached across the seat and took her daddy's hand. "Can we pray for Mommy too? To get all better and come home tomorrow?"

"If that's what you want, Sweetie, it's okay with me."

They rode on in silence for a while. Country roads and farm fields gave way to the lights of Winslow. The football field at the edge of town was bustling with activity. High school sports were the highlight social events for the whole county. Even with the car windows up, they could hear the roar of the crowd. It brought back memories of Tom's high school football days, when his parents were enthusiastic fans in the bleachers. The lump returned to his throat.

He quickly focused his thoughts on his wife. "When Mommy comes home tomorrow, we have to let her rest," he said. "She's going to need our help. You can be a good helper, I know. I saw you helping with dishes tonight at the Smith's."

"I set the table too. I can help Mommy with everything."

"That's good. So you had a good time after school, playing at their house?"

"I like Jenny," Kendy said with excitement. "And Holly. She's a good dog. Jenny said I can come and play with her lots. And she said her Aunt Joyce has lots of puppies for sale."

"Well, don't get any ideas about getting a puppy. We don't have room for a dog in our apartment, not to mention how much a dog costs. But I'm glad you've made a new friend. I know moving here meant you had to go to a new school, but now you have a new friend and that's good."

"Yeah, and I know Hannah and Tracy and Emily and Megan. I like my teacher and my new class. It's good here."

"It is good here. I have a job I like, Mommy has started looking for a job, you are happy at school. Moving here is turning out to be good for everybody." Tom drove the car into the apartment parking lot and turned off the engine. "And we'll go get Mommy tomorrow afternoon and have yummy lasagna for supper, and I won't have to cook it!"

As he followed Kendy up the apartment steps, Tom thought about the Smith family. He could envision a good friendship forming with them. Yes, moving to Winslow was turning out to be a good thing.

Chapter 5

HOSPITAL VISITORS

After Tabitha had finished her breakfast, she slid the hospital tray aside and settled back in her bed. She hadn't been hungry, and the food offered wasn't that appealing. She had eaten only some applesauce and toast. The IV attached to her arm was annoying but she knew it was keeping her hydrated. She also knew there was some kind of pain medication being pumped into her. Thankfully, she was not feeling the extreme pain from yesterday. That pain had been almost unbearable and was why she agreed to come to the ER. It was a good thing, too, because the surgeon told her waiting even an hour could have had drastic consequences.

The nurse had stopped by with some antibiotic pills. The concern now was infection, although the doctor had assured her the cleanup was complete. You just never knew, though, because infection could happen. And if she were to get really sick, then what? Kendy needed her mother, and Tom, how could he go on without her?

A gentle tap at the door brought Tabitha's thoughts back from her worries. "Yes, come in," she called.

A young woman entered the hospital room and stood at the side of the bed. She looked familiar, but Tabitha couldn't place her. Shoulder length black hair, a flowery tattoo on her arm, and a big warm smile. 'Where have I seen her before?' Tabitha wondered.

"Hi, Tabitha," said the woman with a friendly voice. "I don't suppose you remember me. My name's Melissa. I'm a friend of Becky Smith and I saw you at Jenny's pizza party a few weeks ago. I heard you were in the hospital so I'm just stopping by to see how you're doing."

"Oh, that's right. I knew you seemed familiar." Tabitha relaxed a little. "I'm doing okay, I guess. The doctors say I should get to go home this afternoon. Supposedly they are going to get me up and have me walking pretty soon."

"Oh, I know you'll do fine. It always seems like they rush patients to get them moving, but you know, it's usually for the best. Just sitting in bed isn't good for you. Moving is actually good for healing."

"Within reason, I suppose." Tabitha gave a slight shudder. "I imagine it's going to hurt."

"The nurses will be watching, don't worry. If you're too tired or hurting too much, they'll know when to get you back to bed. But you have to build up your strength for going home."

"I suppose you're right."

"So, have you lived in Winslow long?"

"No we just moved here this past summer. Our daughter is in second grade with Jenny Smith. I'm just getting to know Becky and Coop."

"Oh, they're great people. You can't go wrong, making friends with them. I've known Coop nearly all my life. And

Becky, she's a sweetheart. She had every reason to dislike and distrust me, but thanks to the love of Jesus in her heart, she has forgiven me for my bad behaviors and I can say we are friends now."

"What do you mean?"

"Well, let's just say that I've changed a bit in the last couple of years. I had a life altering experience, when I thought I was going to die. But Jesus spoke to me and I've changed my ways. The old me is gone and a new me has come! It hasn't been easy, but Jesus is helping me follow him and become more like him. There's a verse in the Bible, I think its Philippians something. It says I should focus on what lies ahead. So I'm trying to forget the past and I'm moving forward to get to the heavenly prize."

That was a lot for Tabitha to process. "We're not a church-going family, but Becky invited us to come with her someday."

"That would be super! We go to the same church. It's a great place, full of people who love and serve Jesus. You'll like it. The preaching is right from the Bible, and explained in a way so we understand and know how to apply it to our lives. I'm new at this Christian way of life, but the church people have loved me and accepted me, even though I was really a terrible person before. My sins have been blotted out by the blood of Jesus, and the church people only see the new me. No judgment, no hard feelings. I've always felt accepted. Of course, the best feeling is that Jesus loves me, despite my flaws. I take delight in the Lord's presence because he loves me so much."

Tabitha raised her eyebrows and said, "Hmmm. You sure sound committed to this new life you talk about."

"Oh, I'm sorry! I didn't come here to preach! It's just that talking about Jesus is getting so easy for me now. He's my best friend! And I love sharing about him, so others will get to know him too."

Just then a worker came in to take away the breakfast tray. "Hey, Melissa, you sure get around. You must work on every floor. I never know when I'm going to run into you!"

Melissa laughed, hugged the girl and said, "Hi, Mandy. Today I'm not working. I just stopped in to see my friend Tabitha." She turned to Tabitha and said, "This is Mandy Hiller. She goes to my church too. In fact, her dad is the assistant pastor."

"Nice to meet you, Tabitha. I would just bet that Melissa has invited you to come to our church." Mandy bent close to Tabitha, cupped her hand near her mouth and whispered loudly, "She does that a lot!"

Nodding, Tabitha agreed. "She was definitely telling me about her best friend Jesus! She hadn't quite gotten to inviting me to church, but I figure that's coming!"

"Then let me beat her!" Mandy laughed. "Please think about visiting our church. We have two services every Sunday morning at nine and eleven, and there are classes for every age group, too,"

"I know the Smiths and they have invited me too. I have a daughter who is in Jenny's class at school. They seem like a nice family." Tabitha paused and adjusted herself in the bed. "I guess I better talk to my husband and make this church visit happen!" she chuckled, "You all are pretty convincing."

"Great! Then I'll be looking for you." Mandy picked up the breakfast tray and added, "See you around, Melissa."

Melissa turned to Tabitha and said, "I better be leaving too, I'm helping at the food pantry later this morning. Always try to keep busy, doing things that please the Lord. Can I pray for you before I leave?"

"Well, sure, I guess so." Tabitha closed her eyes but opened them when she felt Melissa put a hand on her shoulder. As Melissa prayed, Tabitha felt a comforting warmth flow into her. A peace came over her and she closed her eyes again and listened.

"Father God, come near to Tabitha and bring her healing and strength. Let her feel your presence as she returns home and recovers. Touch her body and her spirit. Speak to her through your children who will minister to her and her family. And Lord, you are with us through all our days. Draw us each closer to you. Thanks for your love and your gift of everlasting life. Amen."

Melissa's hand gave a little squeeze. "So, you just keep getting stronger, and hopefully I'll see you at church soon. I'll be looking for you!"

"Thanks for stopping by this morning. I appreciate it." Tabitha was surprised at how comfortable it was to talk with Melissa. And she thought she might want to learn more about her story.

Chapter 6

ALL IN A DAY`S WORK

Becky shivered and pulled her sweater closer around her. She looked out the kitchen window, studying the sky. Low dark clouds were moving in from the west and the wind had picked up a bit. The weatherman was predicting the first snowfall of the season, but not much expected accumulation. The temperature had dropped since morning.

Movement across the yard caught Becky's attention and she watched as Coop and Jenny came up from the barn, followed closely, as usual, by Holly the collie. Jenny picked up a stick and tossed it and Holly took off on a run after it. Suddenly she stopped, dropped the stick, and trotted off to the fence. A sheep was crossing the pasture, bleating insistently for the dog's attention. Running full speed, the two met at the fence and were soon nose to nose.

Becky smiled remembering the little lamb they had rescued from the neighbor's farm after a tornado destroyed most of their property. Despite a broken leg, the lamb had healed and grown and now the young ram acted like he owned the barnyard. He and Holly had a close bonded friendship. Tinkerbell would come when called and seemed to be part collie himself. Becky had even seen them frolicking together in the pasture like puppies.

'Not a little injured lamb any more, are you, fella? Time is passing and you're a big boy now.' Becky looked across the yard to the fields beyond. The harvest had been good this year, thankfully. Coop had worked so hard getting all the fields plowed and planted this spring. They had had near perfect weather this year, although Coop had irrigated the corn field during hot July. Now the barn was full of hay, and they had sold a good amount of wheat at the elevators in town. The corn stalks were drying and turning their autumn colors of brown and yellow. Coop had already arranged for help with the harvest in a couple of weeks. God had seen to their needs with garden vegetables too, and the storage shelves were loaded. They would all be eating canned beans and corn and carrots this winter.

Yes, it was a lot of work. But the flavor of their own garden vegetables was always far superior to store bought produce. And the simple feeling of accomplishment and pride in knowing she had provided for her family, well, Becky felt it was all worth it. Working with her hands, doing whatever she could to assure the health and well-being of her family, using her energy from sun up until sundown to bring good, not harm, to her husband and children - she was beginning to feel like the woman in Proverbs 31. She knew Coop appreciated her dedication to the family. He had told her so often.

In moments when she felt overwhelmed or extremely tired, she allowed herself to take a break and step away for a bit. Her favorite place to go was the backyard of the old house. Marla Jean had a beautifully laid out flower garden with graveled pathways that wandered amongst pleasing colors and fragrances. Just a slow walk around the garden could soothe and comfort the anxiety of a difficult day. Becky usually made her way to the weeping willow tree and sank into the grass under it. It was an especially peaceful spot for her.

No need for a quiet get-away lately – things had been going well. The first few weeks at home with a new baby had been tough. Nicholas had been born three weeks early, so his arrival had surprised them all. Fortunately, the baby room was already set up and waiting, so they didn't have that to worry about. And he was good-sized, for being early, so that was a blessing too.

Becky reached down and ran her hand across her abdomen. The scar from the cesarean had healed well. When the doctors had discovered that the cord was wrapped around Nicholas's neck and he was breech, they felt that a cesarean was the safest and quickest way to deliver him. Coop and Becky had quickly agreed.

And despite all the strikes against him, being early, being breech, and the stress caused by difficulty with oxygen, Nicholas was doing well. He had readily taken to nursing and had picked up weight almost immediately. Developmentally he was right in the normal ranges. "Thank you again, Jesus. Thank you for my family. Thank you for loving all of us. Please give me wisdom and patience. Amen."

Becky smiled as she watched Coop stoop down and allow Jenny to climb onto his back. Jenny loved piggy-back rides, but she was getting so big now, even Coop was having difficulty carrying her. She had always been tall, but it seemed to Becky that she had grown three inches since school started! With her heavy coat, Coop could barely get his arms around her legs. Jenny's boots clanked against Coop's legs as he jogged across the driveway. Coop pranced like a horse and made whinnying sounds. Jenny threw her head back with laughter and Coop nearly lost his hold on her. Becky sighed with pleasure at the sight. She loved watching the relationship between them grow.

With the coming of winter, they could relax a little and enjoy more family time. She was glad that Coop was a hard worker, but his dedication to farm chores often left him tired and worn out. He never complained about it; in fact, he often talked about the joy he felt working God's earth and tending God's animals. But his ability to fall asleep immediately was a sure sign that he was often physically exhausted. Becky was quick to rub his back to ease the tension in his shoulders from long hours sitting on a tractor. She tried to do as much as she could to help him with chores. Her prime responsibilities were with the children, the garden and the house. During harvest, she worked with Marla Jean and Dana to prepare hearty lunches for the hired workers.

Sometimes Becky was tired too. And she was aware that when she was tired, she could also be short-tempered. Just yesterday she had gotten overly upset when Jenny left the chicken house open over night. It was a simple mistake, and of course Jenny hadn't done it on purpose, yet Becky had criticized her harshly and Jenny had run into her bedroom crying. When Becky realized that she had spoken so sternly, she went to Jenny and they talked. Becky asked for forgiveness for the way she had reacted, and Jenny said she'd try to remember to shut the chicken house door tight. They ended with a hug and both of them felt better.

Daily Becky asked God for the strength she would need to serve her family and meet their needs. Not just the physical needs of the body, but also the spiritual needs as well. She wanted to lead her children and help them grow in stature and in favor with God and man. As she had done so many times in the past, Becky once again thanked God for her husband Coop. Together they were building up the kingdom of God.

Jenny slid off Coop's back at the door, and held it open for Holly to enter. They dropped their boots on the porch, hung their coats on pegs, and came into the house, making straight for the kitchen.

"I smell hot coffee," Coop said, stopping to kiss Becky before washing his hands at the sink. "Just what I need. Snow is in the air."

Jenny stuck her hands under the running water and Coop squirted some soap for her. "It's cold, Mommy. Can we have some hot chocolate? I don't like coffee!"

"When did you ever try coffee?" Becky asked.

"Well, I didn't really. But I just know I won't like it." Coop handed her a towel and she dried her hands. "It smells good when it's making, but not when people breathe it on me! That's yucky! So I know I don't want it in my mouth."

Becky laughed, "It's an acquired taste, I guess!" She poured two cups and took them to the table.

Before Coop sat down, he kissed her lips and said, "Mmmm. Well, Jenny, I happen to like the smell and taste of coffee on your mother's breathe." He kissed Becky again and gave her a big hug.

Becky closed her eyes and relaxed into his embrace, enjoying the feel of his strong arms around her. It was a short-lived moment of peace, however, because she heard a chair sliding across the kitchen floor. Becky opened her eyes in time to see Jenny standing on the chair, reaching up to a high shelf in the pantry.

"What are you doing, Honey?" Becky asked.

"Getting the chocolate powder. I can do the chocolate if you do the milk."

"How long has Nicholas been asleep?" Coop asked.

"Not long enough!" Becky laughed. "Let's just enjoy the peace and quiet while we can. He'll be up soon enough, and I'd like to get the laundry folded before he needs me to feed him."

"I'll help," Jenny offered. "After I drink my hot chocolate."

Becky gave her daughter a smile and tussled her hair. "Thanks Sweetie, that would be great." She stirred the milk while it heated, then sat the hot pan on the cutting board by the stove. "You can put in the chocolate powder now. Just don't touch the pan, it's still hot."

Chapter 7

PROGRAM PRACTICE

Christmas was fast approaching, and the church building was bustling with excited children, exhausted teachers, and anxious parents. Dress rehearsal for the annual Christmas pageant wasn't going smoothly. Nervous toddlers fidgeted with their sheep costumes, chatty five year olds were not following directions and the boy assigned the role of Joseph had a sneezing fit caused, he said, by the feathers on the angel costumes.

Standing just off stage, three mothers sighed in unison. Becky and her best friend Nancy Martin had been through a few programs with their daughters before, but this was Tabitha's first involvement with a church Christmas pageant. Becky and Nancy had recruited her to help. Their job was to watch over the sheep, and the three of them were trying their best to keep order in the flock. Nancy's son Andy saw his mother and crawled over to her. "At least he's staying in character!" Nancy laughed as she bent down to talk with him. "Go back on the stage, Honey. You need to stay with the other sheep."

A fifth grade boy, dressed in his father's old bathrobe and looking very much like a shepherd, came to the edge of the stage and herded the sheep all back together. Using a cane as a shepherd's hook, he gently poked and prodded until the sheep were in the right spot. Andy gave out a loud "Baaa!" and the other sheep joined in.

"Oh, great!" Nancy laughed. "Just what the show needs! A flock of rowdy sheep!"

"Don't worry, Nancy. You know it will all be fine. In rehearsal it always seems like the pageant will be a disaster, but then it turns out fine. And the little bloopers just make the show more interesting."

"You're right, of course. I remember the year Hannah was a lamb. She was terrified! She lay down on the floor and closed her eyes. Everyone thought she was playing the part of a sleeping lamb, when in reality she was just trying to hide from the crowd of people watching! When it was time to leave the stage, a shepherd came over and picked her up and carried her off. It was actually very cute!"

"And look at her now. No more fear." Becky pointed up to risers where the elementary age girls were gathering to sing. Hannah, Jenny and Kendy stood front and center, ready to sing a verse of "Away in a Manger" as a trio. Kendy looked a little nervous, but the other girls were giving her a pep talk. They were experienced at performing in Christmas programs; this was Kendy's first time.

Tabitha smiled encouragingly at her daughter. She was so glad they had started attending church. It was good to see Kendy developing friendships with these girls. The move to Winslow had been difficult at first, but things seemed to be working out. Tom liked his job and Kendy liked her school. Tabitha looked around at the women standing near her and sighed. She liked her new friends, too.

Somehow they all made it through the rehearsal without any major mishaps. One of the wise men had jumped off the stage and twisted his ankle, but his mother said he'd be okay for the performance tomorrow. If not, he could be a wise man on crutches. Another interesting twist, but it would be fine.

Snow was falling as they left the church. Becky drove to her mother's house to pick up Nicholas. Elizabeth had been more than happy to watch her grandson during the rehearsal.

"It's really starting to come down," Becky said as she and Jenny entered Elizabeth's little house. "We can't stay long; I think we better get home before the roads get bad."

Margaret Lawrence came in from the kitchen. "We was jus' a havin' some tea. Cain't you stay an have some with us?" Margaret was Elizabeth's neighbor and tended to visit whenever anything interesting was happening. A baby boy in the house was certainly a good reason to come calling.

"Oh, I'm sorry Margaret, I don't think we'd better. I don't mind driving in snow, if I have the truck, but I brought my little car, and it tends to slip and slide."

"Well, jus' let me have one more snuggle with this little fella, then. He sure is gettin' mighty big! They don't stay little fer long." She sat in the rocking chair with Nicholas and said, "Here now, give me his coat and I'll put it on 'im."

Elizabeth spoke with Jenny, "So, are you all ready for the Christmas program tomorrow? Did you practice your part?"

"I'm ready!" she confidently replied. "I get to wear my new red and white dress. Hannah got a green and white, and Kendy's is mostly purple. We're going to be like a rainbow!"

"Sounds pretty!" I'll be watching and listening."

Margaret joined in, "I'll be there too. I always like watchin' you little chillen."

A few minutes later, buckling Nicholas's car seat into the base behind the driver's seat, Becky whispered up a quick prayer for safety and alertness as she drove home. Jenny got in from the opposite door and fastened her own seatbelt. "Pull it tight, Honey."

"I know, Mommy. I know. See?" Jenny tugged at the belt, which was indeed tight enough. "I hope it snows a lot so we can go sledding. But I hope it doesn't snow too much that we have to miss the Christmas program." She sat back, folded her arms across her chest, and said with a huff, "So what should I tell God? That I want snow or that I don't want snow? It's confusing!"

Becky turned from her seat behind the steering wheel and smiled. Jenny was praying on her own more and more lately. She was showing a real understanding of the importance of a conversation with her savior. "I guess you tell him just what you said to me," she answered with a smile. "Tell him you would like lots of snow, but not until after the program." She turned back to the front and started the engine. Before she put the car in gear she looked again at Jenny. "But also be sure to ask him to help you to be content with whatever comes, snow or no snow, program or no program, because you need to be satisfied with whatever circumstances you are in. Knowing that God has a plan and knows what's best is the important thing."

"Hmmm. I guess. But I just don't want to miss the program. I like singing with Kendy and Hannah. They can't do "Away in the Manger" without me. Kendy would be too scared. I need to hold her hand."

"Well, let's not worry about that right now. Let's just get home safely." Becky pulled slowly onto the street and headed towards the farm. "You know, that kinda of reminds me of what Paul in the Bible said. He was in jail, locked up in chains and beaten, because he was telling people about Jesus, and the soldiers didn't like it. But that didn't stop him from praising God anyway. He said he had learned to be content with whatever circumstances he was in. Whether he was in jail or free, or whether he had lots to eat or nothing, or whether someone was beating him or taking good care of him. It didn't matter to Paul. He said we shouldn't worry about anything, but instead we should pray about everything."

"Okay, then I'll just pray that I can be happy with either snow or no snow."

"Perfect!"

"But I'll also tell him that I want the snow to come after the program!"

"Oh Jenny! I think he knows! But I also know that you will be able to handle whatever happens, because Jesus Christ will be with you and help you."

"I remember a verse Daddy told me. Philippians chapter four. 'I can do everything through Christ, who gives me strength.'"

"Yes, and it was Paul who wrote that. While he was in jail!"

"Oh! I didn't know that! Paul is pretty amazing, to be happy even though he was in jail."

"Yes, he's pretty amazing, alright. He can teach us a lot of lessons. Let's talk with Daddy when we get home and see if we can study more about Paul during our family devotions. I think it would be good for all of us to read about Paul's life."

Jenny looked over at Nicholas and laughed. "But not Nicholas. He's sound asleep!"

"He must have had a lot of fun at Grandma's. He's all worn out!" Becky smiled as she turned onto the gravel road that led to home. "And look, we're almost home, with just a little snow sticking on the road. Thank you Jesus."

"Thank you, Jesus," Jenny piped from the back.

Chapter 8

FELLOWSHIP AND FRIENDSHIP

The children's Christmas program went off without a hitch. Well, almost. But no one seemed to mind, really, when the huge cardboard star extended by a rope from the ceiling kept swinging back and forth over the stage. One of the wise men had set it in motion with a shepherd's staff and was intent on keeping it moving. Just when the star slowed its orbit, the wise man tapped it and the star was on the move again. The angels, standing on risers, had to duck out of the way or be hit on the head by the swinging star. That's when the giggling began, and the show almost ended in a fit of laughter.

Fortunately, one of the teen boys who was assisting backstage took charge, confiscated the shepherd's staff, and held the star in place while order returned to the stage. By the time the congregation rose to join in the singing of "Joy to the World" peace ruled and all was well in the joyful world.

In the fellowship hall, families gathered for refreshments before heading home. Excited children, glad to be free at last, nibbled on cookies and brownies while their parents congratulated one another on a successful program. The teachers and assistants seemed as relieved as the children to have survived another pageant. The room was filled with laughter and smiles.

A photo area had been set up at one end of the room, and families posed in front of a Christmas tree for pictures. With her cell phone, Becky took a picture of the three second grade singers, smiling brightly. "I'll send it to you," she said to Tabitha. "The girls did really well."

"They did," Tabitha nodded. "I know Kendy was scared, but Jenny helped her feel more confident. She's a special little girl, your Jenny. You must be very proud of her."

"She's special, all right. I'm thankful every day that God gave her to me. It was hard, being a single mom for the first six years, but God has blessed us with a great family now, and I couldn't be happier."

"Oh, I didn't know you had been a single mom. So is Coop not Jenny's real father?"

Tabitha stopped short, glanced down and went on hurriedly, "Oh, I'm sorry. I don't mean to pry."

Becky gave her a little hug and said, "No problem. I don't mind talking about it. I met Jenny's biological father while I was a freshman in college. When he found out I was pregnant, he quickly got lost. When Jenny was born, I lived with my mom and she was such a help to me. But the biggest help came when I gave my life to Jesus. When I believed that he didn't condemn me for my previous lifestyle, my whole life changed. I knew that my sins were forgiven. And I knew that, no matter what, I would have a friend in Jesus. I met Coop when Jenny was almost five. He's been God's biggest blessing!"

Tabitha nodded quietly. All this talk about Jesus and sins forgiven and lives changed – she was hearing it from every direction lately. She knew her husband Tom came from a church going family, but after his parents died in a car accident, Tom lost interest in church or religion. In fact, he had been angry at God and wondered if he even existed outside the pages of the story book called the Bible. By the time she met Tom, years later, he was bitter about the whole idea of God. They seldom talked about it, but Tabitha knew that Tom didn't think that a good, loving God would have taken his parents from him.

They had never really considered going to church until Becky and Coop and Nancy and Greg had invited them. Even Melissa Madison, who talked so freely about the changes in her life, seemed convinced that God was a loving source of comfort and peace. And Tabitha had to admit, they all seemed like nice people, ones she would enjoy having as friends. They had been so kind while she was in the hospital with her appendix surgery, and even afterwards, bringing in meals and helping with housework for a few weeks.

Nancy had sent the most beautiful handmade card with words of encouragement. Becky and her mother Elizabeth had come over one day to vacuum and do laundry. Becky even brought some strawberry jam she had made. Coop drove Kendy to her gymnastics class one Saturday when Tom had to work. Everyone seemed to be going above and beyond to make them feel welcome in the community.

So she saw no reason to deny Kendy when she asked repeatedly if she could go to Sunday school with Jenny and Hannah. And she felt comfortable sitting with Becky and Nancy and their husbands during the adult class, even though Tom was still refusing to attend.

Kendy had begged her daddy to come to the Christmas program, and Tabitha was relieved that he had agreed. She knew it was because he wanted to support his daughter and she was grateful for that.

Tabitha smiled as Tom and Kendy approached. She was glad they had this opportunity to have a family picture taken. Giving Becky her cell phone, Tabitha joined them in front of the decorated tree. Becky snapped a few pictures, then handed the phone back to Tabitha. "They are really good," Tabitha said as she swiped through the photos. "Thanks so much."

"Happy to do it," Becky said and turned to Tom. "Would you take a picture of us three moms? One with just us and one with the girls."

Tom agreed and the women arranged themselves for the photo. Tabitha, in the middle, felt surrounded by a group of loving friends. All three women were smiling as Tom took the picture. Then the little girls stood in front of their moms for a final round of photos.

Nancy broke up the party by saying, "Time for us to get home. It's been a busy weekend, and I know a little lamb who needs to get to bed. Hannah, go find your daddy, See him over there talking to Pastor Green? Be polite, but tell him we need to go." Hannah took off, paten leather shoes clicking on the tile floor.

"Hey, Tabitha, have you been thinking about coming to the ladies Bible study that's starting up in January? We'd really love to have you join our group." Nancy was the group leader and was praying that Tabitha would start coming.

"It's going to be a great discussion. I think you'll like it," Becky added. "We'll be studying the Proverbs 31 woman. Nancy found a study guide that looks very helpful."

"It's Wednesday evening, and the girls can go to their own class. It's good to have an hour or so of adult women talk! The first class will be mostly a 'get-to know-you' session, so it would be the perfect time for you to meet some of the other women in the group. And we'll have some light refreshments."

Nancy looked at Becky, who acknowledged the reminder. "Yes, I know, I promised to make something. Not sure what yet, but I'll take care of it!"

"Well, it does sound like a good way to get to know some other people. I'll think about it, and check with Tom. He'll probably say it's up to me, so I'll say a tentative 'yes' for now."

"Great!" said Nancy and Becky in unison. Amidst laughter Nancy added, "There's a men's group meeting at that time too, if Tom would be interested."

Tabitha shrugged her shoulders and shook her head. "I doubt it. He's not much interested in God or things of the church. But I don't think he'll tell me I can't go. I'll talk with him about it first though."

"That's good! That would be what the Proverbs woman would do too! See, you already understand what the class will be about!" Becky gave Tabitha a little hug. "We'd better get going too. If I don't see you before Christmas, have a blessed day. You too Nancy. Merry Christmas"

Nancy embraced Becky warmly. "Merry Christmas to you too. We're still planning on having Jenny over while you and Coop are away. But we'll talk more later." She turned toward Tabitha and hugged her also. "Bye Tabitha. Merry Christmas!"

The women gathered children, coats and husbands and headed home. Each was filled with Christmas spirit. The program and fellowship afterwards had been delightful.

As Coop drove home, Becky mentioned that there was still some gift wrapping to be done. "I'll try to finish up this evening. Maybe tomorrow we can drive around and do some delivering?"

"Sure. You're planning to visit the Hennesey's, right? Who else?"

"Yes, and I have small gifts for Pastor and Mrs. Green and also the Hiller's, and Mom's neighbor Margaret, and Doc and Lila Larson."

"Sounds like a full day of visiting!" Coop laughed. "Because I know you won't just be dropping off packages. You'll want to stay and talk and talk."

"Well, sure! I know the Hennesey's really appreciate the company. Since they moved to Primrose Place, we just haven't spent enough time with them. And they don't have family around, so I feel like we should visit them as much as we can. Marilyn loves seeing how the kids have grown. And Ed, he might not remember who we are, but his eyes light up when he sees Nicholas."

"Then we'll spend as much time with them as we can. Spreading a little holiday cheer! I bet they'll be really surprised when we show them their repaired clock. It's taken awhile to get done, but it runs as good as new now." The Hennesey's mantle clock had been damaged by the tornado that destroyed their home. Coop had salvaged the pieces and found a clock restoration company in Topeka who had done the repairs.

"They're going to love it! That clock was really special to them, a gift on their wedding. It will make them so happy to have it fixed and back home."

"Too bad about Ed. He might not even remember that the clock has a special meaning."

"I know. Dementia is such a hard thing to watch. That's another reason why we should visit more often. Marilyn needs support, and a break now and then. But at least, living at Primrose Place, they have people around all the time. Marilyn would just need to call for assistance, if she needed it. There are caregivers and even neighbors who can help if she calls."

They drove on in silence for a bit until Becky said, "I think I'll take some of my strawberry jam over to Sheriff Bertell. He seems alone a lot too. No family. I remember how good he was to us during all that trouble with Melissa. I know we've thanked him, but let's not forget to show our appreciation at Christmas too."

Coop glanced in the back seat. "Looks like everyone is asleep. So let's talk about our anniversary! Know what? I love you more today than I did three years ago when we got married. And man, I didn't think that was even possible! My heart was bursting with happiness and love when I saw you walking down the aisle. But now, after being your husband for almost three years, I know more about love than I ever did back then."

Becky laid her head on Coop's shoulder and sighed with contentment. "I think I know what you mean. Love grows deeper every day. All the traits that drew me to you, years ago, are reinforced and strengthened with time. I love you. And I love the family we have made. And the team we are, whether working together at the farm or serving the Lord together at church. Being your wife is such a fulfilling role."

"If our love keeps growing, can you imagine how in love we'll be when we are sixty or seventy years old?"

"I can't wait to find out!" Becky laughed. "But let's take it one day at a time. And enjoy every minute. I love you, Benjamin Cooper Smith."

"Going back to the cabin will be nice. Remember the hot tub? And the fireplace?"

"I do," Becky said dreamily. "And I remember getting snowed in, and not minding one bit!"

"Well, hopefully not so much snow this year. But it will be good to get away, just the two of us."

"I hope your mom knows what she's getting into, taking care of Nicholas for that long. It can be exhausting."

"She'll have Dana in and out to help. Mom will be just fine."

"And Jenny will be with the Martin's so we don't have to worry a bit about her! I did overhear that Tabitha might bring Kendy over one afternoon so they can all three play together."

"It was good to see Tom there tonight. Greg and I were talking about trying to get him more involved with the men's group."

"I mentioned it to Tabitha, but she seems to think he would not be interested. She didn't elaborate though, so I don't really know the whole story. But if I know you, you'll soon win him over." Becky chuckled to herself. Coop really did have a way with evangelism. Sharing Christ came as a second nature to him.

"Well, the first step is to pray for his openness. And Greg and I are already doing that. Then we'll just be friends with him, and hopefully he will see our lives reflecting Christ."

"Hanging out with you and Greg, he's bound to notice. You'll be planting seeds with whatever you say and do."

"That's our prayer," Coop said as he pulled onto the dirt road that led to the farm. Gravel crunched under the tires and Jenny roused slightly from her sleep.

"We're home? Good! This dress is itchy!"

"Yup, we're home Sweetie. Just change into your pj's. It's nearly bedtime."

"I took a bath before the program, so I don't need to again, right?"

"Right," agreed Becky. "Just wash your face and hands and brush your teeth, okay?"

****

As Greg and Nancy Martin drove home that evening, their conversation also turned to the topic of the Barkdale family. Nancy shared that she was overjoyed that Tabitha had as much as agreed to come to the Wednesday night ladies group. She mentioned that Tom seemed to be resistant to the idea of Jesus but Tabitha hadn't opened up to explain why. Greg spoke a prayer aloud as he drove. "Father God, we pray for Tom and Tabitha. We ask that you open their hearts to be receptive to your words. And whatever it is that is keeping Tom from wanting to hear about you, soften him. Give us all the right words to say. Help us as we witness. Let your love for Tom and Tabitha be evident in our interactions with them. In your name we ask it. Amen."

Hannah spoke up from the back seat. "And Kendy too. Amen."

****

"Becky and Nancy talked to me again about that lady's Bible study group." Tabitha said, approaching the subject cautiously. "If it's okay with you, I'd like to go. It starts in late January. On Wednesday evenings. And Kendy can go to a class too."

"You're really getting in deep with those church ladies, aren't you?" Tom gripped the steering wheel and looked straight ahead. "Well, I know they all seem like good people, and the Smith's were sure nice to us when you were in the hospital." He paused to think a minute, then said, "Well, it's up to you. I guess there's no harm in it, as long as it makes you happy."

"I'm happy when I'm with Jenny and Hannah. And I like their mommies." Kendy leaned forward from her seat and whispered to her mother, "They make good brownies!"

"I noticed you eating brownies tonight," Tabitha said. "I had one too. They were really good."

Kendy reached into the pocket of her coat and brought out a pile of brownies, wrapped in a napkin. "Hannah's mom said I could bring some home."

"She did, huh?" said Tom. "I hope you got enough for me too! I didn't eat any tonight!"

"She gave me lots." Kendy held them carefully. "You can have one when we get home. But I'll save the rest for tomorrow."

The Barkdale's older model Ford sputtered as Tom pulled into a parking place in front of their apartment. The car rattled and coughed as the engine was shut off.

"Just what we need, another car repair bill," Tom grumbled. "And right after we spent all our savings on doctor and hospital co-pays."

"I'm so sorry I got sick," Tabitha murmured with her head down. "And now the extra Christmas expenses." She sighed and reached for the door handle.

"Well, we knew it would be hard, just moving to a new place and getting settled. We'll bounce back, eventually. I'm taking on some overtime at the hospital, so that should help." Tom opened Kendy's door and helped her out. "Come on Beautiful. Let's get you upstairs. It's almost bedtime."

"Daddy?" Kendy started hesitantly.

"What, Sweetie?" He took her hand as they walked toward the apartment building.

"Thank you for my pretty dress for the program. I'm sorry you had to buy it for me."

Tom stopped and looked directly at his daughter. "You looked so beautiful tonight, and you sang so pretty. I loved you in your new dress. And don't you worry about the money. There's enough for a dress and Christmas presents and Christmas dinner and whatever else we really need. You should not worry one minute about it. I'll take care of things."

"And hopefully after the holidays, a job will open up for me, and then we'll have even less to worry about." Tabitha made a mental note to contact a few places where she had interviewed, to see if they had made a decision. Most companies had said their positions didn't open until after the first of the year.

"I hope God will give you a good job with lots of money," Kendy said, which caused both of her parents to stop and look at each other over the top of their daughter's head. Kendy went on, "Jenny says we should pray about everything. So I'll pray for your new job."

Tabitha raised her eyebrows and tilted her head. Tom held the door open as his family entered the building. As they climbed the stairs to the second floor, he thought to himself, 'Even Kendy is getting in deep with the church kids. I better keep an eye on this. They don't know what they're getting into.'

Chapter 9

SECOND HONEYMOON

The cabin looked just the same as it did on their first visit. The kitchen was stocked with food and drinks. Logs were laid in the fireplace. Warm water awaited in the hot tub. The bedroom was cozy and inviting and the sight of it brought back fond memories.

Becky put her suitcase on the bed and began to unpack. She remembered the thrill of their honeymoon days here. She remembered their first tentative touches, when everything was new. She remembered the excitement of exploring and learning about each other. She remembered the joy of total satisfaction and knowing that her husband was satisfied as well.

She turned from the closet to see Coop standing in the doorway, gazing at her with a look of longing. He crossed the room in two quick steps and took her in his arms. She welcomed his kisses with an eagerness that surprised her. A new excitement was sparked and she fumbled with the buttons on his shirt.

"We are alone!" he exclaimed. "And you are all mine." He pulled her sweater off over her head and buried his face in her chest. Becky moaned as a little trickle of breast milk leaked through her bra.

"We may be childless and alone, but I still know I have a baby to care for, one way or another. Let me pump and then we can continue."

Coop's face contorted into a pout and his shoulders sagged. "You promise?" he asked pleadingly.

"Absolutely!" she replied and kissed him deeply. "I want it as badly as you do, my love. Maybe you could light a fire while I pump. This really won't take long."

"I remember another night in front of that fireplace," Coop said. "When you're ready, we can do a reenactment!" He pulled her close and kissed her once again.

"Sounds good to me," Becky said. She glanced down at the trickle of milk starting to stain her bra. "Now look what you've done! Go! Get that fire going while I do this."

Coop left the room and Becky sat on the bed with the breast pump. While the milk filled the bottles, she looked around the room once more. 'The cabin may not have changed in three years, but our lives certainly have,' she thought. 'God has been so faithful to me. To us.' She sighed with contentment.

In the living room, Coop also was thinking of the changes the past three years had brought. He lit the fire and sat on his haunches, watching as the flames licked the wood and finally took hold. Staring as the fire curled around the logs, he began to sing. "It only takes a spark, to get a fire going. And soon all those around will warm up in its glowing." He hummed the rest of the song as he stood and stretched. He rolled his shoulders in circles and sighed as he felt his muscles relax. The only sound in the room was the crackling in the fireplace. Outside he heard a blue jay call.

Coop went to the window and looked out towards the woods. It was easy to spot the jay as he hopped from one leafless branch to another. Another movement near the edge of the trees caught his eye. A turkey hen scratched in the brown leaves, searching for something to eat. Coop strained his eyes and looked closer, noticing several more birds along the tree line.

He was still bird watching when Becky came up quietly and wrapped her arms around him. "What's out there?" she asked.

"Turkeys," Coop answered, turning slightly to let her look out the window. "See them?"

"I do," she purred. "Just hens though. I wonder where the tom is."

"He's probably around nearby. With all these hens, he's probably a happy fella."

"Oh Coop, do you mean that a male can't be happy with just one mate?" Becky teased.

He turned and took her in his arms. As he kissed her, Coop whispered, "Turkeys, maybe no. But for me, you are all I need. You're the only girl for me."

They moved as one to the couch and, while the flames in the fireplace crackled and danced, Coop and Becky's love also burned hot and complete.

Cuddled together afterward, Coop gently stroked Becky's hair. Her head lay comfortably on his chest and her arms were wrapped around him. "I love you, Rebecca Joy Emerson Smith. With all my heart." he said and kissed the top of her head.

Becky sighed in total contentment. "I know. And it feels so good to be loved by you. I'll never get tired of this."

"I'm sure glad I'm not a turkey!" Coop said with a chuckle.

"Well, that's an interesting comment! Why, pray tell, are you glad you are not a turkey?"

"Because a tom turkey only mates with a female once. Then they are done for a year! I don't want you just once. I'd be happy with once a day, forever."

"Does that mean you are not happy now? Because I know we used to make love once a day."

"Or more," Coop interrupted.

"Or more," Becky agreed with a chuckle. "But now we don't. Life happens, I guess. Does that make you unhappy?"

Coop sat up straight and pulled Becky into a position facing him. "Of course not, Becky. It's just that, when we are together like this, I'm reminded of how good it is between us. You still take my breath away."

She leaned into him and their lips met once again. Coop slowly pulled away with a twinkle in his eye. "You know, what I said about turkeys wasn't quite true."

"What do you mean?"

"Well, actually the tom mates one time with the hen, then moves on to another, and another, and another. So it's actually just the hen that only mates once a year."

Becky playfully punched Coop in the arm. "The hen is off working, laying eggs and taking care of the chicks. No time for fun! The tom just goes on his merry way, finding pleasure for the moment with other hens. Come to think of it," she added thoughtfully, "I'm also glad you're not a turkey!"

"Oh Becky, I could never find pleasure with any other hen but you. We are mated for life! I need no other. Besides, I think I help with the kids, so you are freed up to pleasure me more than once a year."

He was joking with her and Becky continued with a playful comeback. She put her hands on her hips and asked accusingly, "So, let me get this straight! You help me with the kids so I will reward you with sexual pleasures? Is that what you're telling me? No other reason? Just to butter me up for lovemaking?"

Coop turned the conversation around immediately. "I'm just playing with you. You know that. I help you because I love you. I want to do whatever I can to lighten your load, whether it's with the housework or gardening or kids, or whatever. I help you like you help me. Out of love."

"We've always said we are a team. A God appointed team. And of course I know you love me. You love our family and care about every part of our lives. You are a perfect head of our home. And I am happy to be your partner."

"I never want you to think your work with the house and the kids isn't important." Coop put his hands on her shoulders and looked directly into Becky's eyes. "You're the perfect partner. We compliment each other. We complete each other. I need you and you need me. And the three of us, you, me and God, are doing great things in our family."

"You do help me, Coop, you really do. Jenny has a bond with you that is a joy to see. I couldn't ask for a more special relationship between you two. And Nicholas, he brightens up when he's with you."

"Ah, he just smiles all the time! It has nothing to do with me."

"I think you're wrong," Becky answered. "I've watched him. He's starting to look for you when he hears your voice. He wants your attention, I can tell."

"I sure love that little guy!" Coop kissed Becky on her forehead and added, "You have beautiful children."

"You helped with that one!" Becky laughed.

"And I'll help you with the next one," he said as he kissed her cheek. "And the next one." He kissed her nose. "And the next one." He kissed her other cheek. "And the next one." He kissed her chin.

By this time, Becky was giggling and trying to squirm away from him. Coop caught her and gently but firmly kissed her on the lips. He sat down on the couch and pulled Becky onto his lap. "We better get started, my little hen."

Chapter 10

THE BROWNIES

Jenny sat on the floor of the Martin's back porch, struggling with Kendy's boots. She pulled and tugged with a "Grumph" and finally the purple boot gave way. "Those boots are tight!" she exclaimed. "I guess no snow will get in. There's no room!"

"Mommy says she'll buy me new ones when she gets her first paycheck. If she gets a job."

Nancy overheard the conversation and went right to the closet. Rummaging around in the back, she pulled out an old pair of Hannah's outgrown boots. "See if these will fit you. Hannah can't wear them any more, so if they fit you, you can have them."

Kendy's foot slipped in easily, with a little room to wiggle her toes. "They do fit!" she said joyfully. "I can have these?"

"Sure!" Nancy answered with a smile. "They are pink; I don't think Andy will want me to save them for him! Sorry they aren't purple though. I know that's your favorite color."

"That's okay," the little girl replied shyly. "Pink is good too." Then she added a quiet "Thank you." She took the pink boots off and lined them up with Jenny's yellow and Hannah's blue boots already sitting against the wall. As an afterthought she added, "Does Andy like purple? He can have mine!"

Nancy laughed, "Well, he just might! We'll just ask your mom what she wants to do with them. But for now, let's all go in and have a snack."

The three girls hustled into the house and headed to the bathroom to wash up. They laughed as they looked in the mirror at their rosy red cheeks. The overnight snow of just an inch wasn't much good for sledding, but they had fun outside anyway.

"Hey, look!" Hannah exclaimed. "We all have the same hair!"

Three little set of eyes looked at the reflection in the mirror – smiling faces topped with various shades of brown hair. "That's funny! We're triplets!" Kendy giggled.

"I used to have blond hair when I was little. But mommy's hair is brown, and now I'm getting her hair too," explained Jenny. "Yeah, we're triplets! We can be sisters!"

"I know! Let's make a name for us. Like a club. A brown hair club!" Hannah came up with the plan but couldn't think of a good name. "What should we call us?"

"That's easy!" Jenny declared. "Let's be The Brownies!" She threw her arms around the other girls in a giant hug. They danced together around the bathroom, bumping into cabinets and walls and doors but continuing to giggle and dance regardless.

Nancy stuck her head into the bathroom. "What's going on in here? You girls are having too much fun! What's so funny, Hannah?"

"We're The Brownies, mom! The Brownies! See our hair? We're all brown."

"And so you are! The Brownies! That's perfect!"

Hannah caught her breath and asked, "Can The Brownies have brownies for snack?"

"Brownies for The Brownies," sang out Jenny and Kendy and Hannah joined in. Another burst of giggles brought an end to the singing.

"Sorry girls, I don't have any brownies today. We're having peanut butter crackers. Too bad your name isn't The Crackers!"

And the laughter started again.

Chapter 11

THE ROAD HOME

A light dusting of fresh snow lay on the farm fields, barely covering the dirt and slight undergrowth. The roads were clear and Coop maneuvered the truck towards home at a steady pace. "Very different from the last time we drove home, isn't it?" he asked.

Becky, looking out the window at the passing fence posts, said, "I was just thinking about that. Last time there were mountains of snow on each side of the road, and I didn't even know there were fence posts there. We should be about to the place where you drove into the snow bank."

"Hey, it's not like I did it on purpose, you know! It's all because of the vultures that nearly collided with us. Not my fault." Coop looked at her with a grin. "Besides, it turned out okay." He was recalling their joint efforts to free the truck and the fun they had lying snuggled in the snow together.

"If I didn't know better, I would think you planned the whole thing, just to have another chance to cuddle up with me!" Becky gave Coop a playful jab on his arm.

"I will admit, that was a bonus!" Coop took her hand and said, "But no, it wasn't planned." He lifted her fingers to his lips and kissed them softly. "It was fun though!"

"It was," Becky agreed and kissed his hand back. "I don't think we'll have an issue with snow this year. There's hardly been any snow this year at all."

"Winter is far from over, my dear. But yes, usually we have had more snow than this. Makes me a little worried about crops next year. We count on snow almost as much as rain to give the fields moisture. The wheat I planted in September needs cold temperatures and then snow."

"But you're right, there's lots of winter left, and then spring rains. Nothing to worry about. God will provide."

"Oh, I don't really worry. That was a poor choice of words. I'm not anxious. I'm just aware. It doesn't hurt to be reminded of Philippians 4:6 and remember to pray about everything."

Coop started to quote the verse and Becky joined him. "Be anxious for nothing, but in everything by prayer and supplication, with thanksgiving, let your requests be made known to God."

"So we put it into God's hands. His righteous right hand."

"Like we do everything, every day."

They drove on in silence, holding hands and silently praying for moisture, good crop growth, and a fine harvest.

Coop pulled onto the main highway and picked up speed. The roads were completely clear and traffic was moving along normally. "At this rate, we'll be home by supper time. We can pick up Jenny first, maybe grab some carryout from the diner so you don't have to cook, and get out to the farm. I can't wait to see our little man. I bet he's grown in the past week!"

"Let's get enough supper for your mom and Dana too. I'm sure they'll appreciate it – after all they've done for us this week."

Coop chuckled, "Every time I called Mom to see how things were going, she said she was exhausted but happy. She loved taking care of Nicholas, but I think she'll be glad for the break! She said Dana was helping a lot."

"Dana sure knows how to jump in and help wherever she's needed. She's great in the kitchen, sweet and gentle with the kids, strong when doing farm work, and a leader at church. And smart, too. Her college grades have been really good. God has great things in store for her, I just know it."

"It's exciting to watch her growth, in so many ways," Coop said. "She will be making some major decisions in the near future. I've been praying for her."

"Me too. I know she's looking forward to that trip to Nicaragua this summer. I've been praying about it every morning. It's funny, but a few months ago the Lord gave me a desire to pray about the water in Nicaragua. I'm not sure why! But a vision of moving water comes to me every time I pray about her trip. A river or something. Anyway, I pray about water whenever I pray about that trip."

"Interesting," Coop said, pondering her words. "Now I'm curious about how that will play out. There must be some reason."

"It is amazing how God can plant ideas in someone's head and we never know why, maybe for months or years. But he always has a reason. Maybe preparing the way or clearing a path for some of his plans to be fulfilled. We may never find out."

"Or we might! And then we'll say, 'Ahh, that explains everything!' It's great when that happens."

"Remember last year, when Dana and I took the trailer to Joyce's to get Jenny's pony?" Becky waited to see Coop nod. "I remember hearing God clearly whispering to me, saying that Dana should drive home. We never did find out why, or what might have happened if I had been driving, or why it was important for Dana to be driving. Who knows? But the point is, God knows. I listened. And for whatever reason, we got home fine."

"You're right. The important thing is, you were listening and you obeyed. God blessed your obedience. We just might not understand how. But we don't need to. If we're holding on to his hand, listening as he guides us, we know we can trust him."

"So I guess I'll keep praying about Dana and water, even though I'm not sure why!"

"I've been praying about Dana, too. But I've been focusing on safety. Maybe she needs to be safe around moving water. You know, maybe God is speaking to both of us in different ways about the same thing. But I'm also praying about her relationship with Tucker. It seems to be getting pretty serious." Coop looked down at the dash and said, "We're getting a little low on gas. Let's fill up at that truck stop where we ate supper last time. Maybe we can get a snack for the rest of the trip home. And I'll call Mom and tell her what time to expect us."

"And tell her we're bringing supper," Becky added. "If not, I know she'll get busy making something for us. She always wants to be helping. No wonder Dana knows how to jump in where needed. She's your mother's clone!"

Snacking on a package of mixed nuts as they made the final leg of their journey home, the conversation turned to their new friends, the Barkdales. "The ladies study on Proverbs 31 starts next week," Becky said. "I am glad Tabitha will be joining us. It's going to be a great study."

"I know Nancy is leading the class, but I think you are a perfect example of the Proverbs 31 woman." Coop glanced at his wife. "You are worth more than rubies to me, that's for sure."

"Awww, that's sweet!" Becky cooed. She tipped some more nuts into his outstretched hand. "I'm trying to live up to the model given us. Not easy to be perfect, but I'm trying!"

"Well, you're perfect in my mind, anyway." He started to lick the salt from his fingers but Becky grabbed his hand and pulled it to her lips.

"Here, let me help." She began to slowly remove the salt with her tongue. "Always want to help my husband," she said with a twinkle in her eye. "Doing whatever I can to make his life easier."

Coop gave a little moan and pulled his hand away. "You better stop, or I'm going to have to pull this truck over and thank you properly!"

"Oh goodness no, that's not necessary. I want to get home and see my babies. No time for playing around!" Becky sat back with a laugh.

"Can't think of anyone I'd rather play around with!" Coop chuckled. "But I want to get home, too. Getting away has been good, but I do miss those kiddos."

"I'll remind you of that when Nicholas is hungry at two in the morning!"

They rode on in silence for several miles crunching cashews and pecans to pass the time. Suddenly Becky said, "I wonder what the story is with Tom."

"What do you mean?"

"Oh, I don't know. But there's just something up with him. Tabitha has suggested that he isn't a believer. He doesn't even want to hear about God or church activities or even just coming to church on Sundays. I have the feeling there's been some kind of tragedy or drama or something. But she hasn't talked about it."

"Maybe she will open up more, when she gets comfortable in your women's group."

"I hope so. She seems really sad and maybe conflicted when she talks about Tom. There's something deep going on."

"Here comes the Proverbs woman again – kind and compassionate to those in need. And it sounds like Tabitha is in need of a friend like you, to lead her to a relationship with Jesus. Greg and I will work on Tom from our side. You'll see. Soon the whole Barkdale family will be convinced of God's love for them, and give their hearts to Jesus."

"I pray you are right. What a celebration we'll have!"

"Thank you, Father, for the gift of your son," Coop prayed aloud. "Thank you for loving Tom and Tabitha, even if they don't know it yet. And thank you for working in their lives even now, preparing their hearts to accept that gift for themselves."

"Amen," said Becky softly. "Amen."

Chapter 12

HE HEARS YOUR HEART

Jenny was looking out the front window, waiting for her parent's arrival, when Coop pulled the truck into the Martin's driveway. Two other little brown heads flocked either side of Jenny and all three girls began to wave frantically. Jenny was first to the door and flew to her mother with a welcoming hug.

Nancy came from the kitchen, drying her hands on a sunny yellow towel. Little Andy followed behind, carrying a metal mixing bowl filled with kitchen gadgets. He dumped them out on the living room floor and sat down with a plop. One by one he threw items back into the bowl, each one landing with a metallic 'ping.'

"So glad you made it home safely," Nancy said as she moved away from the noises made by her son. She gave Becky a hug and asked, "Did you have a nice time?"

"Very," said Becky. But she added, "I really missed my kids though." She turned to Jenny and her friends. "I bet you girls had fun! What have you been up to?"

Jenny answered first, but each girl had something to add. "We're The Brownies! That's our club name! Cuz all of us have brown hair."

"And we played in the snow and ate snacks, but not brownies. And then we made puzzles and did gymnastics in the basement and we told ghost stories at night but not too scary. Kendy didn't sleep over that time, so she didn't hear the stories. But next time we are all going to have spooky story time." Hannah had a lot to say.

Kendy, always a bit shy, stood quietly by, smiling. "I had fun in the snow. And Hannah gave me her old boots."

"Well, it's nice to see you girls all playing so well. Sounds like you all had fun. Jenny, please go gather your things, so we can head for home."

All three girls took off for Hannah's bedroom to help with the packing.

"It's nice to see Kendy here," Becky said to Nancy. "Has she been over a lot? That must have been a houseful."

"Yes, she was here the other day when we had a little snow to play in. But Tabitha is out on a job interview this afternoon, so I offered to keep Kendy until she gets back. Those three girls are like peas in a pod. Never stopped giggling!"

Andy flipped his mixing bowl over and began banging on it with a whisk. Nancy looked down at him and laughed. "Sometimes the noise got a little out of control, but we managed!"

They moved into the kitchen. "Want some coffee?" Nancy asked.

"Um, no thanks. Honestly, I just want to get home. We picked up supper from the diner, and Marla Jean is waiting for us. And I want to cuddle Nicholas and nurse him and tell him how much I missed him."

Jenny came from the bedroom, carrying her little suitcase. Hannah was carrying her cat Marmalade and Kendy carried a picture she had drawn for Jenny. Nancy got Jenny's coat from the closet and helped her into it. "Thanks for being such a good girl, Jenny. We all enjoyed having you here."

Jenny threw her arms around Nancy's neck and whispered, "Thank you for taking care of me. I love you!"

Becky smiled, enjoying the connection her daughter had with Nancy. "Yes, thank you, Nancy. I never worried one bit about Jenny. I knew she was having fun. And I knew you'd watch over her just like I would. You're the best!"

"Any time. I mean that. We love having Jenny here. Now get home to your little one! I'll call you in a day or two to update you on some things about the class."

Little girl hugs led to more giggling, but soon the Smith family was settled in the truck, ready to head towards home. A car was waiting while Coop backed the truck out of the driveway, and Becky waved to the driver as they passed. "That's Tabitha, coming to pick up Kendy. She had a job interview today. I hope it went well."

"I helped Kendy pray for a job for her mommy. All The Brownies prayed about it. In our fort we made in the basement." Jenny was still animated. "We took all these blankets and we built the biggest fort ever, in the whole basement. And we had a pretend cookout and made pretend s'mores, but it was really just ice cream sandwiches, but we pretended it was s'mores and we ate in the fort. But we prayed before we ate them, and that's when we prayed about the job for her mommy. Kendy doesn't pray out loud yet, but I told her God can hear her heart."

Becky was sure God could hear her own heart singing with joy.

Chapter 13

THE PROVERBS 31 WOMAN

Nine ladies gathered every Wednesday in a church classroom. Long white tables formed a square in the center of the room. Bibles and reference books were scattered across the tables, along with water bottles, coffee mugs and usually snacks of some sort. It was a good time of relaxation for everyone. Most of the women had young children and were happy for some adult companionship. A couple of the women were older, retired and overflowing with compassion for the young moms. They'd been there, done that, survived and had a lifetime of advice to share.

Tabitha had been hesitant to talk much at first. She had been intimidated by the women, thinking that she didn't really fit in or belong in a group like this. A Bible study group was all new to her. She felt like there was a lot to learn, and surely she had nothing to share yet. No wisdom, that's for sure. But she did have a lot of questions and as she felt more comfortable with these ladies, she began to open up.

Intimidation was a common feeling for Tabitha. She looked around the room and saw ladies who all seemed so confident and put together. Well dressed, perfect hair, an air of success, these were all attributes Tabitha felt far from. But as Tabitha settled in, she began to feel included and even welcomed. She liked Nancy a lot, even though their lifestyles were so vastly different. Tabitha remembered the feeling of awe she had experienced when she first drove up to Nancy and Greg's house. It was practically a mansion, compared to her shabby little apartment. Yet Nancy didn't let that stand in the way of their friendship. She had included Tabitha in so many things with the church, and they were becoming good friends. So maybe income and lifestyle didn't really matter.

The study of Proverbs 31 was leading to some spirited conversation. Nancy had explained that the purpose of their class was to bring each woman into a closer and more exciting walk with God. She said that the goal was to help them become women who desired to honor God with their words and actions. That sounded logical to Tabitha; she just didn't know how it was going to work, or what she'd have to do to be that type of woman. It did seem like a good person to be, with or without Jesus being her 'savior' whatever that was supposed to mean.

To Tabitha, being a good person was all that was necessary. This 'turn your life over to God' talk she'd been hearing at church, well, she thought that was just a bunch of cultish brainwashing. Even the idea of sin and hell was a little far fetched. She didn't consider herself a bad person. She felt that she did mostly good things, surely lots more good than bad. But this study of the woman in Proverbs was showing Tabitha ways she could be even better.

Tabitha was becoming more confident about her relationships with all of the women in the group and felt camaraderie with them on many levels. That all changed when the discussion centered on verse 18. When the other women began talking about how they balanced their home life and their business life, Tabitha grew silent and withdrawn.

Among the other women in the group, some were nurses, some had been teachers, one was a tax preparer and two owned and operated small businesses in Atkins. Nancy was doing part time work as an editor from a small office in her home. And although Becky did not work outside the home, she did talk about her plans to expand her vegetable garden and sell some of her produce at the Farmer's Market. Everyone seemed to have made an impact on their family finances. Except Tabitha. After nearly nine months in their new home and despite dozens of applications and interviews, Tabitha had yet to be offered a job.

Jenny noticed Tabitha's solemn demeanor and asked, "What are your thoughts, Tabitha? How has this verse been true in your life?"

"That's just it!" she exclaimed. "I mean, I've tried and tried to get a job here. I want to help with my family's finances. And I'm not lazy; I really do want to work. But so far, nothing. I feel like a big failure. Like I've let Tom down. Like we're soon going to be so far behind we will never pull ourselves out. I just don't understand why it's been so hard to get a job. I've never had this problem before." There was a quiver in her voice and she bit her lip to stop talking before the tears took over.

Harriet, one of the older women, said, "You know, there's other ways to help with family finances besides having a paid job. Like we've talked about in other sessions, money management, cutting back on inessentials, budgeting, saving, reusing….these are other things you can do. It doesn't have to mean just a nine-to-five job."

"I know, Harriet, and I do all that. I shop with coupons and watch the sales. We eat leftovers and don't throw anything away. Kendy wore boots that were too small, because we couldn't afford new ones." She looked over at Nancy and added, "Thanks to Nancy and Hannah, we worked out a trade. But without that help, Kendy would still be squishing her feet into those little boots from last year."

She lowered her head to hide the embarrassment. "I just don't understand why I haven't been hired. By somebody. Anybody. I've applied at all the doctor's offices and clinics and hospitals. I know I'm only an LPN, not a full Registered Nurse. But you'd think somebody would be willing to give me a job. By this point, I'd take pretty much anything."

"I think it's time we should earnestly seek the Lord's help with this," said Nancy. "Let's go to prayer. Tabitha, would you come sit here? We'll all gather around you and lay our hands on you while we pray."

The ladies began to pray and oh what a time it was! Praying led to singing, singing led to tears, tears lead to an outpouring of the Holy Spirit. As the women came seeking and knocking, Jesus opened the door and ushered in peace and contentment.

Harriet prayed that Tabitha be presented with a perfect opportunity to use her skills and talents. Vicky prayed that the employer be impressed to give Tabitha's resume a closer look. Ellen praised God for having a plan, and thanked him for working it all out. Andrea asked the Lord to move in powerful ways, to clear a path as Tabitha sought employment, to move obstacles that might be in her way. Rose put a petition before the Lord, asking that he speak to the right people so that the perfect job would become available. Becky prayed for patience as Tabitha waited for him to show her the direction to go. Nancy closed the prayer with these words:

"Father, we thank you that you are all-knowing. Thank you for orchestrating all things. We ask you to honor our prayers for a job for Tabitha. Lead and guide her to just the place she needs to be. Let us recognize your goodness and mercy in the fulfillment of today's heartfelt petitions. In your mighty working name, Amen."

This was followed by a murmured chorus of Amens from their closely connected group. Harriet gave Tabitha a reassuring hug and whispered, "God's going to bless you through this. I just know it. You'll see."

Tabitha sighed and looked up at her, smiling. These women seemed so sure of God and prayer and trusting Jesus. Maybe there was something to it, after all. At least it was worth considering.

Chapter 14

HANDPRINTS

Coop came across the driveway, banging his hands against the legs of his jeans. He was trying to dispel most of the dust before he got into the house. Spring plowing was a dusty, dirty job. But he was almost done and would soon be planting. This was his favorite time of the year. Planting brought along with it hope. Hope for a good crop. Hope for a harvest that would sustain them financially.

He stood with his hands on his hips and took a deep breath. Coop loved the smell of spring. Fresh air filled his lungs. A hint of blooming flowers left a faint fragrance in the air. A light breeze ruffled the ends of his hair, reminding him that he needed a haircut. He'd see if his mom had some free time tomorrow afternoon.

Before he went inside, Coop let his gaze fall over the wide expanse of his farmland. Fields and pastures, ponds and hills, the cattle, the sheep, the chickens. And the land – oh he was blessed to be steward of all this. He hoped his dad would be proud of the work he had done. Coop had tried so hard to keep things running like his dad would want.

Every morning, Coop prayed as he walked to his early chores. Today's prayer had been memorized and repeated many times. "A new day has dawned, God's gift to us. The fruits of the land are ours to enjoy. We thank you Lord, and ask that you help us become good stewards of the day. May all that we do and say and think and imagine be pleasing to you, oh Savior. With upright hearts, we praise you. Amen."

Coop had been working in the fields ever since he was strong enough to load hay bales. He started driving the tractor before he drove a car. The rhythm of farm life had become second nature to him. Working with his dad had brought them close together and taught him how to make farming a sustaining enterprise. Not that they were making a lot of money at it, but their needs were met and their family was thriving.

Coop was blessed with scholarships that helped pay for his years in college. He had planned to attend Seminary and become a pastor. But when his father was diagnosed with cancer, Coop had to leave college in his senior year and help with the farm work. Thoughts of Seminary and church leadership were put on hold. Coop didn't come back to the farm begrudgingly. He came because he loved his dad and mom. He wanted to help. Very quickly he learned that he actually enjoyed farm life. And he believed that God wanted him here, continuing with the farm after his dad passed away.

Yes, it was hard, dirty work. But the rewards were many. Watching the corn seedlings pop out of the freshly turned soil always gave him a feeling of pride and accomplishment. He loved the anticipation, yes, the hope, that growing things brought. Gazing out at row upon row of corn and soybeans and knowing that farmers feed the world gave him a real sense of pride. The golden wheat moving freely in the breeze was a sight of beauty. No wonder the songwriter wrote about 'amber waves of grain.' It really did look like ocean waves.

Coop did like knowing that he and God were working together to provide for his immediate family as well as the community of consumers who would benefit from his efforts and the Lord's provision.

A verse from Psalms popped into Coop's mind. 'The Lord will indeed give what is good and our land will yield its harvest.' "Thank you Lord," Coop said as he pulled open the screen door to the porch. "Thank you for the harvest that is to come."

As he took his boots off, Coop thought of another type of harvest. The harvest of souls. He thought of the members of his family who would be one day gathered together in heaven. His parents, sister Dana and brother Michael, with his wife Stacy. Becky and Jenny and hopefully Nicholas. All of Becky's family. Dana's boyfriend Tucker. The circle kept expanding. Coop thought of a pebble tossed into a lake – the ripples came out from the center, widening and spreading until they finally reached the shore.

A New Testament verse came to mind. 'The harvest is plentiful but the laborers are few.' That verse led Coop's thoughts to his sister and her upcoming trip to Nicaragua. She and Tucker were so excited about this mission trip. Coop had been praying for the relationships they would be building there – relations with the people of Nicaragua primarily. Talk about a harvest that was plentiful! The reports from the Nicaraguan villages told of hearts eager for the gospel. Dana and Tucker talked about the physical work they we going to be doing, but mostly they were excited about the relationships they would form with the people. The thought was, in order to best spread the gospel, you first have to have a relationship with the people. A friendship and trust, a willingness to share and teach and listen to each other. This is where Dana would excel. She was a people person.

He chuckled as he remembered that Dana had not always been open and accepting of others, especially others that she considered unworthy. He thought back a few years, when Dana had warned him not to get involved with the waitress at the diner, because she was ungodly and would bring him nothing but trouble. How things had changed!

True, that waitress did cause a lot of drama for Coop and his family. But in the end, what some had intended for bad had turned out for good. Misty had eventually received Christ as her Savior and turned her life around completely. She had changed her name to Melissa and was now testifying to the goodness of God every chance she got. She faithfully attended Bible study and was bringing new people into the church. She served on community outreach committees and participated in service opportunities.

Even Dana had acknowledged the big change in the woman. They were in the same young adult Sunday school class and Dana had occasionally commented about the spiritual growth she was witnessing. Coop thought back to the early days of his relationship with Misty/Melissa. Although he had tried to witness to her, she had turned away from his message. Yet God had reminded Coop that his job was to plant the seeds and Jesus would take it from there. And apparently that's exactly what had happened.

Once again Coop had to thank God for the goodness of his plan!

He heard singing and laughter from inside the house and stood smiling a moment before entering. His family was another source of joy and proof of God's good plan. Becky and Jenny were in the kitchen, singing a made up song about the goodness of God. How coincidental!

Becky started, "God is good to me, God is good to me, God is good to me because…" and Jenny filled in the rest of the line. "He made my pony Benny!" Jenny stood in front of Nicholas, who was sitting in his high chair. She made a horsey noise, "Neigh, neigh, neigh," and Nicholas burst into laughter. As soon as his laughing settled down a bit, Jenny said, "Neigh!" again and the laughter started all over.

Moments like this made Coop's heart swell. He walked over to Becky and put his arms around her. "I love our family," he said, "and I love you!" He kissed her warmly and she responded, then playfully pushed him away.

"I love you too," she said, "but I will love you even more when you get cleaned up! You smell like dirt and tractor fuel!"

"Ahh, the life of a farmer's wife! Always insisting her husband wash up for supper!" He kissed her forehead and laughed, "Complain, complain, complain! Supper smells good; what is it?" He lifted the lid of the crock pot and inhaled. "Man, I didn't know I was so hungry."

"Put that down!" Becky insisted. "Get out of here until you're clean!" She swatted him with a dish towel and he quickly returned the lid and headed to the bathroom. He stopped to tousle Nicholas's hair, and then thought better of it. Better not share his dirt with the baby!

"Hi, Jenny. I liked your song," he said on passing. "Let's make some more verses when I get clean."

"Okay, but hurry up. I have a good one for next."

"Yes, Ma'am!" Coop laughed while giving Jenny a salute. He turned sharply and marched down the hall, Jenny laughing as he went.

Sitting at the table, holding clean hands, the family prepared for prayer. Jenny stopped them by asking, "Can we do a song prayer?"

"What do you mean, a song prayer?" Coop inquired. "Explain it please."

"It's the song Mommy and I were singing. It can be a prayer, can't it?"

Becky nodded and said, "It sure could be. The words of the song could be a prayer. That's a good idea. We could do it."

Jenny added, "And everybody can add a verse. I want to be last."

Becky began by singing "God is good to me because… He made my family."

On Coop's turn, he sang "God is good to me because…. He makes the fields grow."

Then it was Jenny's turn and she sang, "God is good to me because…..He carved me in his hand." Then she added "Amen!"

"That's a good one," Coop said. "How did you think of that one?"

Becky was serving steaming hot beef stew in bowls but was intently listening.

"Grandma told me it," she said. "When I was sleeping at her house when Mommy was in the hospital."

"Really?" questioned Becky. She set a bowl of stew in front of Jenny and said "Be careful, Honey, it's pretty hot." Then she went on, "That was almost two years ago. You remember that?"

"I do. I remember because I dreamed about it. And when I woke up I told Grandma the dream I had, and she explained it."

"Do you remember the dream?" Coop asked and he looked over at Becky. This was quite a revelation.

"It was a dream about a picture. On the wall. There were lots of handprints. Big ones and little ones, and all colors too. The whole wall was covered. And when I got real close to the hands, I could see faces. Every hand had a face in it. It seemed funny. But when I told Grandma she told me about the verse."

"Oh, maybe you mean the verse from Isaiah where God says that he has engraved you on the palms of his hands." Coop was grateful that Elizabeth had helped Jenny to understand and remember that important verse.

Jenny blew on her stew before taking the first bite. "That's it. Grandma said engraved means like carved."

"You really do have a good memory, Jenny. God has blessed you with a good mind. I'm so happy you are remembering all these good lessons." Becky tasted a spoonful of stew and reached for the salt shaker. "Daddy and I pray for you every night, that you will use your gifts in ways that always please God. You're doing a good job of it so far!"

Jenny smiled sheepishly and said "Thanks," then got down to the business of eating.

Coop buttered a slice of bread and changed the subject somewhat. "Speaking of gifts, God sure gave me good weather for the plowing. I can't remember a week of plowing that was more perfect than this. Tomorrow I start the planting. And I hear there is rain in the forecast for next week, so that will be perfect too."

The conversation continued through the meal and soon every bowl was empty and stomachs were full. Nicholas's face and hands were washed and he was put on the floor to play. Jenny went off to her room; she said she wanted to draw pictures at her desk.

Becky and Coop went about clearing the table and rinsing dishes. As Becky loaded the dishwasher, she said to Coop, "Mom needs to get an appointment with the eye doctor. Last time she was in, he said the cataracts were nearly ripe enough to do surgery. I'll call and set up the appointment. The surgery will be two appointments actually, a couple of weeks apart."

"I remember when Dad had his done. It seems like a pretty simple procedure. Just in and out surgery."

"I know," Becky said with a shudder. "But just the thought of somebody digging around in my eye – yuck! I think I'll ask Mom to stay here a couple of days while she recovers."

"Good idea. She might need your help. There's eye drops to do, as I remember."

"Right. And I just don't think she should be alone, especially when she's wearing a patch and doing drops. I'd just feel better if she were with us."

In Jenny's bedroom later that night, Becky sat braiding her daughter's hair. It was still damp from her shower, and was easy to gather into a braid. Coop had just finished reading the

Bible story for the night and Jenny asked, "Want to see my picture now? It's on my desk."

"Sure," Coop said and picked up the picture she had drawn with magic markers. He showed it to Becky as she put a hair tie on the end of Jenny's braid.

"See, it's God's hand. It's real big. Real real big. Because he's got the world in his hand." In the center of the hand, Jenny had drawn a circle and made an attempt to put in land and oceans. "I can't make the countries so good, but it's the earth. Like my globe." She pointed to the globe sitting on top of her bookcase. She had gotten it from Grandma for Christmas last year.

After prayers, Jenny started their nightly routine. They called it 'Best Part.' Every night they would all say what had been the best part of their day. This ritual had been going on ever since Jenny could talk, when it was just Jenny and her mom. Now Coop was included.

"My best part is the dream about the hands. I'm carved in God's hand." Jenny looked at her own hand and then kissed it.

"Well, I think that's my best part too. Remembering that God has me in the palm of his hand. And he has you too!" Becky bent over and kissed Jenny's hand.

"I make that three votes. Palm of his hand for me too." He planted a kiss in Jenny's hand too. "Goodnight sweet girl. I love you."

"Love you too," said a sleepy Jenny. "And Mommy I love you too."

Coop and Becky left the room hand in hand, singing softly, "He's got the whole world in his hands."

Chapter 15

WAR IS WAGED

Coop and Greg had invited Tom to men's group several times but he had not yet agreed to attend. They decided to take a different approach. Having discovered that Tom liked fishing, Coop suggested they all get out to the lake for a day on the water.

"Come on, it'll be great!" Coop insisted. "Greg has a boat, we've got extra gear. I haven't been out to the lake for years. Usually I just fish my little pond, but lake fishing is so much better. Let's do this. When are you free? Greg and I can go just about any time."

Greg added, "I'll even let you drive the boat. It'll be fun!"

"It does sound like fun. I haven't been fishing since I was a kid." Tom pulled out his phone and checked his work schedule. "My next day off is Friday. Would that work?"

"I'll make it work," Greg said. "I can pretty much set my own schedule at the office, so I'll just make sure to clear everything off Friday"

"And since all the planting is done, there's not so much for me to do at the farm. Just watching things sprout and grow. And praying for rain. It's been a dry spring. But I'll plan on Thursday. If we are fortunate enough to get rain, we'll reschedule." Coop asked Greg, "How early do you want to get started?"

"I'd like to say sunrise, but maybe we should wait till the girls are off to school. That way our wives won't feel quite so deserted." Greg laughed and added, "Don't know how many fish we'll catch, but that might not be the point anyway! Just getting out on the water, having some guy time, that'll be great!"

"How about I pick you up around nine?" Coop asked Tom.

"Sounds good. And if we don't catch anything, that's fine with me. I'm not a fan of cleaning and eating my own fish. Had a terrible experience as a kid with fish bones. It's made me leery about ever eating fish again.

"No problem," Coop said. "We usually just throw them back anyway. Once in a while Greg takes one or two home with him. Becky isn't a fan of fish either, so she's happiest if I don't bring any home. But she knows it's important to get out and get my mind off of farm work for a few hours. We all need a break now and then, I think."

The plans being made, Coop and Greg spent the next few days in prayer. Tom went about his normal work week, unaware that heavenly warfare was being waged on his behalf.

Chapter 16

GOD MOVES IN MYSTERIOUS WAYS

Harriet was trying to remain calm, but she was excited. She paced around the table in their Bible study classroom, glancing every few seconds towards the door. She had been all a-twitter when she arrived, practically busting at the seams to share her news with the ladies. But she insisted on waiting for Tabitha, and wouldn't say anything to the others until Tabitha was there too.

Finally Tabitha came into the room, and Harriet hurried across to meet her. "Oh, Tabitha, Honey, I have some wonderful news for you. Just wait till you hear how God has been working things out!"

"What are you talking about?" Tabitha asked. The other women gathered around, eager to hear what Harriet was so excited about.

"You might not know this, but my husband is on the Winslow school board. And they had a meeting last week. One of the things on the agenda for the meeting was about filling a position at the elementary school. It seems that the school nurse has turned in her resignation! Her husband got a job transfer and a big promotion and suddenly they have to move out of state. So, they are looking for a nurse to fill the position for the rest of the school year. I told him about you, and he said you should fill out an application online. Isn't that great? Just last week we prayed over you and already God has answered our prayers!"

Amidst praises of "Amen!" and "Thank you God!" Tabitha raised her voice.

"That's nice, but does he know I'm not an RN? They might want a degreed person, and I only have my LPN."

"Funny you should mention that!" laughed Harriet. "I told him about that, and he said to just finish the semester, they would be happy to have anyone who was even half-way qualified. So this sounds perfect for you, don't you think? You can fill out the application tomorrow and get right on it."

"Well, then, I will! And thank you for telling me about the opening. We'll see what happens."

"But wait, there's more!" Harriet was bubbling now. "Harrold said there might be a chance you could get continuing education hours and work towards your nursing degree and the school board will help pay for it!"

"That sounds wonderful!" Nancy joined in. "We'll start our class tonight with a prayer of praise and thanksgiving for Tabitha's new job and her new degree!"

"Well, wait. That's a little premature, don't you think?" Tabitha pulled back from the crowd gathered around her. "Nothing says I'm going to actually be offered the job. Let's not jump the gun. I'm grateful for the opportunity, of course, and thanks for putting in a good word for me, Harriet. But it's a little too early to celebrate."

Becky put her arm around Tabitha's shoulders and pulled her close in a hug. "Okay, for now we will praise God for this possible job. We'll thank him for opening the way for you. And we'll trust him to care for you, whatever happens."

"And next week, after your interview and getting the offer and signing the contract, then we'll celebrate!" Harriet announced with confidence.

The ladies took their seats and bowed for prayer. Nancy said "Thank you, oh Father, for watching over your children. Thank you for preparing Tabitha for this new opportunity. Thank you for the job opening that makes this possible. We know you will be with Tabitha through the application and interview process. Thank you for the way you have planned this and worked it all out. Thank you for hope and mercy and guidance. As we study your word tonight Lord, open our eyes and ears and hearts to learn more about you. We want to become Proverbs women. We are listening closely, learning about your plans for our lives. We all want to be women who are worth more than rubies. And you have shown us the way. Teach us now to walk in your ways. Oh God, you are so good. You are a good, good Father. Amen."

Before the class got underway, Becky had a thought she wanted to share. "You know, Nancy, your prayer made me think about something. The school nurse is moving away right? And moving in the middle of the school year. I doubt that was something they planned. So isn't it neat that her husband was told about the transfer, just when we were praying that a job would open up for Tabitha. It's like it was God's plan all along. He worked out the husband's job offer, transfer and relocation. It was all set in motion long before we prayed about it. Like so many other times, he knows what we need, even before we ask. Sometimes even before we know ourselves! Like Romans says, 'He works all things out for our good.' That's just so amazing to think about!"

The ladies nodded and smiled in agreement. Tabitha sat back in her chair, marveling at the faith and insights that these women were sharing with her. A sense of calm and peace settled over her. For the first time, she considered the possibility that there was a God who was in control, who had a plan, and who was working all things out for her good. For the first time, she breathed a prayer of "Thank you, God," and meant it.

Chapter 17

A LITTLE TENSION

Becky was working in the garden, chopping at some stubborn weeds with her hoe. The ground was hard because they needed rain. It was strenuous work and her shoulders and back were already aching. She stood up and leaned on the hoe, taking a little break. The sun was climbing and it would be time for lunch soon. She really hoped to get this weeding done before lunch, but it didn't seem likely.

Dana sat on a blanket nearby, shaded by the side of the house. She was reading to Nicholas and singing to him. 'God bless you, Dana,' Becky thought. 'You don't know how much I appreciate your help with the baby.'

Holly the collie came around the corner of the house and went to lie down beside the blanket. She had become very protective of the baby and could often be found nearby. Dana reached over to give Holly a pat.

Becky heard the four-wheeler out in the driveway and knew that Coop had come in for lunch. She looked at the weeds still to be pulled and sighed. 'Never ending chores,' she mumbled to herself. 'Well, maybe after lunch, while the baby naps.' She rolled her shoulders to relieve the tension in her upper back. 'Wish I could get a nap.'

She heard the screen door on the front porch slam and closed her eyes, shaking her head. "He has never learned how to shut that door properly," she complained to Dana. "Well, let's go in and get some lunch. Would you mind carrying Nicholas in? I'm all dirty and sweaty."

"Sure, no problem," Dana said with a smile. "You should just give up hoping he'll stop slamming screen doors. Mom tried to teach him, but he just can't get it into his head." She laughed but was surprised to see a scowl on Becky's face. She picked up the baby and his books and threw the blanket over her free arm.

"Well, it's ridiculous, if you ask me. How hard is it to close a door properly?" She walked with a huff towards the house. Dana followed, still pondering where Becky's attitude had come from.

Coop's boots, covered with dust, were on the floor of the porch. His hat, also dirty, perched on the hook by the door. When Dana walked past, Nicholas reached for the hat, which sent it falling to the floor in a cloud of dust. Becky picked it up, put it back on the hook, and sighed deeply. Another chore to do, sweeping the porch floor. Almost pointless, with all the dirt he brought in with him.

Dana put Nicholas down on his activity mat and said, "I'm headed off to school in a bit. I'll grab a granola bar on my way. See you all later."

"Thanks for your help, Dana. Have a good afternoon."

Coop came into the kitchen, smelling like soap. His hair was wet from a quick washing and he had put on a clean shirt.

He looked at Becky and teased her, "You're a hot mess! What have you been doing this morning? Rolling in the dirt?"

"I've been working in the garden, trying to get rid of the weeds that are trying to take over. Thanks for your help, by the way. I thought you said you'd get the tiller out and go between the rows this morning."

"Oh, I didn't forget. I just needed to go out and check on the cows first thing. I'll get to it." He sat down at the table and asked, "What's for lunch?"

Exasperated, Becky said, "Well, gee, I don't know. But I'm sure I'll find something for you. I would like to wash up first myself."

Coop looked at her and noticed the tension. "Sure, you go clean up. I'm in no hurry."

As Becky walked to the bathroom, she bristled, 'Would be nice if he offered to fix lunch for us, instead of just expecting me to do it.' She splashed water on her face, soaped up her arms and neck, rinsed and dried off. She stood in front of the mirror and looked at herself. 'What has gotten into you?' she asked her reflection. She picked up her hairbrush and forcefully brushed out her wind-tangled hair. 'Snap out of it. Lord help me, this attitude is not pleasing to anyone.'

Walking through the bedroom, Becky realized that she hadn't made the bed yet. Then she remembered how tired she had been that morning. The night had been interrupted several times by Nicholas, who couldn't seem to get to sleep, despite nursing and rocking. 'No wonder I'm snapping about things,' she thought. 'I'm tired. Really tired. Maybe I just need to forget the garden and take a nap while Nicholas sleeps.'

Nicholas was getting fussy on the floor, but Coop was on the phone and didn't seem to notice. Becky bent over and picked the baby up, cooing to him as she walked to his bouncy seat. "Can you just play here for a few minutes, Sweetie? Mommy has to fix lunch. They you can have your milk and take a nap.' She gave him a rattle and turned to fix lunch.

Coop was finishing his conversation. "Great, I'll see you about nine then."

"We can have ham and cheese sandwiches, okay?" Becky asked.

"Sure, that's good. Can you grill them? I love the cheese melted."

Becky signed and turned to the stove. She got out a skillet but banged it down on the burner a little harder than she intended. Coop looked up but didn't say anything.

"Who were you talking to? And what are you doing at nine o'clock?

"It was Tom. I'm picking him up at nine to go fishing with Greg."

"That's tomorrow? I knew you were going, but you never told me what day."

"I didn't? Well, yes, it's tomorrow. It'll be good to get out on the water, a whole day of peace and relaxation. Can't wait."

"I'll bet!" Becky said, trying to hide the sarcasm but not succeeding. Coop finally caught the bite in her words.

"What's up, Becky? You sound upset."

"I do, huh? Well I wonder why?"

"Okay," he answered hesitantly. "I wonder why too. What's bothering you today? You're not acting yourself."

"I guess you forgot that I'm going with Mom to her eye doctor's appointment tomorrow. She wants me to be with her because she'll have her eyes dilated and she doesn't want to drive home herself. And she wants me there because the doctor is probably going to talk about her cataracts and she thinks I should hear what he has to say, or she'll probably forget. So I need you to be home with Nicholas. But apparently a peaceful day on the lake is more important than my mother." She was busy buttering slices of bread and didn't look up while she talked.

She felt rather than saw Coop get up and come stand behind her. He put his hands on her shoulders and said, "Becky, look at me." Reluctantly, Becky put the bread down on the counter and turned to face him.

"Becky, of course your mother is more important than my day at the lake. But I will admit, I did forget about her appointment. I'm sorry about that. I made these plans with Tom and Greg and didn't check with you first. That's my mistake."

"I don't suppose you'll be home by eleven-thirty, will you?" she asked.

"No, I know we won't be home that early. We're not leaving till nine, as it is. What about mom? Have you asked her to watch the baby?

"No, I didn't ask her because I figured you could do it, since most of the field work has been done for now. I guess we didn't communicate very well." Becky turned back to the stove and put the bread on the skillet, then added cheese and ham.

"I guess you're right. We need to do better at talking things out. We used to be real good at that. I wonder what happened, to make us miscommunicate. I don't like to see you upset like this."

"Well, for one thing, I'm tired. I haven't slept well in ages, and it's just getting to me, I guess. And sometimes I feel overwhelmed with all the work I have to do. I know you work a lot too, and I really shouldn't complain. But I do get tired. And the idea of a day relaxing on the lake, well, it sounds nice, but really foreign to me right now. I can hardly get a nap in once in awhile, much less a whole day to myself."

"Then we're just going to have to be sure you get more time to yourself. And I'm going to do a better job at communicating with you, so we don't let stuff like this build up again. And after lunch, you are taking a nice long nap."

"You mean, after I clean up the lunch dishes, change the baby, feed him and put him to bed. I feel exhausted just thinking of everything I have to do before I can take a nap."

"I can do all of that, you know. I can even give Nicholas a bottle so you have more nap time. And I'll call mom, to see if she can baby-sit for a few hours tomorrow."

Becky was hesitant, but gave in to his arguments. "Okay, I appreciate that. I really do need a good long nap."

"And I appreciate you!" Coop kissed her on the cheek. "And I promise to do better with making plans and remembering appointments."

"Thank you, Coop. I'm sorry I was such a grouch. I could have found better ways of expressing myself, I guess."

"I really think it's because you are so tired," Coop replied. "Lack of sleep can change a person. It clouds everything. So here's what I want you to do. Eat lunch and go right to bed.

I'll do everything else. And you just sleep, as long as you can. As long as it takes for you to feel refreshed and yourself again."

"Don't tempt me," she joked. "I might sleep for twenty-four hours!"

"Better not do that!" Coop laughed. "Then you would miss your mother's appointment!"

"Well, I don't want to do that!" She gave Coop a hug and quick kiss. "Let's eat. I'm hungry and tired!"

****

It was the best afternoon nap Becky had had since Nicholas was born. She woke when she heard Holly barking and Jenny coming home from school. When Becky walked into the kitchen, she found Nicholas playing happily on the floor, Jenny having a snack at the table, and Coop peeling potatoes for supper.

Chapter 18

FISHERS OF MEN

Friday dawned with a glorious sunrise, a light breeze and not a drop of rain in sight. As soon as Jenny was on the school bus, Coop kissed Becky and Nicholas goodbye, tossed his fishing gear into the truck and drove over to Tom's apartment. Tom was waiting at the front steps of the building. He stood, picked up a cooler and waved at Coop.

Coop slowed the truck and waited for Tom to jump in. "Good morning! What's in the cooler?"

"I brought us some sodas and water. Thought we might need it, once the sun gets hot."

"Good plan. I brought some granola bars and apples. Greg will bring the bait. Ready for a good day?"

"For sure!" Tom laughed. "Tabitha is sure in a good mood. She's going on a job interview today!"

"Is that right? Where?" Coop asked, but he was already pretty sure he knew.

"She came home from that ladies group Wednesday night, got right on the computer and filled out an application for a school nurse job, and they called her already this morning.

I guess the job just opened up, and they are in a hurry to fill it. She has an interview at one."

"That's terrific! I know Becky and I have been praying about a job for her. Actually, Jenny has too. God's at work."

"Well, I don't know for sure about that. But I do know that she's been looking for a job ever since we moved here last summer, and nothing has opened up until now. She's had lots of interviews, and has tried so hard, but nothing. And now this."

"He always has a plan, Tom. We don't always understand his ways. In fact, we seldom do!" Coop laughed as he drove out of the apartment complex. "But he sees the whole picture. He's got all the pieces and knows how they fit together."

Tom was quiet as he settled into his seat. He had a lot to think about.

He was still deep in thought when Coop turned the truck into Greg's neighborhood. A soft whistle left Tom's lips as he looked over the large houses with well manicured lawns. "Nice neighborhood. I've never been in this part of town before. What does Tom do, that he can afford to live around here?"

"He's a partner in a big law firm in Atkins. He deals mostly with family law. But don't be overwhelmed by the houses in this neighborhood. Greg and Nancy live modestly. Yeah, they have a nice house, and a pool even, but they are just normal, down to earth, God loving Christians. Nothing pretentious about them, that's for sure."

"I know Greg has never acted like a high and mighty lawyer. I had no clue. Just a nice guy." Tom nodded as Coop pulled into the driveway of a two-story colonial home. It was nice, but surely not on the scale of some of the larger homes they had passed.

Greg was already sitting in the driver's seat of his SUV. His boat was on a trailer hitched up in the back. Coop put his fishing gear and snacks along with Tom's cooler into the boat and secured everything for the trip. Then he hopped into the back seat of the SUV and Tom got in front. As they buckled their seatbelts, Greg said, "Let's pray before we hit the road." The trio bowed their heads and Greg said, "Lord Jesus, we ask for you blessing on us as we spend time together today. Give us your protection on the highway and on the water. We thank you for your wonderful world of nature. For lakes and rivers, wildlife and fish, trees and flowers, and bright blue skies. Be with us now. Guide our conversations. May everything we do and say be pleasing to you, oh God. Amen."

Coop echoed the "Amen" from the back seat. Tom grunted.

"Have you ever driven a motor boat before, Tom?" Greg asked.

"Yes, a long time ago. My dad had one and I drove when I was a teenager. We used to take the boat out on the lake a lot. Dad loved fishing. I actually haven't been since he passed away." Tom grew silent.

"I'm sorry to hear about your dad," Coop said. "My dad passed about five years ago. He had cancer. I was just twenty-four. How old were you?"

"It was fifteen years ago. I was twenty-one, just out of college. Mom died two days later. Stupid drunk driver." There was a tinge of anger in his voice, mixed with sadness and longing. "Everything changed."

"I'm sure it did. Twenty-one is a tough age anyway. How did you manage? Do you have brothers or sisters? Or did you have to take care of all the final arrangements yourself?" Greg was curious but didn't want to push too hard.

"I'm the baby of six. So the older kids took care of things, mostly. My parents weren't well off, so there wasn't much of an estate to settle. Life insurance paid for the funerals, with very little left over for us kids. It was tough. I took it hard."

"I still have both of my parents, Nancy too." Greg said. "Coop and Becky have both lost their dads."

"So I'm the only orphan," Tom said with a chuckle. "It took a while to get used to that word!"

"Well, unfortunately, it's going to happen to all of us, if we are lucky enough to live that long. I see my mom aging and Becky's mom too, so I'm reminded that this world is not our home. We will all face death, one way or another. I'm just so glad we have forgiveness of sins and a home in heaven to look forward to. I know I'll meet my whole family there, whenever the Lord calls me home. That will be quite the day!" Coop paused for a moment, then asked, "Were your parents Christians, Tom?"

"I guess that depends on your meaning of the word. They went to church and we prayed at meals. But other than that, they never talked about God much. Some of the older kids still go to church, one even teaches a Sunday school class, but not me. I haven't been to church since the funeral. We buried Dad and Mom both the same day. And other than going to see Kendy in the Christmas program, I haven't darkened the door of any church since then."

"I've been going to church all my life. Can't imagine where I'd be without Jesus as my best friend." Coop fell easily into a conversation, sharing his testimony. "I have heard all of my life that God has a plan for me. For a while, I thought he wanted me in ministry, preaching in a church somewhere, or maybe on a mission field. But then dad got sick, I came home, and discovered that my ministry is right here in Winslow. I feel like I'm right where God wants me to be."

Greg added, "And it's clear that God is using you, Coop. You have a real gift for sharing scripture, and making it relevant to today's issues."

"Maybe that's my problem," Tom admitted. "I've never seen the relevance. Oh, I prayed and prayed when Dad died and Mom was hanging on. But God didn't listen. He didn't care. Mom died anyway, and I was alone. So what was the use of praying? Why did I even bother to ask God for help? He didn't care. If there even really is a God, he just didn't care about me."

"I can tell you are still angry about that," Coop said. "But we all have to realize that bad things happen, even to good people. It doesn't mean God doesn't care, or doesn't exist. It does mean that he is with us through it. We aren't really alone, when we have Jesus in our lives."

From the front seat, Greg carried on the conversation. "He will never leave us or forsake us. That's repeated in the Bible over and over. Old Testament and New."

"Right! And Tom, even when you felt alone, God was still there. You just didn't know it. And now, here you are, years later, talking with us about God's love for you and his plan for your life. I think that was part of his plan!"

"Could be," Tom admitted. "We'll see."

Greg pulled off the highway and slowly drove down a graveled roadway to a parking lot. A few other cars were parked with empty trailers. Greg backed his trailer down the boat ramp until the boat was in the water. Coop jumped out, released the boat from the trailer and climbed aboard. Tom got in while Greg parked the SUV.

Before long, the boat was anchored in the middle of the lake, three poles were extended out over the water, and the fishermen were watching for movement on their bobbers, waiting for the tug on their lines. Not a lot of fish were caught and all were released. But the time passed in comfortable companionship.

They took turns steering the boat to different locations in the lake, hoping to find just the right spot to catch a big one. That monster fish eluded them, however, but it didn't seem to matter to the men. They were having a good time, getting to know each other and sharing the day.

Over and over, Tom heard his new friends tell of the goodness of God. Coop and Greg talked about Jesus like they knew him as a friend, a teacher, a guide and a protector. But it was when they talked about salvation and the forgiveness of sins that Tom paid the most attention. This was not a topic he ever remembered hearing in church as a child. And his parents had never told him about it either.

There was something different about these men. Tom had never been around anyone who spoke with such conviction. They really believed in this God they talked about. They believed in prayer and a plan. And they were such good people. It was easy to feel like they really cared about him, while at the same time, they didn't judge him for his uncertainties. By the time the boat was headed back to shore, Tom knew he had made some true friends. And he also knew he had questions.

They were almost back to Greg's place when Tom's phone buzzed. "Hi, Tabs. What's up?" "How'd it go?" "Really?" "That's great!" "Monday, you mean like three days from now?" "Yes, that is terrific!" "Okay, I'll be home in about an hour. I'm so happy, Tabs. And proud of you!" "Love you too. See ya soon." With a big smile on his face, Tom put away his phone. "You'll never believe this," he said to his new friends.

"Let me guess," Greg said. "Tabitha got the school nurse job?"

"And she starts Monday? That's quick." Coop pounded Tom on the back in congratulations. "I'd say God is good!"

"Yeah, she's going to work with the nurse who's there for a week before the lady moves. This is really happening fast." Tom let out a big sigh. "And it came at just the right time. I'm not sure how much longer we could make it on just my salary. This is good. Real good."

"God knows what he's doing. I see his hand in this, don't you?" Greg pulled into his driveway. "Perfect timing in every way. God is faithful."

Chapter 19

HIDE AND SEEK

April and May had been unusually warm and dry. When Coop plowed the fields, dust rolled behind the tractor and drifted across the fence lines. A fine layer of dust seemed to settle on everything: cars, clothes, lawn chairs and children. Now, the planting was done and corn was beginning to grow. The little green sprouts were pushing their way out of the soil in military precision, lined up in a mesmerizing pattern of little green dots that got a little taller every day.

The Brownies didn't mind the dust and heat though and happily gathered in the back yard of the big house. Grammy's daffodils had passed their peak and the irises were forming buds. Marla Jean had put Jenny in charge of watering the flowerbeds and she had faithfully completed her job throughout the past weeks. Things were looking good in the back yard.

Of course, Jenny, Kendy and Hannah had managed to get themselves pretty wet while watering flowers. No one minded, though, because the temperatures had been steadily climbing to unexpected highs. It wasn't too hot for a footrace, however, and running was Kendy's favorite thing to do whenever she visited Jenny at the farm. With all the open space, she could run freely. Not like the small playground area at her apartment in town.

As usual, Kendy won the race.

"You did it again!" Jenny exclaimed, panting to catch her breath. "I run fast at the first but then I get tired and have to slow down. If we did a short race, I can beat you. But with long races, you always win."

"And I always lose, no matter what," said Hannah as she put her hands on her knees and gasped for air. "But that's okay. I can jump off the diving board and you guys can't yet."

"I guess God gave us each different skills," Jenny said. "You are the best swimmer, and Kendy is the best runner, and I'm…." she trailed off. "I don't know what I am."

"Horse rider!" shouted Hannah. "That's a skill I can't do. Even Benny scares me to ride. You are good with horses."

"And with dogs, too," Kendy added. "You know how to teach Holly the best tricks."

"I learned that from my Aunt Dana. She used to have a dog named Riley who had lots of ribbons for all the tricks he could do." She looked around the back yard and said, "Speaking of dogs, where's Holly? Are we ready to start her lesson?"

A hot wind blew in from the south. The girls, sitting in the shade of the weeping willow tree, called out for the dog. "Holly, come!" "Holly." "Come here Holly."

"Wait," Jenny commanded. She put two fingers to her lips and gave a shrill whistle. Wide-eyed, Kendy said, "Whoa, that was loud!"

"Yeah, warn us next time, would ya?" Hannah laughed. "We need to cover our ears first."

Holly came running round the corner of the house and trotted right up to Jenny. She threw her arms around the collie's neck and buried her face in the long white hair. "Well, it worked, didn't it?" Jenny nuzzled Holly a bit longer and then said, "Let's get busy, before it gets any hotter. Holly doesn't like to be hot."

"Maybe you should give her a haircut," Hannah suggested.

"Nope! Doc Larson says she will stay cooler if she keeps all this hair. So no haircuts. Just a trim now and then. Her feet mostly! Her toes get really hairy!"

That comment brought about hoots of laughter. Holly sat and looked at each girl, tilting her head as if to say, "What's so funny?" That made the girls laugh even more.

"Let's get on with it," Jenny said, finally catching her breath. "Did you bring the stuff?"

Hannah nodded and reached into the back pocket of her jeans. She pulled out a pair of pink panties. "Will this work?" she asked with a giggle.

Jenny stared at her with raised eyebrows. "Panties? You brought panties?"

"You said bring something personal. I can't think of anything more personal than panties!" Laughter ensued and soon the girls were rolling on the grass. Holly jumped and leaped, barking and showing much excitement.

"Settle down, girl. We've got work to do." Jenny turned to Kendy. "What did you bring, Kendy? I hope it's not panties!"

"I brought this purple ribbon I put around my pony tail sometimes. Do you think it will work?"

"As long as it smells like you, it should work. Let's try it! First, rub you item all over yourself. Get lots of your smell on it." Each girl got busy, rubbing arms and necks and hair. Kendy held her hair ribbon in front of her face and sniffed.

"I don't smell anything. Are you sure this is going to work?"

"Holly's nose is much stronger than ours," Jenny exclaimed. "You'll see. Now let Holly smell it."

Kendy held out her ribbon and encouraged Holly to come and sniff. Holly nosed the ribbon and Kendy said, "Good girl. That's my ribbon." Kendy petted Holly and smothered her with praise while hugging her tightly. After a little more sniffing, Jenny gave instructions.

"Now, I'll keep Holly with me, and you two go and hide. I won't let Holly see where you go. In a couple of minutes, I'll tell her to go find Kendy, and I'll let her sniff the ribbon and we'll see what happens."

And so began the game of hide and seek. Kendy and Hannah both hid well out of sight. Even Jenny didn't know where they had gone. But it wasn't long before Holly gave a bark of joy and Kendy called out, "Holly is amazing! She found me!" They rounded the corner of the house, running and jumping as they came. "I can't believe it! I was watching her from behind the bushes by the front porch. She sniffed around the front yard a little, and then came right up to me. I was hiding good so I don't think she saw me. She must have followed my smell. I can't believe it!"

"Told you she is the smartest dog in the whole wide world!" Jenny exclaimed with pride.

"My turn," shouted Hannah. "Come here, Holly. Come smell my panties!"

"Oh gross!" Jenny laughed. "Next time we play hide and seek, please bring a different personal item!"

Hannah agreed with a shrug. She loved on Holly and gave the collie plenty of time to recognize her personal smell.

"When you hide this time, don't go where Kendy was. Pick a different spot."

"Okay, but why?"

Jenny explained, "Because we don't want Holly to think everybody hides in the same place. She needs to learn to follow the smell, not the memory of what worked last time."

The girls went off to hide and Jenny sat beside Holly. "This time, you need to go find Hannah. She smells like this." She let Holly sniff for a minute, then said, "Now, go find Hannah. Go get her, Girl!"

Holly took off with a bound and Jenny sat waiting for a response from the front yard. No sounds of barking or shouts of success were heard. Jenny was just about to give up and go searching when suddenly a celebration broke out in the front yard. First Holly's barking, then Hannah's voice, then Kendy's laughter. Jenny ran around the house to see what was happening.

Hannah lay on the front porch, covered with a blanket. Holly was standing over her, barking joyfully. Holly pulled at the blanket, revealed Hannah, and began to lick her face. "What a good girl you are, Holly," laughed Hannah. "You found me!"

Hannah used her arm to wipe doggie slobbers off her face and neck. But she didn't stop laughing. "It worked! She sniffed me out!"

Aunt Dana opened the screen door and came out on the porch. "What's going on out here? Sounds like you Brownies are sure having fun!"

"We're playing hide and seek with Holly and she is finding us every time!" Jenny hugged Holly and continued, "She followed the smells and found everybody. The first time even! She is so smart!"

"That's incredible!" agreed Dana. "Can we watch?"

Jenny nodded and said, "It's Kendy's turn again. Let's go in the backyard and do like we did before."

"Tucker and I will meet you in the backyard. He'll want to see this too." Dana turned and went back into the farmhouse. She found Tucker Fredrickson in the kitchen perched high on a step ladder. Dana's mother stood at the base of the ladder, holding on as if to steady Tucker, so he didn't fall.

Tucker gave the light bulb a final twist and said to Dana, "Hand me that cover, would you please?"

She reached the light globe up over her head and Tucker took it. "Thanks for doing this for Mom," Dana said. "It's been out for a couple of days, but Coop has been so busy in the fields, he hasn't been over here to change it."

"Yes, thank you," said Marla Jean as she stood back from the ladder and let Tucker climb down. "I was going to do it myself, but Dana wouldn't let me. Something about falling and breaking a hip!"

"Absolutely, Mom. You should not be climbing ladders. You never know."

"I'm just not used to being told I can't do things anymore. Things I always used to do without even thinking." She folded up the step ladder and began to carry it away but Tucker stopped her.

"Here, let me take this."

Marla Jean sighed in resignation. "See what I mean?"

"After you put that away, come out on the back deck. The Brownies have something they want to show us." Dana gave her mother a hug. "You come too."

Tucker held the back door for the women, then gently took Dana's hand as they stood on the deck looking down at the girls below. Jenny lifted up Kendy's hair ribbon and showed it to them. "This is Kendy's ribbon," she called up. "Holly is going to smell it and then go find Kendy."

Kendy circled the house to the left and Hannah went right. Jenny held Holly's attention until the girls were well out of sight. Then she let Holly sniff the ribbon and said, "Go find Kendy!"

Holly took off without hesitation and ran to the left. Soon they all heard the shout "She did it! She found me!" as the pair came back into the yard.

"Amazing!" Tucker said. "That's just terrific. I know Uncle Steve and Aunt Joyce have had lots of collies, but I've never seen any of them do that!"

"I had a collie, Riley, that could do all kinds of tricks. But this is better than a trick. This could actually be useful." Dana called down to the girls, "Good job! Can she go get Hannah now?"

The game continued and Hannah was discovered in just a short time. "Holly's really good at this game!" she cried out joyfully. "She's so so smart!"

"I hate to cut the game short, but I need to head home. Walk me to the truck?" Tucker asked Dana.

They were quiet as they left the house. The only sound was the crunching of gravel under their feet. Saying goodbye was always hard, but this time seemed especially so. It would be at least a month before they would see each other again. Summer crop tending was right around the corner and Tucker would be needed at the farm. Between helping at home and on his uncle's farm, there would be plenty to keep him busy.

"I am going to miss you so much," Dana whispered into his shoulder.

"We'll be together again before you know it. We'll be so busy for the next few weeks, time will just fly by." He tried to reassure her, but knew his feelings doubled hers. "And then we have Nicaragua."

"I know. Just not sure how I'll last till then!" Dana laughed.

"I'll be praying for you, Dana." Tucker gave her a big hug. "You just be quiet and listen. I know it's hard, but he will speak. We just don't quiet ourselves enough to hear him. So promise me you'll make some quiet time, just to listen for his voice. Promise?"

Dana had been wrestling with uncertainty about her future. Even after a few semesters of college, she still didn't feel like she knew what she wanted to do, or what the future held for her. Except for Tucker. She was sure about that. There had been signs. Now she just needed a sign to show her what God planned for the next step in her life.

"I promise."

Dana stood and waved as Tucker's truck kicked up dust along the road. When finally the dust settled and he was completely out of sight, Dana headed for the barn. Coop always said the barn was his prayer closet. She had often found peace and direction while sitting on a bale of hay in the loft. She hoped to find some clarity there again today.

Chapter 20

THE LOST COIN

A t bedtime, the three Brownies spread sleeping bags on Jenny's bedroom floor. Becky came into the room to settle them in for the night. As part of Jenny's routine, Becky was prepared to read from a devotional book for children. Tonight's lesson was the Parable of the Lost Coin.

Becky read a paraphrased version of Luke 15. "A woman had ten coins. One day she noticed that one coin was missing. She began to look everywhere for it. She turned on all the lights in her house. She swept the floor, every corner, and looked under the bed and behind the dresser." Becky pointed to Jenny's bed and said, "I wonder what we'd find if we looked under your bed. Do you have any coins under there?"

Jenny giggled, "If I get coins, they all go in my piggy bank. None are under my bed." She paused and turned back to the story. "Did the lady ever find her coin?"

"She did!" Becky exclaimed happily. "And oh my goodness, she was so happy! She ran out and told all her neighbors that the lost coin was found. Everyone was celebrating because the woman found her coin."

"Where was it hiding?" Hannah wanted to know.

"Well, the Bible doesn't tell us where she found it. But the important thing is, she didn't stop looking until she found it, and then she was very happy."

"I'd be happy, too, if I found some money," Kendy laughed. "And I'd hold on to it tight and never lose it again."

"Well, the best part of this story is what Jesus said next." Becky turned back to the book. "Jesus said that there is happiness like that in heaven whenever one sinner changes his heart and gives his life to God. The angels are overjoyed! They sing and dance and shout and clap their hands. Everyone celebrates because the lost has been found."

Kendy, being unfamiliar with Bible parables, asked a question. "You mean a sinner is a lost coin?"

"This story is called a parable, Kendy. Hannah, can you explain what that means?"

"A parable is a story Jesus told. And whatever words he said, had a different meaning than just what the words said."

"That's pretty much right! Can you add anything, Jenny?"

Jenny was eager to answer. "Oh I know, I know! A parable is to teach us something. Like, I mean, this story isn't just about a lost coin. It's a lost person, and Jesus keeps looking until he finally finds him, and he doesn't give up or quit when he gets tired."

Kendy's brow was furrowed as she tried to figure this out. "I don't really get it. I mean, the coin is a person who is lost? I thought you said Jesus knows everything. So he could never lose anybody. He would know where he is."

Becky smiled and gave Kendy a little hug. "That's okay, Kendy, let me explain it another way. The person who is lost is not really lost like hidden under the bed and nobody can find him. In this parable, the word lost means his soul is lost. He is a sinner and he is far from God. He will be lost forever if he doesn't change his heart. If he asks Jesus to forgive his sins, and he changes his heart, now he is part of God's family. Jesus finds him and welcomes him into the family of God."

Jenny jumped in, "And everybody celebrates. God and Jesus and the angels and everybody in heaven is happy and singing. Because now that person isn't lost any more. He's found!"

"And the Bible says there's more celebrating in heaven because of the lost soul that was found than because of the lady finding her coin." Becky looked around at the girls. She knew that Jenny and Hannah had both given their hearts to the Lord. But she wanted to offer Kendy the opportunity to have her sins forgiven too. She didn't want to pressure the girl, or make her feel uncomfortable. But it seemed that the time was right. The Holy Spirit was working already. Kendy's lower lip was quivering.

"You mean everybody who is a sinner is lost? And Jesus is looking for him?"

"That's right, Kendy. Jesus doesn't want anyone to be lost. He wants everyone to be part of God's family."

"But am I lost? Am I a sinner? That's a bad guy, right? I'm not bad." Kendy was trying to figure this all out.

"The Bible says everyone has sinned. We've all fallen short of God's glory. But if we ask for forgiveness, Jesus is faithful and will forgive us."

Jenny joined the conversation. "And then we get to be in God's family and go to heaven!"

"And we can walk on streets of gold!" Hannah put in.

"And see Jesus face to face!" Jenny took Kendy's hand. "It's easy! You should do it. Ask Jesus to forgive your sins. Then all us Brownies will be in heaven forever!"

Kendy was laying quietly thinking about all this long after the other little girls were snoozing peacefully.

Chapter 21
PILLOW TALK

Before Becky and Coop fell asleep they had prayer together, as was their custom. They held hands and worshiped, praising God for his moving among the Barkdale family. It was easy to see that Tabitha was nearing the point of a decision. The Proverbs 31 study was finished and she had agreed to start attending the next Wednesday evening class, which was a study of the book of John. She had been asking deeper questions and getting more involved in the discussion. Even Tom had been convinced to come to the men's Wednesday night class. Although he came mostly because of his friendship with Coop and Greg and hadn't yet gotten very involved in the teachings, at least he was being exposed to the word of God. That, in itself, was a first step and certainly a reason for rejoicing. And now, with Kendy's questions tonight, they prayed that indeed a little child would lead them.

****

Tom and Tabitha lay together in their bed, cuddled close and enjoying being with each other. In the last month or so, their level of stress had lifted considerably. With the added income from Tabitha's new job, their money troubles weren't quite so pressing. The friendships that had developed with the Smiths and Martins had given them a social connection that had been missing ever since they had moved to Winslow. Even their attendance at the Wednesday evening Bible studies had added a new dimension to their marriage.

Tabitha rested her head on Tom's shoulder and said, "Thank you for taking me out to dinner tonight. It was nice to do something special, just the two of us. It's been a long time since we could afford to eat out."

"We need to get out more often. Now that you have a job, things should loosen up some financially. Not that we'll ever be able to afford a mansion in Greg and Nancy's neighborhood, but maybe we can move out of this apartment in a year or two."

"That would be something to work towards. But I don't need a mansion like Nancy. I will admit I was a little jealous the first time I took Kendy over there. But I don't need a house like that! Too much work to keep clean!"

Tabitha's head rose and fell as Tom chuckled. When the laughter died down, Tabitha was silent for a while. Then she continued, "Did you know that she has a cleaning lady come in once a week? And a part-time nanny who takes care of their son while Nancy works in her home office? Must be nice."

Tom stretched his arm about Tabitha to hug her. "Much as I'd like to, I honestly don't see us ever being able to afford maids and nannies. But I promise to love and cherish you and

Kendy all the days of my life. You'll have to be satisfied with that, I'm afraid."

"You silly man," Tabitha laughed. "I don't need all that fancy stuff. I'm just a simple woman with minimal needs. As long as I have you and Kendy, I'll be happy." She kissed him and they cuddled for a few minutes. Then Tabitha added, "The Martins are such down-to-earth people. They don't put on airs of superiority at all. Just common, regular people. You can't tell by their behavior that they are rich."

Tom stroked her hair softly and said, "Just good people. Like the Smiths. And thanks to Coop and Becky for keeping Kendy overnight so we could have some time together, just us." He kissed her forehead.

"Truthfully, I think the girls came up with that plan. They've been talking about wanting to have a sleepover, and this was the perfect night for it. It sure was nice of Becky to offer to keep them until church time tomorrow."

"Speaking of church, I was thinking that I would go with you in the morning."

Tabitha sat up a little straighter and smiled. "Really? I think that's a great idea. I would love to have you with me."

"Yeah, well, I was thinking about you, sitting there with Becky and Nancy and their husbands, and wondering if you felt weird without me being there with you. So I thought I'd go along, so you don't feel like the odd man out."

"I appreciate that!" Tabitha said, laughing. "I have sometimes wished that you were there. But not just for my sake. For you too."

"What do you mean?"

"There's just something about being there in church. Something that feels right. Like, I mean, it's hard to describe, but I feel like my heart is a little fuller when I'm there. I have learned a lot about God, and living a Godly life, and trying to see his hand working in my life. I mean, those ladies prayed for my job situation and looked what happened! I've never known so many people who believed in prayer. It makes me want to believe too."

"One thing's for sure," Tom said thoughtfully. "The Smiths and the Martins are great people. Honest, trustworthy, kind. If those are characteristics of Christians then that's the kind of people I want to hang around with. And if it's God or Jesus or Bible reading or praying that makes them good people, then I think it's worth checking into."

Tabitha tentatively asked, "Think we ought to pray about it?"

"If you want to. But you do it. I'm not sure what to say."

"I don't think Jesus is going to judge us on what words we say. I think he'll just be happy we are talking to him!"

"You're probably right, but still, you do it."

Tabitha took his hand and they both closed their eyes. She prayed, "Hello God. It's me, Tabitha. And Tom is here too." She squeezed his hand and went on with a chuckle, "But I guess you know that! You know everything, right?" She took a deep breath before saying, "We want to thank you for Coop and Becky and Greg and Nancy. They have been good friends to us. And thank you for working things out with my new job. We don't know how you did it, but we do think you had something to do with it."

There was a long pause as she thought of what else to say. "So God, we see how Becky and all them are good people, and we like what we see. And we want to be like that too. So show us what we need to do to be like them. I guess that's all for now. Amen."

Tom said "Amen" and opened his eyes. "You know what Coop would say about that prayer? He'd say that we shouldn't want to be like him, or Becky or any of them. He'd say they are following Jesus, and that's what we should do too."

"You're probably right. See, you should have said the prayer. You would have done it better." Tabitha pulled the covers up to her chin and turned to face him with a smile.

"Naw, you did just fine." He kissed her and added, "I'll do it next time."

Tabitha's heart swelled with joy and her smile filled Tom with peace.

Chapter 22

KENDY'S PRAYER

Kendy packed her pajamas into her little backpack. She glanced over her shoulder and saw Jenny and Hannah in the bathroom, brushing their teeth. She hurried out of the bedroom and went into the kitchen. There she found Becky, cleaning up after breakfast. She stood near the table, not quite sure what to say.

Becky looked up from her work and noticed Kendy standing meekly with her hands gripping the back of a kitchen chair. "Is something wrong, Kendy?" she asked. She dried her hands and walked over to the little girl. "Do you need something?"

"I need to ask you something," came her hesitant reply.

"Sure, Sweetie, anything."

"Can we talk some more about being lost and found?" Kendy looked up with tears misting her eyes. "I don't want to be lost. I want to be part of God's family."

Becky drew Kendy close in a hug. "Sure we can talk about it. Do you think you want to ask Jesus to come into your heart?"

Kendy nodded. "I do want to. I want to go to heaven and see Jesus. I don't want to be lost," she repeated. "But how do I do it?"

Becky took Kendy's hands in her own. "We can pray. Jesus is listening. Ask him to forgive your sins and come into your heart. It's as simple as that."

Kendy bowed her head. She spoke with a new confidence as she prayed "Dear Jesus, I love you and I want to live with you and be in your family. I'm sorry for the wrong things I've done. I want to be better, and I need you to help me. I want you to find me and take me to heaven." She paused and thought a moment, then went on. "Please forgive my sins and come live in my heart."

Jenny and Hannah stood in the kitchen doorway, holding hands and smiling.

Chapter 231

THE ONE THAT WAS LOST

Pastor Green's sermon was about the good shepherd who counted his sheep in the pen and found only ninety-nine. One sheep was lost. One sheep was not safely in the fold. One sheep was in danger. One, just one. But the Shepherd left the flock, locked up and safe for the night, and went out to search for the one that was lost. That one lost sheep was so precious to the Shepherd that he looked and looked, despite darkness and danger, despite the seemingly foolishness of leaving the flock, despite the odds of bringing the lost sheep home. He looked high and low until he finally located the one sheep and brought him home to safety.

The pastor was clear with his explanation. "Jesus, the Good Shepherd, wants all people in the safety of the fold. He does not want even one soul to be outside, lost and in danger. The prophet Isaiah says, 'We all, like sheep, have gone astray. Each of us has turned to our own way.' But Jesus is searching. Jesus is calling. Will you answer the Shepherd's voice? Will you come to him today? He offers you forgiveness. He has paid the price for your sinful wanderings. He will gather you in his loving arms and carry you to safety."

From the choir loft, harmonies filled the sanctuary. The anthem was "Softly and Tenderly" and the words spoke of Jesus, calling 'You who are sinners come home.' Dana wiped a tear from the corner of her eye as several people in the congregation moved slowly and determinedly into the aisle and down front to the altar. Her heart swelled when she recognized Tom and Tabitha Barkdale, holding hands and walking forward.

Dana searched the congregation until she made eye contact with her brother Coop. He was standing, hand outstretched and smiling broadly. Becky, standing beside him, had her arms raised in praise. Her eyes were closed and she seemed to be whispering. Dana knew she was thanking God for the salvation of her friends.

Pastor Green moved among those kneeling at the altar. Some of the elders of the church came forward and put their hands on the shoulders of those seeking forgiveness and salvation. Dana smiled again as she watched Melissa Madison stand beside Tabitha. Her tattooed arm reached forward and she touched Tabitha, who turned and looked up at her friend. As she had many times before, Dana thanked God for the amazing transformation in Melissa's life. Who would have imagined, just a few years ago, that Melissa would be standing here, praying for the souls of others?

But God desires that none should be lost. All have sinned and fallen short of his glory, but he is good, and faithful and merciful. His gift of everlasting life is available to everyone who seeks. Dana thought about Melissa and how she had fully embraced Christ's love and continually sought his direction for her new life. She thought about the people of Nicaragua, and so many others who needed to hear the gospel. She thought about the people in her own community who needed Christ.

Brandon Hiller, the assistant pastor, took the microphone and prayed aloud for those seeking salvation. "This is a day for forgiveness and reconciliation," he said. "Let us celebrate God's love for the lost who have been found."

Murmurs of "Amen" and "Thank you, Jesus" could be heard throughout the sanctuary. A few more people moved forward to pray. Tears of joy flowed down many cheeks as people all around the sanctuary were moved to praise or repent. A feeling of revival was stirring and hearts were being touched.

Dana felt the presence of the Lord nudging her softly. She heard a still small voice, urging her to go forward. And so she moved out from the other ladies in the alto section. She went to the altar and knelt down, head in her hands. She let the tears fall as she asked for clear direction. And it came.

She rose with clarity and purpose. And a desperate need to talk to Tucker.

Chapter 24

MARKED SAFE

"Can I have those pictures from the Christmas program, Mommy? All the Brownies and their families?" Jenny was in the kitchen, helping her mother by sweeping the floor. Becky was preparing to mop.

"Well, yes, I have extras. What are you planning to do with them?"

"It's a surprise!" Jenny was excited but whispered because Nicholas was napping. "I'm making a new art project. I need pictures for that. You'll see."

"Finish sweeping and I'll get the pictures. You can do your art in your room while I mop the floor. I can't wait to see what you make this time."

Soon Jenny was at work with paper and scissors, glue and markers. She was humming 'He's Got the Whole World in His Hands' as she worked. Carefully she cut three large paper hands, one purple, one red, and one green. She glued one family picture on each hand and wrote the name of each family in her most careful printing. When she was finished she stood back to admire her work. Satisfied, she pinned the three paper hands on her bulletin board.

Later that night, at bedtime, Jenny showed the pictures to her parents. "The Martin family is on green paper, the Barkdale family is on purple, and the Smith family is red. It's to match our dresses," she explained. "And see what I wrote up here, for the title?"

Letters across the top of the bulletin board said.

'S A V E D and S A F E.'

"Nice work," Coop said as he hugged her. "I see you used the hand idea, like in your dream we were talking about before."

"Yup, and all the families are in God's hand now. So we're safe, all of us."

Becky agreed. "Our names are written in the Lamb's book of life. We are all marked safe because our sins have been forgiven by Jesus and we have him living in our hearts now."

"That's my Best Part for tonight," said Jenny as she was climbing into bed. "Being safe, and knowing all The Brownies are too. And all our families."

"I would agree," nodded Coop. "That's a very good thing."

"Time for prayers," Becky said as she took Coop's hand and Jenny's hand and they all bowed their heads.

Coop prayed, "God bless our families and our friends."

Becky added, "Thank you for your love and the salvation you gave us by dying on the cross for our sins."

Jenny finished by saying, "Thank you for keeping us all in the palm of your hand, and for marking down our names safe in your book of life."

Chapter 25

SCHOOL'S OUT FOR THE SUMMER!

The screen door slammed and The Brownies burst into the house in a fit of giggles. Holly was dancing around their ankles, barking with joy as she caught the joyful enthusiasm of the two girls. Moving quickly, Jenny led the pack down the hall and to her bedroom. The girls threw their heavy backpacks on Jenny's bed and grabbed hands. Dancing together in a circle, they sang, "School's out for the summer! School's out for the summer!"

Hearing motherly footsteps coming down the hall, Holly jumped up on the bed and sat quietly with her paws crossed. "Well, my goodness, girls, you certainly sound excited!" Becky said when she entered the room. She looked over at Holly and laughed "Don't you sit there looking all innocent, little lady! I know you were in on this ruckus too!"

"We can't help it, Mommy! Second grade is done. All the Brownies are third graders now! And it's summer time!" Jenny plopped down on the bed beside Holly and buried her face in fur. "No more school, Holly. Just play time and trick time and fun, fun, fun."

Hannah looked sad. "I'm going to miss Mrs. Novak though. She's the best teacher ever."

"I hope we are all in the same class for third grade too. And with Mrs. Bennett. I like her when she has lunch duty. She always smiles." Jenny kicked her shoes off and Holly hopped down to lick her toes.

Kendy took her shoes off too, and Holly gently started licking. Kendy giggled and said, "This is so strange. But I kinda like it!"

"Not me!" protested Hannah. "My shoes are staying on!"

Kendy asked Becky, "Where's Mommy? I thought she was going to be here. I saw her car." Tom and Tabitha had purchased a second used car when Tabitha started working. They had tried synchronizing their work and driving schedules, but it just hadn't worked out, so they needed the second car. Craig Cashman, Melissa's friend from church, had helped them find a good deal.

"She's getting ready to put drops into Grandma's eyes. They are in the living room. You girls ran right past them!"

"We didn't exactly run, Mommy, just walked really fast." Jenny stood and said, "Let's go watch."

Tabitha was removing the bandage and patch that covered one of Elizabeth's eyes. "So, you need to wear the patch the rest of the day, and tonight, but tomorrow you can take it off except for night time or if you take a nap. The doctor doesn't want you to rub it or scratch it accidentally while you sleep." She put the cap on the bottle of drops and continued, "The drops need to go in every six hours. I don't mind doing it for you, but you should be able to do it yourself, once the patch comes off."

"Or I can help," Becky put in. "Mom's staying here with us for a few days so she won't be alone. I appreciate your being here to help this afternoon. It's good to know a nurse!"

"Not quite a nurse yet, but I'm working on it!" Tabitha handed Elizabeth a tissue. "Just dab the drops off your cheek. Don't rub," she instructed. "Glad I could help." She replaced the patch and secured it in place. Holly sat and looked at Elizabeth, head tilted in confusion.

"Grandma looks funny, doesn't she?" Jenny laughed. "She's a pirate!"

"Grrr! Ahoy Mattie!" Elizabeth joked. "Are you ready for a snack? I'm hungry!"

"I'll hold your hand to the kitchen, Grandma," Kendy said. "So you don't bump anything!"

Tabitha looked over at Becky and smiled. Her parents, Kendy's only grandparents, lived five-hundred miles away and seldom visited. Tabitha liked that Kendy had adopted Elizabeth as a grandma. It solidified the feeling that moving to Winslow had been a good idea. In fact, she felt more and more that God had led them here. Winslow was home now, and these people were more than friends; they were family.

They had a church family now too, and people who showed real compassion and encouragement. Tabitha loved the women in the Wednesday night group. She learned so much from them and especially appreciated the prayers they said on her behalf. She believed it was those prayers that opened up the school nurse job and led her to the position. And now, thanks to the school board, she would be taking classes part time to earn her nursing degree. It was getting easier and easier for Tabitha to see God's hand in all this and to declare that God is good.

Everyone sat around the kitchen table, munching on delicious cantaloupe melon from Becky's garden. "Our first one!" Becky proclaimed. "But there's at least ten more coming."

"Have you decided about the Farmer's Market?" Elizabeth asked. "Do you think you'll do it next year?"

"I do. Coop is going to enlarge the garden space next spring so I'll have room for more tomatoes. That'll give us enough for our own canning, plus I can sell some at the market. Cucumbers too. I think I'll stick to those two crops for the first couple of years, just to see how it goes."

Becky cut some melon into cubes and put them on the tray of the high chair. Nicholas ate them eagerly, filling his cheeks until juice ran down his chin. Elizabeth wiped it off with a napkin and said, "Slow down, little man. You're going to choke."

A cube of melon fell off of the tray and landed on the floor under the highchair. Holly was there instantly to clean up the sticky spot on the floor.

"She likes cantaloupe!" Kendy laughed. "And she cleaned the floor! We need to get a collie, Mommy. Then you wouldn't have to sweep the floor!"

"Oh, I don't know about that. There's a lot to taking care of a dog. Feeding and brushing and going to the vet. And besides, in our apartment, we don't have room for a collie. They need big yards for running and playing. It wouldn't be fair to make her live in an apartment." Tabitha stroked Kendy's hair lovingly.

"Maybe we can move to a house and get a collie later," Kendy said hopefully. "Or maybe I could have a kitty. One of Jenny's cats is going to have babies. Can I have one?"

"We'll see, Honey. We have to ask your daddy."

After the snack, the girls went outside and Elizabeth retired to the living room while Becky and Tabitha stayed to clean up the dishes.

"Thanks for coming to help with mom," Becky said. She rinsed dishes and put them into the dishwasher. "I know I could have done those drops myself. But it was nice to have you over. We don't get enough time to talk, just the two of us."

Nicholas banged his hand onto his tray. "Well, the three of us, I mean!" Becky chuckled. "We can't forget you, can we?" She wiped his hands and face with a washcloth and took him down from the chair. He crawled off to Holly's bowl of water sitting on the floor near the back porch. "Oh, no you don't!" she said, swiping him up just in time. "That's Holly's water. Let's play somewhere else!"

She gave him some toys and sat him on the living room floor near her mother. Holly came and lay down beside him. "Thank you, Holly, you keep watch over Nicholas for just a minute. We'll be done in the kitchen soon."

"That boy can sure move fast. We'll have lots of fun when he starts to walk," Elizabeth chuckled.

"It won't be long, Mom. He's already pulling up and walking around things holding on. One of these days he's gonna just take off! And I'm thankful for every milestone he meets. He may have been premature at birth, but he's right on target with development."

Tabitha was wiping down the table when Becky returned. "We're going to need to get going. Tom will be home pretty soon. He's going to bring home a pizza, to celebrate the last day of school."

"Sounds like a great idea. I made lasagna yesterday and we'll have leftovers tonight. It's been a long day, with getting mom to surgery early this morning. But thank the Lord, everything went well, and she didn't feel a thing. It's kinda weird, to think of somebody operating on your eye, but she did great."

"The miracle of modern medicine!" Tabitha exclaimed. "She should be able to see much better, especially after she has the second eye done. Probably won't even need glasses, except maybe readers."

"God is good," Becky said.

"He is! I know he is!" Tabitha echoed with a smile.

****

The Brownies were having a great time at Vacation Bible School. For two hours every day, they participated in music and story time, art and recreation. They learned new songs, memorized scripture, and made some new friends.

Becky was the teacher for the third-grade girls and she was having a great time. The theme for the week was 'Fishers of Men' and the focus was on knowing Jesus and telling others about him. On the second day, Becky overheard the Brownies talking.

"My daddy went fishing, but he didn't catch any men!" Kendy said, which made the other girls giggle.

"His fishing pole wouldn't be strong enough to catch a man!" laughed Hannah.

"That's not what it really means, you know," explained Jenny. "It means catching people like saving them. Like Jesus saves them. Like us – Jesus caught us and saved us and now we are safe.

"Oh yeah, and our names are marked down in the big book in heaven," Hannah added.

"Okay, I get it," Kendy said. "So does that mean Jesus is the fisherman?"

Jenny answered, "Yes, but we can be fishermen too. 'Cause when we tell other kids about Jesus, it's like we are helping Jesus save them."

Becky agreed but explained further. "When we tell others about Jesus, we are helping Jesus. But he is the only one who can save them. It was because of his great love for us that Jesus died on the cross and took the punishment for our sins. That's how he saves us. He saves us from punishment that we deserved. But he took all that punishment so we could be saved."

"I'm sorry he had to do that," Kendy said.

"That's just it, Kendy. He didn't have to do it, but because he loved us so much, he wanted to do it."

"Like my pictures at home. Saved and Safe." Jenny smiled and hugged her friends. "All safe!"

"Our memory verse for today is John 3:16," Becky announced to the class. "Let's read it together." The girls all looked up the verse in their Bibles. Jenny saw that Kendy was in the New Testament but hadn't found the verse yet, so she helped Kendy find the right place. "Matthew, Mark, Luke and John," she whispered to her friend. "Here it is; find chapter three." "Thank you." Kendy found the verse and together all the girls in the class read: "For God so loved the world that he gave his one and only Son, that whoever believes in him shall not perish but have eternal life."

"Like I said, Saved and Safe!"

Chapter 26

A LITTLE FLIRTING FUN

Summer was in full swing. The winter wheat had been harvested, grain taken to the elevators and straw baled and stored in the barn. Amidst all the farm work, the Smith family praised God for his goodness. The spring months had been dry and a low harvest had been expected. But then the rains came, late in May and just in time for grain growth.

As usual, Coop hired a crew of day-workers to help him during the rush of harvest. As usual, his mother, sister and wife gratefully fed the men an abundant lunch every day. And also as usual, one of the workers, Marco Lopez, flirted with Dana. They had become good friends over the years, with a playful banter back and forth. Marco knew that Dana was interested in Tucker, but still enjoyed teasing her and watching her tease him back. They both knew it was all in fun.

With Dana's trip to Nicaragua just weeks away, Marco had a lot to talk with her about.

"But why you wanna go there? Nothing there but poor people and dirt." Marco brushed the farm dust off his pant legs and stood back up to his full height of four foot ten inches. Dana took a step down from the porch of the farmhouse to be on more of an equal standing with him. Still, she was taller by a couple of inches.

"It's those poor people we want to go and help. If we can work alongside them, the hospital will get built faster and more people can be treated. And at the same time, we will have a chance to share the good news of Jesus' love. Everybody needs to know about that, no matter how poor or rich they are, or where they live or what language they speak."

"You not know much Spanish good. How you talk to them?"

Dana smiled, "Well, we will have several Spanish speakers on the team to help. But anyway, you and your mother have taught me some Spanish. I can get by."

Marco laughed, "You have to say more than enchilada and taco and queso and pollo."

"Hey now, I can say ?Como estas hoy? And Encantada de conocerte." I'll get by! She reached over and brushed some hay off Marco's shoulder and he grabbed her by the arm.

Playfully, Marco said, "Maybe you need me come along. Teach you more words!"

"If you're serious, I will give you the phone number for Tim Swift. He's the one in charge of the mission trip. He'll tell you what you need to do."

Marco dropped her arm and said, "I no have money for that. Need to stay here and work, work, work!" He looked at her teasingly and jokingly said, "Besides, vacations are for rich kids."

Dana let a huff of air escape from her lungs as she said, "Hey! I'll have you know, this is not a vacation. And I'm not rich. And I'm not a kid!"

Marco let his gaze move slowly up and down her body. "You right about that! You a woman, for sure!"

Dana pretended not to notice his innuendo, yet there was a slight blush on her cheeks. She knew it was all in fun, but still, it was a little flattering. "I'm on my way to class," she said, diverting his stare. "Big final in business math today. Then class is over and I can get ready for Nicaragua."

Marco quickly opened her car door, bowed to her with a flourish and said, "Good luck, pretty lady!" Dana got in and adjusted her seat belt. He watched as she pulled the belt tightly across her chest, accentuating her cleavage. Dana let her long blond hair fall forward, covering the seat belt strap and the breasts she had inadvertently emphasized. She waved and started the car. Marco watched as she drove away.

'Too bad I can't go with you to Nicaragua,' he thought. 'Could be lots of fun.' He walked across the gravel driveway and headed for the outbuilding near the barn. He could hear Coop working on one of the combines. He wanted to ask Coop if he needed any help. At least that was the excuse he was using to visit the Smiths.

It was true, he needed money. He needed a job, but his reputation as a hard working farm hand was widespread. He could have gotten hired on just about anywhere. There was just something about working on the Smith farm. The family was always so nice, and man oh man those women could cook! Always an abundance of delicious food at the Smith's, and sometimes even enough to take home to Momma. But Marco had to admit, Dana was an added attraction.

Marco knew his flirting with Dana was getting him nowhere. He had seen Tucker around enough times and was aware of how Dana looked at him. But she was so cute and he couldn't help but be intrigued. Oh well, for now, flirting was fun enough.

****

As Dana drove towards Atkins Junior College, she flipped on the car radio and sang along to the gospel songs playing on the Christian station. Music about the deep love of Jesus calmed her spirit and took away the worry she felt about the math test she was taking this afternoon. She determined to do her best, to put her concerns into God's strong right hand, and put all thoughts of panic out of her mind.

Not that Dana was really a panic-driven girl. She was usually pretty level-headed and calm. Yet, she wondered what her future would hold, and she was not clear on the direction God wanted her to go in her life. But she was determined not to worry any more about it. She just wanted to listen to the Lord's leading. She was thankful that just a few weeks ago, God had given her a clearer direction. She could still feel his presence as he whispered to her and promised to always be with her. She felt, more than ever before, that this mission trip to Nicaragua was about to be a turning point in her life.

A year ago, she thought she had gotten a sign from God regarding Tucker. It was probably just a silly coincidence, but it felt real at the time. Dana was trying to hold on to that feeling, trying to believe it was real. But so much had happened in the last year. She wondered if God was saying, 'Here's a sign. Trust me and I'll get you there. Just remember, my timing is perfect.'

As she pulled into a parking space and gathered her text books, she glanced down at her cell phone. Noticing that she had a text from Tucker brought a smile to her face.

"Praying for you and your test today. Fear not! The Lord is with you." He always knew just what to say.

Dana sent a quick text back. "Thanks," and got an immediate response.

"I'll talk with you later. More details about Nicaragua. Won't be long now. The time will go 'swiftly'."

Again Dana smiled. A 'swift' was their sign. Tucker never forgot.

Dana walked through the parking lot towards her class. Her mind went back to their first conversation about swifts. Was it over a year ago? How was that possible?

The memory brought a rush of warm feelings. To think of Tucker, being dive bombed by an angry swift protecting his family! And to know that at that very same time, she had been watching swifts on a nest in the barn. Well, yes, maybe a silly coincidence, but still, it felt like a sign. And then, to top it all off, this trip to Nicaragua was being lead by a man named Tim Swift. That clinched it!

She couldn't lose the feeling that the Nicaragua trip was meant to be, that she and Tucker needed this time together to really get to know each other, that this was God's answer to her prayer for direction.

Even though their initial plans had been put on hold for a year, Dana still felt that it was in God's control and part of his plan. During that time, Dana and Tucker had exchanged phone calls several times a week. They had met up and spent time together at family gatherings throughout the year. Whenever Becky went to visit her sister Joyce, Dana begged a ride. She and Tucker had gone horseback riding, strolled around the Frederickson's farm, and worked together to build a picnic table in the back yard. They had tended the collies that Joyce raised. They had gone on a couple of real dates, to a movie and a county fair. Dana had enjoyed dinner with Tucker at his home and spent time with his parents and two little brothers.

She felt very comfortable with Tucker and a natural friendship had grown into maybe a little bit more. Beyond holding hands and an occasional hug, their relationship had not been physical at all. They had discussed it. Both believed in the sanctity of marriage. Both expressed their feelings on sexual abstinence before marriage. They were of the same mind.

This mission trip, postponed for a year because of travel concerns and unrest in the country, was set to happen in just a few weeks. The time was getting closer, and Dana was filled with anticipation about what the trip might mean to the people she would meet, the work they would do and the message they could spread. And to the relationship growing between Tucker and herself.

But first to get through this math test!

Chapter 27

CALL ME BERT

Elizabeth Emerson puttered around in her kitchen. She had eaten a sandwich for lunch, cleaned the dishes, read the mail and taken out the trash. There wasn't anything else to do except watch television, and she'd had about all of The Price is Right that she could handle. She had a book to read, but it hadn't grabbed her attention fully so she wasn't eager to get back into it.

As she looked around her living room, her eyes fell to a picture hanging on the wall. It was a beautiful scene of a sunset on the ocean. A verse from Isaiah 41:13 was printed across the picture.

> *'For I am the Lord your God*
> *who takes hold of your right hand and says to you,*
> *Do not fear; I will help you.'*

Elizabeth started humming an old hymn, one the choir had been practicing for Sunday's service. "Take my hand precious Lord, lead me home," she sang. She wandered to her back yard, looked at the flowers that were blooming, and watered the surprise lilies that were just emerging from the ground. She gazed upon an area in the yard where Jenny's swing-set used to be. She remembered all the time she spent giving her granddaughter pushes and playing with her on the slide. Times had changed; Jenny had outgrown Grandma pushes. The swing was now at Becky's house, used primarily by Nicholas.

She sighed in remembrance and walked back to the house. 'Grandkids growing, nothing is the same. I don't feel needed by them now that they've moved to their own house. And Becky has Coop, which of course is wonderful, but it does leave me out in the cold more often than I like to think about.' She reached for the doorknob and winced when she turned it. 'Oh, this old arthritis! I'm starting to feel my age. Getting old is a privilege, I know, but I wish it came with less aches and pains.'

In the kitchen, she soaked her hands in some warm water, then took some pain medicine. 'I need to stop feeling sorry for myself. I need to get out and have some fun.'

"I know!" she said out loud. "I'll drive over to the diner and get some ice cream!"

She put on a clean blouse, quickly combed her graying hair and applied just a little lipstick. She wasn't fussy about her appearance, but did always try to look presentable when she went out.

Al Turner, owner of the diner, looked up from the table he was cleaning and greeted her. "Hey Elizabeth! How good to see ya! You haven't been in for a while. How ya been?"

"Yes, it surely has been a while. It's good to see you too. I've been fine. Had cataract surgery a month ago, but I'm fine. Can see real good now." She looked around and noticed Sheriff Bert Bertell sitting at the counter with a cup of coffee. He tapped his cap in acknowledgement. "I'm in the mood for some ice cream so I thought I'd stop in and see what kind you have today." She took a seat at a table near the window. There were only a few other people in the diner and the one waitress was bringing a tray of food out to one of the tables. Hamburgers and fries did look good. She thought maybe she should eat here more often. Cooking for one person wasn't much fun. But maybe eating at the diner alone wouldn't be much fun either.

"We've got the usual suspects, chocolate, strawberry and vanilla. Plus we have some butter pecan, rocky road, and mint chocolate chip. Any of those sound good to ya?"

"Oh yes! Mint chocolate chip is my favorite. I'll take a bowl please."

Al went off to get the ice cream and Elizabeth did some people watching out the window. Doc Larson and his wife Lila walked past, noticed her and waved. They strolled hand in hand, headed in the direction of the vet's office, which was right next door to their home. Suzie Davis from the church choir walked past with her granddaughter Kayla, deep in conversation. Elizabeth remembered praying for that young girl when she had been very ill a couple of years ago. She smiled and thought 'Thank you for answered prayers.'

Elizabeth was surprised when Sheriff Bertell approached her table. "Good afternoon, Ms. Emerson. Mind if I join you?"

"Oh my no, I don't mind at all. Do have a seat. But please, it's Elizabeth. Not Mrs. Emerson. I'm just Elizabeth."

"I've always liked the name Elizabeth. Actually, it was my mother's name." Bert took a seat.

"It was my mother's name too! Only everybody called her Lizzie. So I was always Elizabeth."

They grew silent for a moment and Al came over with a big dish of ice cream. He leaned close to Elizabeth and said "I gave you an extra scoop! So maybe you'll come back and see us more often. We need more pretty ladies in this place." He smiled and turned to the sheriff. "You want some too?"

"It looks good, but no. Maybe a refill on the coffee though." Bert had a knack of reading people. He thought the reason for an extra scoop went beyond a good business tactic. He glanced at Elizabeth and realized she had a little pinkness in her cheeks. Was she blushing?

"Bring another spoon for the Sheriff," Elizabeth instructed. "I've got plenty enough to share."

Bert tried to protest but Al brought the spoon anyway. "Please, eat some, really, it's more than I need." Elizabeth pushed the bowl to the middle of the table.

"Feels like a date at the old soda shop!" Bert said. "Back in the good ole days!"

He chuckled and took a bite. "Mmm, that is good ice cream. Thanks for sharing with me."

"You're most welcome. Sheriff, I'm not sure I ever really thanked you for how quickly you helped my daughter and Coop when there was that trouble a few years ago. Becky told me how kind you were though all that mess. How you listened and asked just the right questions. How you made them both feel comfortable. So thanks."

"No need for thanks," he said. "Just doing my job." He changed the subject by asking, "How's your eyes doing? I heard you had cataract surgery."

"I make it my business to know what's going on around town. And I knew you hadn't been at your house for a few days, so I checked around. Asked Coop, actually, when he came into town one day."

Elizabeth smiled and said, "Well, yes, it was about a month ago. Everything went well, and I can really see a lot better now. I thought I might have to stop driving at night, but since the surgery, it's much better."

"Good to hear that," he answered between bites. "And how's that new grandbaby of yours? A boy, right?"

"Nicholas Benjamin. But he's already a year old. And starting to walk. Sure keeps us on our toes!"

"They do grow fast!" Bert took one more spoonful of ice cream and said, "That's it. I'm done. No more for me!"

'It seems like yesterday my girls were just little. And now look, grown and mothers themselves." She looked at the sheriff and asked, "Do you have children, Sheriff? I don't know if I've ever heard."

"No, no kids for me. Was married for a little while, long ago. But no kids." He stood to go. "Thanks again for the ice cream, Elizabeth. That was mighty kind of you."

"My pleasure, Sheriff. Better than eating alone."

The sheriff tapped his cap again and said, "Bert. Call me Bert. And the pleasure was all mine."

This time he was sure there was a blush growing on Elizabeth's cheeks.

Chapter 28

GIVING THANKS

Coop walked the corn fields in late June and discovered the stalks were standing up to his shoulders. The old saying that a good crop of corn would be 'knee high by the fourth of July' was just that, 'old.' This year's crop was predicted to far outgrow that standard.

He looked up at the deep blue sky and watched white puffy clouds float slowly by. "Thank you, Lord, for all your blessings. For the rain that you sent at just the right time to save our crops and make them grow. For the wonderful harvest of wheat and the promise I see in this corn field. For the new calves that are growing strong. For the sheep shearers coming next week and the money we will get selling the wool. Every little bit helps, and it comforts me to know that you take care of our every need."

As he walked towards the barn, he continued to pray. "I place Dana in your hands, Lord, as I have done so many times before. Watch over her and keep her safe. Give her wisdom and courage as she meets the struggles in Nicaragua. Teach her your ways; help her to walk in your paths. And may she bring the light of Jesus to the people she meets there."

He had tried to talk to Dana that Sunday she had gone forward and prayed at the altar. All she would say was that she knew God was telling her the answer was in Nicaragua. She didn't know exactly what that meant and Coop didn't either. But that didn't stop Coop from praying. He knew that God's plan would be revealed in his good time.

Chapter 29

MY BAGS ARE PACKED, I'M READY TO GO

"I'm all packed," Jenny said as she zipped up her back pack. "I put in jammies, clothes for tomorrow and my swim suit."

"Toothbrush?" ask Becky. "Hairbrush?"

"Check and check," Jenny answered. "And flip-flops and sunscreen." She adjusted the backpack over her shoulders and added, "But not toothpaste b'cuz I can always borrow Hannah's."

"Then I think you're ready. Let's go tell Aunt Dana goodbye. She'll be on her way to Nicaragua tomorrow and you won't see her for two months. By the time she gets back, school will be starting and you will be in third grade!"

"Huh? That's a long time." Becky was reminded that time seems to crawl by for children, but it flies for adults. Every year seemed to go faster and faster the older she got.

Dana's suitcase was sitting on the screen porch of the farmhouse. A little silver padlock secured the zippers together.

A brown leather name tag hung from the handle. Becky and Jenny opened the door and entered the kitchen.

Dana was seated at the table with her head bowed. Standing behind her was Dave Cole, the leader of Dana's Sunday school class. His hand rested on Dana's forehead. Melissa Madison had placed her hand on Dana's shoulder. Marla Jena stood to the side, with her hand outstretched to her daughter. Dave was praying.

Becky motioned with a finger to her lips and instructed Jenny to stand quietly. They both closed their eyes and prayed with the others in the room.

"For traveling mercies, we ask your blessing Lord. For safety in the mission field, Lord we ask for your mercy. For relationships formed and souls saved, Lord hear our prayer. We ask these things in the name of Jesus. Amen." Together the group echoed "Amen."

"Hi Dave, Melissa," Becky apologized. "I'm sorry I didn't know you were here. Hope we didn't interrupt anything."

"No, not at all," Dave answered. "We decided kind of at the last minute to come over and have prayer with Dana before she leaves."

"That was good of you," Becky said. "Coop's out in the field or he would have liked to join you." To Dana she said, "Jenny came to say goodbye."

Jenny gave her aunt a big hug. "I'm packed up too," she said. "I'm going to spend the night at Hannah's. We're going to go swimming."

"That'll be fun," Dana said. "You just be careful in the deep end. I know you've been taking swimming lessons, but remember to be careful."

"Is there swimming pools in Nicaragua?" Jenny asked. "Can you go swimming there?"

Dana chuckled, "Well, I don't think we will be close to any swimming pools. But there's a lake nearby, and a river. I did put my swimming suit in my suitcase, so I'll be ready if we have time for some fun."

"Then you be careful too, Aunt Dana. Don't let any alligators get you."

"I promise to be on the lookout," Dana laughed. "Love you, sweetie. Have fun at Hannah's."

"Kendy is sleeping over with Hannah too. Our first Brownie slumber party of the summer!"

Dave laughed, "Oh my, I hope Greg and Nancy survive a house full of girls!"

"Slumber parties are lots of fun," Melissa joined in. "I remember a few great times when I was a kid."

"Me too," said Becky. "My sister Joyce and I always had sleepovers for our birthday parties. Mom was very patient with all the noise, but I know now that it really wore her out!"

Becky motioned to Jenny, "We better get going, Jenny. Hannah and her mommy are expecting you soon." Becky made her way toward the door.

"One more hug!" Jenny said as she gave Dana a big squeeze. "I love you. Tell lots of people about Jesus!"

"That's the plan, Jenny. Everybody needs to know about Jesus. Everybody." Dana and Melissa shared a knowing look.

"Everybody," Melissa said with a smile.

****

Early next morning, the church van from Rockford arrived with the mission team on its way to the airport. Tucker was quick to exit the van and greet Dana and her family. He picked up her suitcase and carry-on and said, "I see you packed lightly. That's good. We aren't going to need much. The people there get by with so little." He loaded the bags into the back of the van. "Are you ready for the adventure of a lifetime?"

"I sure am! This is going to be amazing!

The leader of the mission team, Tim Swift, got off the van and led the group in prayer before Dana hugged her mom and brother and sister-in-law one last time. Dana patted Holly on the head and said, "You be a good girl, Holly. Take care of everybody while I'm gone." Coop and Becky stood hand in hand as they watched Dana walk toward the van. Tucker's arm was laid across her back, guiding her gently toward the adventure that lay ahead.

Chapter 30

TRANSFORMATIONS

Craig Cashman backed his trailer up to the cattle loading area and got out of the cab. He usually didn't haul cattle, but this opportunity came a week before when Coop had asked him if he was available to move several of his beef cows to the livestock auction in Lennox, two hours away. After checking his schedule, Craig agreed.

Craig walked to the enclosure and rested his arms on the top railing. He watched as Holly and Coop worked as a team to herd the cattle into the small loading pen. Holly weaved back and forth, moving the cattle toward the opening in the gate. Occasionally she nipped at the ankle of a cow who was wandering from the group. Holly worked slowly, pushing the cows toward the pen. She listened to instructions from Coop, knowing when to move left or right, when to lie down, when to give the occasional uncooperative cow an intense stare. With a few whistles from Coop and a couple of barks from Holly, all of the cows were secured in the loading pen. Coop locked the gate and walked through the cows to talk with Craig.

Craig had watched the process in awe. "That was amazing. I've never seen a dog do that before."

"She's pretty special. She's really good with sheep, but getting better with cows, especially a small group like this. She's bred to be a herding dog, and it's practically second nature with her. It took some training, of course. She had to learn what my commands meant. But she caught on fast."

Craig shook his head. "Unbelievable. I thought dogs mostly played fetch and learned to sit and come. This dog is something else!"

Holly came and sat at Coop's side. He patted her on the head and said, "You're a good girl, aren't you Holly? Yes, you are!"

It took very little time to get the cattle up the ramp and into the trailer. Coop secured them into stalls and made sure everything was ready for travel. After final instructions from Coop, Craig set the GPS in the truck and turned to Coop with a request. "I think we should pray before I leave."

Coop nodded in agreement and took off his black cowboy hat. He banged it against his leg to remove some of the dust and dirt that always collected when he was working. "I think that's a great idea! Glad you thought of it!"

"You know, a couple of years ago, I never would have thought of praying. It certainly wasn't something I put any importance into. But now, since I've become a Christian, I talk to God all day long. It's really changed my life."

"God is good!" Coop replied and slapped Craig on the back.

They bowed their heads as they stood beside the trailer loaded with cattle. Craig began, "God, I ask that you would be with me as I drive these cows to Lennox. Keep me alert to trouble on the road. Keep the cows calm. Help me not get lost." He paused and Coop took up the conversation.

"Heavenly Father, go with Craig as he drives to Lennox. Be with him on the highways, on the bridges, during turns and up and down hills. Keep him alert and attentive. Get him safely to the cattle-yard and home again. And Lord, if it be your will, it would be a real blessing if the cattle brought a good price. As always, we thank you in advance for how you take care of us. You have provided for our needs in the past and we trust you to do it again in the future. We love you, rely on you and thank you. Amen."

"Amen," echoed Craig. "Well, thanks, I guess I better hit the road. Want me to text you when I've got them all delivered?"

"Yeah, that would be great. Okay, buddy, have a safe trip. Talk to you soon."

Craig took off slowly down the gravel road. A dust trail followed the trailer but soon dissipated. Craig checked the time. He should be in Lennox before noon. He'd drop off the load, get some lunch and head home. He was hoping to be home before five because he was on the committee charged with setting up the fireworks for the town's Fourth of July celebration. He should have plenty of time to make it to Lennox and back before the meeting.

It was a beautiful day for a drive. Craig put down the window and laid his left arm in the sun. He watched the farm scenes roll past him one after another. Fields of corn, tall and heavy with ears, gave way to acres of grazing cattle. Large barns and silos dotted the hillside. Well manicured homesteads, small in the shadow of immense outbuildings, indicated that the farm family took great care of their land. "Thank you for farmers, God. And ranchers," he said as he drove along. He thought of the big steak he hoped to eat for lunch and his stomached growled.

He was driving under the speed limit, never went over it. This small load of cattle seemed calm and the drive was going well. Craig glanced at the clock; he was making good time. He made a turn and merged onto a four lane highway. Traffic was a little heavier here, but seemed to be moving well.

In his side mirror Craig watched a red car approaching quickly. The driver was definitely in a hurry, obviously going over the speed limit. Craig watched as the car wove from lane to lane. Then it passed him and continued its journey, passing cars and trucks as it traveled up the gently rising roadway. Craig could see it in the distance as it crested the hill. Then the red car was no longer visible. By the time Craig got to the top of the hill, the red car was totally out of sight.

It wasn't long before brake lights were seen ahead and Craig slowed the truck to a crawl. A police car, sirens blaring, sailed past him in the left lane. Then traffic stopped completely. Cars pulled to the left and right to allow an ambulance to get through. Next came a fire truck and two more police cars.

Craig had moved his truck to the right shoulder and sat patiently half on and half off the highway. No one was moving now. Some people even got out of their cars and started conversations with other drivers.

Even though he didn't know what was going on up ahead, Craig prayed for whatever the situation was. He remembered some accidents he had driven by in the past and realized that he had never prayed about any of them. Only since his conversion had he started thinking about praying for those in need.

Craig opened a Coke and took a long drink. He left the truck running, so he would have air conditioning in the cab. It wasn't an overly hot day, but cars and pavement and engine heat would soon become an uncomfortable combination. He hoped the cattle in the trailer would be okay.

"Oh God," he prayed, "Watch over the people in trouble up ahead. Be with the police and emergency helpers. And if it is your will, make this traffic move soon so we can be on our way."

Craig let his mind wander. As he often did lately, he prayed for his sister Pat. There had been rumors that the nursing home where she worked was going to close. Pat was worried that she was going to lose her job. Since she was nearly fifty, she was afraid that her chances of finding a new job were few and far between. She had never married and lived alone all her adult life. Her budget was tight and she didn't have much money in savings. She already feared the financial strain being unemployed would bring. So Craig prayed for peace for his sister. He prayed that if she did lose her job, another job would come along quickly. And he prayed that through it all he would be a witness to her and help her see God's plan for her life.

He had encouraged Pat to come to church with him, but she had to work on most Sundays. So Craig added in his prayer that Pat's new job would not include Sundays. "It's a silly thing to pray for, I guess. But I know the Bible says somewhere that we don't get what we don't ask for. Or something like that. So God, no Sunday's, okay?"

His thoughts drifted to his cousin JJ. After surgery for kidney cancer, JJ had been recovering well. He had returned to his job as an electrician, but was only working part time. JJ's wife Bev was a school teacher. They lived in a small house on the outskirts of Atkins. They had one son, Frank, who had left home right after high school and hadn't kept in touch with his parents. Nobody knew what happened to him. JJ said he had been trouble since the day he was born, and refused to talk any more about him. It was like he disappeared, or maybe never even existed in the first place.

Bev had shown a bit more concern when Frank left and never contacted them. She said they should talk to the sheriff and get somebody to look for him. But JJ said since he was eighteen and left on his own, nobody would waste their time looking for him. He was an adult and would just have to make it on his own. So that was that.

As he sat in the gridlock of traffic, Craig prayed for Frank. He prayed that he would make good decisions, that he would be safe, that someone would come and witness to him.

Craig also prayed for his cousin. He had tried to talk JJ and Bev about Jesus after he was saved, but they had been only mildly interested. Mostly curious about the change in Craig's lifestyle. Even Melissa Madison had invited them to church, but they resisted.

Melissa Madison! What a story she had! Craig shook his head once again in wonder. It was hard to believe that she had been changed from a criminal, a drug user, a thief, to a child of God! And thanks to her witness, Craig himself had come to Christ.

So Craig concluded his prayer time with praise to God for his great love and for his salvation plan. He prayed that somehow he would be able to convince JJ and Bev to accept Christ and be saved. 'I need to get over there and visit them, at least. They might need some help with something. I should go visit. Maybe Pat would like to go along. I'll call her later.'

Up ahead, Craig could see the traffic begin to move slowly. He clicked on his turn signal and inched back onto the road. Before long, two lanes of traffic were merged to the right and directed to use the next exit as a detour. They followed in single file on a gravel country road, making quite a stir of dust as they passed through town after small town. People stopped and watched as if it were a holiday parade, waving and laughing at all the traffic. It was the most excitement these little towns had ever seen!

Finally the line of vehicles made its way back onto the highway. They picked up speed and moved ahead at a normal pace. Craig never did see what the problem had been although he assumed it was an accident of some sort.

He was more than an hour off schedule. But rather than worry about it, Craig was glad he had the chance to have a good prayer time. He'd been trying to be more consistent with his devotional time and prayers, but sometimes it was hard. With odd work and travel schedules plus all the community things he was into lately, his days were pretty full. He wanted to do better, and today's road delay had been the perfect opportunity. He was grateful.

****

Coop checked his watch again and prayed that everything was going smoothly for Craig and the cattle. He should have heard from Craig by now. He said a quick prayer for his safety and went out to the garden where Becky and the three Brownies were hunting for cucumbers. Becky carried a basket and walked among the hills, checking to make sure the girls didn't pick every cucumber in sight. "Let's leave that one," she instructed Hannah. "It needs to grow some more."

"How about this one?" Kendy asked, lifting some leaves to display a cucumber about two inches long.

"We'll wait on that one too," Becky answered. She held up one of the cucumbers in her basket and said, "More like this one. Keep looking, I'm sure you'll find some more."

"Remember that big big zucchini we had last year?" asked Jenny as she stretched her hands wider and wider. "With all the seeds?"

"I remember it!" laughed Kendy. "Your dad played like it was a baseball bat!"

"Yeah, he did!" Jenny laughed. "We used those seeds to plant more zucchini, and they are really growing. See? Here's a good one."

"And here's one," added Hannah. "Can we pick zucchini too?"

"Okay, each of you find one zucchini, but then we need to finish the cucumbers." Becky looked over at the swing-set, where Coop was pushing Nicholas in his bucket swing.

"Have you heard from Craig yet?" she called to him.

"No, not yet. And he should have been there and all unloaded at least an hour ago. Hope everything is okay."

"I'm sure he would have called if there were a problem," Becky reassured him.

"You're probably right," Coop caught Nicholas by the feet and held him. "You want to go higher?" Nicholas grinned and banged his hands on the swing. "Say more please."

To Coop's great delight, Nicholas used his hands and signed the words as he said, "Mu pees."

"That's my boy!" Coop exclaimed and sent Nicholas flying high. "You taught him that, didn't you?" he asked Becky.

"I did, though to be honest, it wasn't my idea. I noticed that his teacher at the church nursery taught some of the older kids, and I thought I'd give it a try. He learned it fast."

The girls finished their picking and Becky carried the loaded basket into the house. The girls ran ahead to wash up. Coop offered his fingers to Nicholas, who gripped them tightly and took several tentative steps. "You're doing great, little man!" exclaimed Coop. "You'll be walking on your own in no time." When they got to the steps, Coop let Nicholas crawl up on his own. Then he picked the boy up and carried him into the house. "Let's wash your hands. Mommy is fixing a snack."

Becky sat a plate of freshly sliced cucumbers on the table. Jenny got a plate for everyone. Nicholas was cleaned up and secured into his high chair.

"I'll pray!" exclaimed Kendy.

Becky nodded and smiled, happy to see that Kendy was getting comfortable with the idea of prayer.

"Thank you Jesus, for our cucumbers and zucchini and seeds and the Brownies! Amen!" Kendy said enthusiastically.

Everyone chorused the 'Amen' and munched on cucumbers. Even Nicholas enjoyed his snack. He tossed one slice down to the floor and Holly gobbled it up. Everybody likes cucumbers!

Chapter 30

THINKING BACK

Craig pulled his rig into a long parking space at the Lennox truck stop. He'd been at this particular truck stop before, on a cross-country run a few years ago. Walking in, he recognized the layout right away. Most all the truck stops were primarily the same. Truck accessories and tools, restrooms and showers, a gift shop with tee-shirts and audio-books, a section for overpriced snacks and sodas, and a clerk at the counter wishing him welcome. He wound his way through the store front and walked up to the lunch counter. He sat on a high stool and looked around while he waited for the server.

It was pretty busy here, which was a sign of good food for sure. He quickly spotted some other truckers; most were sitting alone, nursing hot coffee until they got on the road again. In a couple of booths, two drivers sat together. A family with three small children sat in a booth at the back and a family with teenagers sat at a round table. One teen caught his eye. She had long dark hair that shone in the iridescent lighting and a flowery tattoo on one arm. She reminded him of Melissa.

He smiled at the memory of sitting in another truck stop with Melissa, only she was Misty then and had just cut her black hair short. She was on the run, trying to get away from the police who were hunting her down. That chance meeting had been the beginning of a journey towards Christ, only neither one of them knew it at the time. So much had changed since then. And all for the good.

The waitress came by and brought coffee. Just what Craig needed. A good cup of coffee. Nothing better when you're facing road fatigue. He ordered his meal, including a sixteen ounce steak, and settled back to watch the television hanging behind the bar. The volume was muted but he read the captions. 'Two killed in rollover accident.' Craig sat up a little taller and leaned forward. The pictures of the accident showed clearly a red car upside down in the median. Two other cars were involved in the accident, but only the red car was on its top.

He recognized the car. 'That explains the traffic detour,' he thought.

The waitress appeared with his food and noticed his attention on the television. "How sad," she said. "Two teenage boys from Lennox. Out for a drive and then," she snapped her fingers, "Lives changed, so fast."

Craig shook his head from side to side. "We never know when our last day will be. Just have to be prepared for eternity."

"That's the truth," she answered. "Well, enjoy that steak." She walked away, leaving Craig to look down at his plate of food. Besides his steak, he had ordered mashed potatoes and carrots. Everything looked delicious. He prayed and dove in. Half an hour later, completely satisfied after his meal and dessert of cherry pie, he stood and placed a Bible verse tract on the table. He had started doing that after Melissa had told him that it was a good way to witness without being pushy or confrontational. So now, whenever Craig read a scripture that jumped out at him, he would copy it down on little cards. He always had a few in his pocket, to leave whenever the Lord led him to do so.

He walked across the graveled parking lot, boots crunching rocks as he went. He made a call to Coop before starting on his way.

"Hey, I was beginning to wonder if you were alright," Coop said when he answered the call.

"Yeah, I'm fine. Just had a delay because of an accident on the highway. The cows are delivered, I had a great lunch and I'm ready to head home. If all goes well, I still have plenty of time to get to my meeting tonight."

"Great. I'm glad everything's okay. Thanks again for doing this. I appreciate it."

"What are friends for?" Craig joked. "Okay, I'll get going. See you soon."

"Praying for a safe trip home. Later, my friend."

"Later." Craig pulled himself into the cab and started for home. He didn't forget to ask God to go with him.

Chapter 32

BOMBARDING HEAVEN

An impromptu prayer meeting was in session. An emergency in Nicaragua had come up and Marla Jean called for prayer. A group gathered around her kitchen table. Pastor Green and his wife were there, as were Dave Cole, Melissa Madison and several other members of the young adult Sunday school class. Becky and Coop had come over from their own house and were setting up extra chairs in the kitchen. Nancy and Tabitha were welcoming guests as they arrived. Soon the room was filled with prayer warriors.

Pastor Green opened the meeting with an introduction. "Folks, thank you for coming out to the farm for this prayer time. We are going to come together to stand for Dana and the others on the mission trip. Becky, would you tell us what you know so far."

Becky nodded and began, "We got a phone call from someone on the prayer team from the Baptist church in Rockford. The mission team in Nicaragua is dealing with some dangerous weather situations and asked for prayer. You've probably heard about the tropical storm brewing in the area. If the storm worsens and makes landfall, as is expected in the next twenty-four hours, there's likely to be serious flooding and property damage, probably even loss of life. So the team asked for everyone to be in prayer about the situation."

Coop added, "We know the power of prayer. We know that where two or three are gathered in his name, God is there. Dana and Tucker and the rest of the team need intercession. That's why we are here."

"So let's get right to it," said Pastor Green. "We want to bombard heaven with our prayers. Feel free to pray as you are led. Listen to the Lord's prompting and pray aloud or within your own heart, as you are comfortable. I'll begin."

Heads were bowed, some couples held hands, and Pastor Green opened his heart. "Lord God, Father of heaven and earth, Creator of the world, Master of the universe, we come to you now with hearts of love and adoration. We worship you for all the good you have done in the past. For how you have answered prayers. For ways in which you have protected us from harm. For your perfect plan and for always being with us. We ask now that you be with Dana and her friends on the mission team in Nicaragua. Cover them with your wings and keep them safe from the storm. And if it be your will, calm the storm. Speak the word and the winds and waves will obey you. You've done it before, Jesus, when the disciples were in the boat on the Sea of Galilee. We know you are in control of all things. So you are mighty and able. Lord, we ask your help. We ask for your intervention. You are a good Father. We call on you now."

He paused and it was silent for a moment. Then Dave Cole said, "Yes, Lord, you are all knowing and all powerful. If it is your will, you can turn the storm. Send it back to the sea, where no harm will come to the people of Nicaragua. We know you have the power – you are King of Kings and Lord of Lords. And we pray in your holy name."

When Becky prayed, she felt led to ask God for protection from the flood waters that might come. "Lord, you've asked me to pray about Dana and the water in Nicaragua. I ask now that you will keep her safe from any flooding that she may encounter. Hold your hand on Dana and the others on the team. Lift them above the raging flood waters. Lead them to a place of safety."

Coop followed in Becky's line of thinking. "God, creator and sustainer of all life, I pray for my sister and the others with her. I ask that you protect them from whatever dangers come their way. Flood waters, raging rivers, deep pools. Please God, keep them safe. We remember the verse in Isaiah that says, "When you pass through the waters, I will be with you; And through the rivers, they will not overflow you." We pray these verses over Dana and the team today. Hold them with your mighty right hand."

Another minute of silence followed. Some softly whispered prayers could be heard but no one spoke loud enough to be heard. They were talking to God and did not need others to hear.

Marla Jean began to hum. Soon she sang the words to a familiar hymn and others joined her. "What a friend we have in Jesus, all our sins and grief to bear. What a privilege to carry everything to God in prayer." The song was full of hope and reminded everyone that prayer is always the answer, to whatever situation they may find themselves.

Tom and Tabitha didn't know that song but sat quietly listening to the words. The phrase 'In his arms he'll take and shield thee' spoke to Tabitha. She felt goose bumps rise on her arms. In her mind she prayed, 'shield Dana in your arms, Jesus. What an awesome feeling that must be, to be wrapped in Jesus arms.' She sighed and Tom glanced at her. She flashed him a smile and determined to tell him later what she had been thinking about.

They were not comfortable enough to pray aloud in front of so many people. Nancy had told them that prayer was just talking to God, but they were still self-conscious about doing it 'right.' Yet Tabitha felt nudged by the Lord to repeat the prayer that was in her mind. So she took a deep breath and after the song was done, she prayed aloud. "Shield Dana in your arms, Jesus."

Across the room, Nancy smiled and prayed silently, rejoicing that her new friend was finding a voice for Jesus.

For the next hour, the little kitchen was filled with the presence of the Lord. Everyone sensed that God was right there with them. Prayers and praises were uttered, voices were lifted in song, and tears were shed. There was a moving of the Holy Spirit and everyone felt it.

Under the weeping willow tree in the back yard, the three little brown-haired girls were also praying. Their prayer meeting was much less than an hour, but they each took a turn. "Jesus would you please tell that storm, 'Peace, be still' like in the Bible story you did for the disciples?" Jenny prayed. "You can say 'Peace, be still' and make the storm stop. We know you can do it Jesus. Because you are strong and powerful. We will be so happy if you do something to make the storm stop. Thank you. Amen."

Hannah said, "Please keep Aunt Dana safe from the storm. Help her not be hurt if trees fall down. And the houses too. Amen"

Kendy was already feeling more confident in prayer. She had gotten over her shyness and insecurity because Jenny and Hannah had encouraged her to 'just talk to God like you talk to us.' So she prayed, "Hi God, this is Kendy. You know Aunt Dana? She's going to be in a big storm. But I know you can keep her safe, because you are God, after all. So keep her safe, please. She is special to Jenny and to me and Hannah too, so take care of her so she can come back home soon. Amen."

"Let's sing something," suggested Jenny.

"Like what?" Hannah asked.

"Like that song we can add verses too. 'God is so good.' But we can say 'God keeps us safe' and other things we make up."

So The Brownies sang and sang. "God answers prayer." "God calms the storm." "God hears our prayers." "God is so great." "He loves me so." "God keeps us safe." "He holds my hand."

They had almost run out of ideas until Kendy thought of one more. "God is my friend."

Holly the collie sat with them under the tree, looking from girl to girl as they sang. When the song ended, Holly tilted her head as if waiting for another verse. Jenny rubbed her head and said, "Did you like our song, girl?" Holly barked.

"She did! She liked it!" laughed Kendy.

"It was a good song," Hannah put in. "I'm glad we made up good verses."

"Want to go play with the kittens?" Jenny asked.

"Sure!" was the answer in chorus. The Brownies scurried off to the barn to find Muffin and her new kittens.

Chapter 33

FROM DESPERATION TO EXHILARATION

All over town, people were watching the television as pictures and videos of the tropical storm made the evening news the next day. The broadcaster talked of strong winds, lots of rain and some structural damages. The biggest problem was because of the storm surge, which brought flood waters inland. Dozens of homes along the coastline of Nicaragua were destroyed. Debris was floating out to sea as the waters rescinded.

No mention was made of the missionary team from Kansas. None of the team had contacted their families back home. Not hearing from them had everyone, especially Marla Jean, on edge. It was hard to remain hopeful, with no information. The newscast talked about downed power lines and blocked roadways. 'Maybe that's why we haven't heard anything,' thought Marla Jean. She said yet another prayer on Dana's behalf.

In town, people were praying too. The church was always open for prayer and there had been a parade in and out all day. Elizabeth was there, kneeling at the prayer rail in the sanctuary. Other members of the choir came by and knelt alongside her. After a bit, Kaye the choir director came in, went to the piano and began to play hymns softly. It set a mood of quiet reflection.

Near the back of the sanctuary, Melissa and Dave sat together, holding hands and sharing prayers. Just as Dave was closing his prayer, Melissa got a ding on her cell phone. She looked at the message and immediately said, "Oh praise God. Thank you Lord."

"What's up?" Dave asked.

"It's a Facebook post. Somebody on the mission team posted and it's being shared all over. It says 'Marked Safe from Tropical Storm Izelda' and it's from the whole mission team. I need to tell Pastor and spread the word! Dana is safe!"

Dave squeezed her hand and said, "Awesome! God heard our prayers!"

Melissa noticed Elizabeth at the altar and hurried up to her with the news. "Oh that's wonderful!" said Elizabeth. "I'll call Becky right now, and Marla Jean too. They will be so happy."

Dave went to the piano to tell Kaye and she started playing 'The Doxology.'

> *Praise God from whom all blessings flow.*
> *Praise Him all creatures here below.*
> *Praise Him above the heavenly host.*
> *Praise Father, Son and Holy Ghost.*

The atmosphere in the sanctuary instantly changed from one of desperation to one of exhilaration. Dana was safe! The whole team was safe! The good news spread outside the church and soon everyone had heard. Dana and the team were marked safe.

****

Sheriff Bertell drove his cruiser slowly through the church parking lot. He was surprised to see so many cars here at this time of the day. It wasn't unusual to see a couple of cars at odd times, but this looked like quite a gathering. He wondered what was going on.

He had made it his business to know the vehicles that belonged to residents of Winslow. Right away he spotted Elizabeth Emerson's light blue Honda parked near the church entrance. He smiled slightly remembering mint chocolate chip ice cream and a pinkish glow on Elizabeth's face.

Bert pulled his car up beside Elizabeth's and got out. He saw her leaving the church and stood near her car, waiting.

As Elizabeth walked closer, she noticed the sheriff. "Good evening, Sheriff," she said. "Is anything wrong? I know I wasn't speeding!"

"No, no, nothing like that. I just noticed your car and thought I'd stop and see how you're doing. Everything alright?"

"Better than alright, Sheriff. We've been praying really hard for Dana Smith and the others who are on a mission trip to Nicaragua. I'm sure you heard about the terrible weather they were having there. Lots of rain and wind and flooding." She waited and the sheriff nodded his head. "Well, we just heard that they are all safe. We don't know any details, just that they are all safe. That's the answer to prayer we've been waiting for."

"Well, I'm glad to hear it. Dana is a right sweet girl. I'd hate for anything to happen to her. So that's why all these cars are here?"

"Yes Sheriff, it is."

"I think you forgot something," he said, with a little twinkle in his eye.

"Forgot?" Elizabeth looked around. She had her purse; her keys were in her hand. Whatever could he mean? "No, Sheriff Bertell, I don't think I forgot anything."

"You forgot that I asked you to call me Bert!"

"Oh, you scared me! Yes, you did ask me to call you Bert. I didn't forget, exactly. I'm just not comfortable being so casual with a person in authority. I mean, Pastor Green is always Pastor. I could never call him John. Just doesn't seem right."

"Well, maybe in my case, you could forget the authority part. Unless you're in trouble with the law, which I don't see is the case, I could just be a friend. How's that sound?"

"I guess I could try," Elizabeth said. "But I might forget again."

"Then let's practice! Say, 'Good evening, Bert.' He paused to let her respond.

With a little giggle she said, "Good evening, Bert. Lovely weather we are having, don't you think?"

"Yes, Elizabeth, it is a beautiful evening. We're supposed to have a full moon tonight. And no clouds, so it should be a perfect night. Do you have any plans?"

"Well, Bert, I'm going to go home and write a thank you note to God in my praise journal. I like to thank God whenever good things happen. And Dana being safe, that's really good."

"I'd say it really is." Bert made a move away from her car. "Well, Elizabeth, drive home safely. No speeding, you hear? Goodnight now."

"Goodnight, Bert." When Elizabeth got into her car, she had to sit still a minute and take a deep breath. She hadn't realized it, but her heart was beating a little faster than usual. She let her breath out slowly and shook her head slightly to clear her thoughts.

"Silly old lady," she said to herself. "Don't be ridiculous."

Chapter 34

HENS AND CHICKS

"Remember what you told me about praying for Dana, and God kept bringing water to your mind?" Coop asked Becky. "I've been thinking about that. Isn't it awesome? You were praying about Dana and water, long before there was a flood anywhere near her. God knew what was ahead for Dana and he had you praying about it when we didn't even know anything about a flood."

The kids were already asleep in their beds and Coop and Becky were taking advantage of some quiet time to cuddle together in the living room. Becky's feet were tucked up under her and she leaned against Coop as he sat with his arm draped over her shoulder. Times like this were few and far between so they wanted to take advantage while they could.

"True," Becky responded. "And I'm so glad I listened. It seemed silly at the time, but it was part of God's plan all along. Incredible."

"So that maybe teaches us two things," Coop went on. "One, to listen to the little nudges God gives us. And two, that God's plan is far above our understanding."

"And three," added Becky. "That God's plan is good!"

"Amen!"

They sat quietly for awhile, just enjoying the togetherness. A rustling sound came through on the baby monitor. Nicholas was rolling in his crib, repositioning himself. But he stayed asleep, and Becky breathed a sigh of relief.

"Speaking of God's plan, I was wondering," Becky trailed off, hesitating just a little. "I was wondering if maybe it's time to think about adding to the Smith family pretty soon. Nicholas is one now. If I went off the pills, we could just see what God has planned for us. I mean, if you want more kids, and I think you do, maybe we should talk about it."

"Oh, you bet I would like more kids. I love being a daddy!" Coop gave her a hug. "But do you think your body is ready? I mean, you had the miscarriage, then a little scare with Nicholas. Do you want to put yourself through that again?"

"If it's God's will, then of course. I mean, I have learned to trust him, even when things were hard or uncertain. Every experience, no matter how difficult, has been a learning opportunity."

"Spoken like a real Proverbs woman!" Coop said. "Wise and always learning. And willing to do whatever it takes to care of her family."

Becky smiled and kissed him. "If I go off the pill, then it really puts everything in God's hand. He'll figure out the right time. And he knows what's best."

Coop pulled her close and kissed her neck. "I like that plan. Maybe we should start working on it tonight?" He stood and pulled Becky to her feet. "Come with me to the bedroom, my little hen," he teased. "We can make some little chicks and increase our flock."

"Oh I'll come willingly, my love, but it will take a while for the pill to clear my system, once I go off. So don't plan on little chicks right away."

"No problem, we can just practice."

"And practice makes perfect!"

"Yep! You, me, Jenny, Nicholas and whoever or however many little chicks God sees fit to give us. Perfect." Coop pulled her to himself and surrounded her with his arms. He kissed her deeply and Becky relaxed in his embrace. With all of the emotional ups and downs of the past few days, being in the arms of the man she loved was very comforting. And perfect.

Chapter 35

PREPARATIONS

Jenny was up at sunrise on the morning of the Fourth of July. She had chores to do and she wanted to get them done early. This was going to be a busy day. She dressed in cut-off jean shorts and a Mickey Mouse t-shirt, stomped her feet into her boots and headed to the kitchen. The sun was peaking through the kitchen window above the sink, bathing the room with a pinkish glow.

Coop was already drinking his first cup of coffee. "Hey Jenny, you're up early," he said, tousling her hair. "Want some toast?"

"Sure! One piece please. With cinnamon and sugar."

"Will do. What are your plans for this morning?"

"First I'll get the eggs. Then Mommy needs some green beans picked. After that, I want to go looking for Muffin. That momma cat keeps moving her kittens. I want to find where she's hiding them this time."

"Just remember to be careful climbing the ladder to the hay mow. I know you can do it now, you've grown so much, but always be careful."

Jenny nodded in agreement and poured herself a glass of milk.

"You also need to brush down Benny really good. He's gotten a little messy, rolling around in the dust."

"That's his favorite thing to do, rolling in the dust out in the pasture by that dried up creek place. He goes there and lies in the dust all the time. Don't know why he likes it!"

"Maybe the dust keeps the flies away."

"Yeah, maybe. But I wish he wouldn't. I wish I didn't have to brush him today. I want to find those kittens."

"Chores first, then playtime," Coop instructed. "Remember, Benny is your responsibility."

"Can't I just wait until tomorrow? One more day can't hurt." Jenny put her elbows on the table and held her chin in her hands. "I just want to find the kittens."

"Jenny, just think a little. What is the most important thing? Looking for kittens or living up to your promises? Finding the kittens, or caring for an animal that depends on you? Doing what you want to do, or doing what is right?"

"I remember you told me once about when you didn't do what your daddy told you to do. And your daddy taught you a lesson." She wasn't ready to admit it yet, but she was thinking about her responsibilities.

"And do you remember the verse my dad taught me?"

"And then you taught me. Yes I remember. 'Keep your tongue from evil and your lips from telling lies. Psalms 34:13.' But I wouldn't be telling a lie if I didn't brush Benny."

"No, but you would be breaking your promise to care for your pony. So isn't that just about like lying? Saying you'd do something, but not doing it. It's almost a lie."

"Okay, I get it. Benny first, then the kittens."

Coop buttered four pieces of toast and added cinnamon sugar to one. He put strawberry jelly on two slices for himself and sat the fourth slice to the side. Jenny sat at the table with her toast and waited for Coop to take his place.

"I'll pray!" she said enthusiastically. She stretched her hand to Coop's and said, "Thank you dear God for the pretty sunrise and for toast and cinnamon sugar. I know all good things come from you, so thank you. Amen!"

She took a bite of her toast and chewed thoughtfully. "Oh! I should have prayed that we don't have a tornado today. Like that one year."

"You remember that day, don't you? It was quite a storm! But remember where we were?"

"I know! We were in the basement and lots of people were there because they came for the picnic but then the tornado came so we went down there and we had candles and cobbler and ice cream." She took another bite. "And we sang songs and you were Goliath and Hannah was scared but I knew we were safe in the basement and God was with us." She chewed another bite of toast. "Oh, and that's the day we got Tinkerbell!"

"Goodness, you really do have a good memory. And look how big Tinkerbell is now! That was two years ago."

"He was always a silly little lamb. He followed Holly around everywhere. I think he thought Holly was his mother, even though she's a dog!" Jenny swallowed the last bite of her toast and washed it down with a drink of milk. She pointed at the single piece of buttered toast left on the table and asked, "Could I have that toast too? I'm more hungry than I thought."

Coop slid the toast over to her. "I thought you might be. That's why I made it for you!"

"Thanks Daddy. You always know what I need, even before I do."

"Jesus is like that too, you know. Philippians 4:19 'And my God will meet all your needs according to the riches of his glory in Christ Jesus.' He knows our needs and supplies us with good things."

"Like my prayer," Jenny declared.

From down the hall, they heard Nicholas call, "Momma! Momma!" From the sounds of things, he was standing in his crib, jumping up and down as he held on to the railing.

"One of these days, he's going to jump right out of that crib!" Coop laughed. "I'll go get him and let your mom sleep in a little."

"She's not sleeping, Daddy. Listen."

Sure enough, they could hear Becky softly singing as she moved about her bedroom getting dressed. Another day had begun. A day with lots of activities and excitement.

"You can go say hi to Nicholas," Jenny said as she took dishes to the sink. "I'll put these in the dishwasher and get to work outside."

Coop stood looking at his daughter, amazed once again at how she was maturing into a responsible young lady. And she had just turned eight!

He walked into the baby's bedroom and found him standing in the crib, trying to throw his leg over the rail. "Oh, no you don't!" he exclaimed as he scooped his son up with a flourish. "No climbing out of the crib, young man!"

Becky stood in the doorway watching as Coop danced around the room with the baby. Nicholas threw his head back and gave a loud belly laugh. Becky smiled and sighed with satisfaction. This was a sight that filled her heart with great joy. 'God, you have met the desires of my heart,' she thought. 'I am blessed by your goodness.'

"Good morning to my favorite men," she said.

Coop walked towards her, said good morning and held Nicholas out at arms length. "Mommy is here to rescue me!" he said. "He was trying to climb out of his crib. I think he knows he needs a diaper change." It was obvious that the diaper was heavy. The baby's pajama bottoms were drooping and nearly falling off.

Coop looked over at the crib and said, "I'll lower the mattress down a notch or two. We definitely don't want him climbing out."

"Good idea," Becky said. "Here, give him to me. I'll change him and get him dressed. You probably need to get outside anyway. I guess Jenny is up and out already?"

"She is. We had some toast together. That girl is sure growing up. Time is flying by."

"Sure is." Becky laid Nicholas on the diaper table and began to undress him. "You know what today is, don't you?"

Coop stood behind her and put his arms around her waist. "Of course I do. Four years ago today I kissed you for the first time. But I knew before then that I was falling in love with you. The kiss just sealed the deal."

Becky laid her hand on Nicholas's tummy and turned to face Coop. Their embrace was full of passion, memory and promise. As their lips parted, Becky put her head against

Coop's chest. He stroked her hair and said, "I've said it before and I'll say it again: I love you more and more every day."

"I never mind hearing it, over and over. I love you more every day too." Just then Nicholas squirmed on the table and kicked his legs. "I guess I better get him changed," Becky said and reluctantly turned back to the diaper table.

Coop kept his hands on her shoulders and whispered in her ear. "Just another minute, Becky." He nibbled on her earlobe and made her giggle.

Becky leaned her head back and encouraged Coop to continue planting soft kisses on her neck. "Ohhh," she moaned. "You are making me melt." She felt a new wash of warmth move up her neck and bring a blush to her cheeks.

Nicholas grabbed hold of Becky's hand and brought her fingers to his mouth. With one quick chomp of his seven baby teeth, the mood was broken. Becky pulled her hand free and jumped back. "Ouch! Nicholas, don't bite Mommy. That hurts!"

Her sharp reaction startled the baby and his lower lip began to quiver. His eyes widened, his mouth opened and he let out a wail comparable to a tornado warning. Becky turned her attention to him and said, "I'm sorry sweetie. I didn't mean to scare you. But you can't bite Mommy."

Nicholas pulled his knees up to his chest, puckered up his lips and cried out again. Becky picked him up and held him close, patting him on the back and trying to sooth him.

"Hey, we'll continue this discussion later, when it's a little quieter. I need to get out to the field anyway." Coop kissed his son on the head. "You settle down, little man. You're okay. But no more biting!"

"Don't forget, we're going over to the Martin's at about 3:00. I'm taking watermelon and making potato salad."

"Great! Yours is the best. Another reason I love you so much!"

Chapter 36

CELEBRATING WITH FRIENDS AND FAMILIES

The Martins and the Smiths had started a tradition of spending the Fourth of July together every year. Starting with a picnic and ending with a night of fireworks at the high school football field, the day was filled with family activities. Jenny loved playing with Hannah in the Martin's pool and had become a pretty good swimmer. When the picnic was held out at the farm, the girls went horseback riding. Hannah was learning to handle Jenny's pony Benny while Jenny had bravely moved up to riding the larger horse Nell. Coop and Greg Martin usually took turns supervising the girls while they walked their horses in the pasture.

The size of the gathering had grown this year, because the Barkdales were invited also. The three young families and their children made for a very busy afternoon. In addition, this year grandparents were also in attendance. Elizabeth and Marla Jean sat in lawn chairs in the shade, chatting with their new friends, Greg's parents Alan and Janet Martin and Nancy's parents Fred and Judy Grandville. It was a good thing the

Martin's house was so big and could easily hold such a large gathering. But the weather was nice so they spent most of their time outside.

The celebration was in full swing. There was no chance of running out of food. Everybody had brought something to share, and there was plenty! A serving table had been set up in the shaded area of the patio and it was loaded with goodies. Potato salad and coleslaw, chips and dips, a fruit bowl with assorted berries and grapes, baked beans, watermelon, as well as hot dogs and cheeseburgers – there was more than enough to go around. Three trays of brownies were displayed at the end of the table, ready for the taste testing contest.

Each of The Brownies had been responsible for coming up with her own version of the standard brownie recipe. Kendy had used walnuts and chocolate chips as a frosting and Hannah's recipe called for slivers of peppermint candy. Jenny had bravely decided to try something new, zucchini brownies. The grandparents would have the difficult task of judging the contest.

Becky had to keep her eye on Nicholas anytime they were outside because he was very interested in the pool. The Martin's little boy Andy was three now, and had grown up with the pool in his backyard. He had a respect for the water that little Nicholas hadn't learned yet.

"Sorry I'm not much help with the food," Becky apologized to Nancy. "I just don't want to take my eyes off of Nicholas."

"Not to worry, I've got this under control. All the grandmas have taken care of setting up the food. Just about everything is out on the table now. The girls need to get out of the pool and dry off before we eat." She called to Hannah, Kendy and Jenny who were having an underwater tea party.

When the girls came up laughing and sputtering, Jenny said, "We don't need to eat anything. We already had tea and crumpets!" Hannah burst into fits of giggles and Kendy joined in.

Becky and Nancy exchanged knowing looks. Their two little girls were best of friends and laughter was often their chosen means of communication. Sometimes just a look or a nudge got them going uncontrollably. Becky was thankful that her daughter had such a good friend, one whose parents shared the values and morals she and Coop lived by as well. It was like all four parents tried to live lives pleasing to the Lord, and surrounded all the children with godly truths.

And now the Barkdales were fitting in so well. It was fun to watch the three girls together. Kendy, quieter than the other two, was starting to open up. Becky was glad to see how her daughter had welcomed a new friend. She and Hannah always included Kendy in their activities now. The Brownies - Becky smiled every time she thought of that name.

After Coop led the group in prayer, everyone got down to the business of eating. Plates were filled, seats found at the table and in lawn chairs. Coop took two hamburgers to start, but Greg said, "How many you gonna eat this year, Coop? Your usual ten?"

"Ah, come on, I've never had ten! Maybe six!"

"Or seven," piped in Becky and everyone laughed.

The conversation moved easily from children's activities and school news to farm work and weather, then on to church programs and the plans for the Sunday school class that the Martins and Smiths co-taught.

"I've noticed that attendance has been down this summer," Greg said. "I know that's to be expected, with school being out and everyone is taking vacations when the kids are free. But it's about time to start planning the fall curriculum and socials."

"I've been giving it some thought," Coop said. "What would you think about a study of Paul's letters? The longer books are talked about a lot, but there's so much good stuff in Galatians and Ephesians that sometimes gets overlooked. Even Colossians and first and second Thessalonians. I don't think we've had studies on those books in a long time. Not in depth anyway."

Nancy poured some more water into Andy's cup and said, "That's true. And one of my favorite verses comes from Ephesians. I think that would make for a good study."

"Let's each give it some thought," Coop said, addressing Greg but including the wives as well. "We should have a planning meeting in a couple of weeks."

Tabitha asked, "Nancy, what's your favorite verse in Ephesians?"

"Well, there's the armor of God verses, and the verses about marriage and parenting, and the verses about spiritual gifts. But I think my favorite is chapter four, verse thirty-two where it says, 'Be kind to one another, tenderhearted, forgiving one another, even as God in Christ forgave you.'"

Tabitha was thoughtful before she said, "Yes, that's good. Sort of sums up the Christian life."

"Right. And when I think about how much Jesus loves us, that he was willing to die for our sins, I can't help but want to live like him. Forgiveness isn't always easy, but if Jesus can forgive the sins of the world, I can forgive those that sin against me. It's a good way to live."

"We have so much to learn, Tom and me, I mean." Tabitha looked at her husband and he nodded in agreement. "You all seem to have integrated scripture into every part of your lives. We haven't managed to do that yet."

"It's easy to fall back into our other way of life," Tom added. "We never thought about God, or following his commandments, or trying to live a holy life. Now, we're trying, but we forget a lot."

"That's understandable," said Greg. "We have been in church all our lives." He nodded towards his parents, smiling in appreciation. "Thanks to godly parents and lots of opportunities to listen and learn from good preaching, we have been immersed in scripture. You'll get there, too. It just takes some time. Don't give up."

Becky joined the conversation. "And don't compare yourselves to others. None of us will ever condemn you for not knowing as much about the Bible as we do. We've each been at this Christian walk a lot longer than you. And Jesus certainly doesn't condemn anyone either, like it says in Romans 1:8. "Therefore, there is now no condemnation for those who are in Christ Jesus." It took me a while to understand that verse, because I condemned myself and figured everyone else did too."

Becky cut up a hot dog into wedges and set it in front of Nicholas. He popped a piece into his mouth and chewed, smiling as he reached for another bite.

"Isn't it great to think about how very much God loves us? That he was willing to sacrifice his son and that Jesus was willing to suffer on the cross like he did – and all because of immeasurable love." Coop smiled at the group, knowing that they all believed as he did.

Jenny interrupted him by saying, "Daddy, Daddy, we learned a verse about love. In Sunday school. We can say it!" She looked at the other Brownies and led them. "Dear friends, since God so loved us, we also ought to love one another. 1 John 4:11."

Hannah said, "We learned a song about love, too. Let's do it!" The three Brownies stood together, holding hands and swinging their arms back and forth. "Let us love one another, for love is from God." When the song was over, they took bows amidst claps and cheers. Even Andy and Nicholas were clapping.

The grandparents were beaming with pride. "The Sunday school teachers have done a great job with these children," Elizabeth said. "It is so comforting to know that our younger generation is soaking up the love of Jesus."

"And sharing it with others," Marla Jean added.

The hot dogs and hamburgers were grilled to perfection, the potato salad and deviled eggs disappeared quickly, and watermelon juice dribbled freely down chins. When everyone had eaten their fill, or beyond, it was time for the brownie contest. When it came down to the final decision, the score was tied at two votes each. Everyone agreed that all were winners and all were delicious and all were worth eating. Nancy and Becky had all they could do to limit the little boys Andy and

Nicholas to just small bites of each flavor. The dads polished off several brownies of each variety.

Soon the picnic trappings were cleaned up and the group headed for the football field to watch the fireworks.

Chapter 37

RIPPLE EFFECT

As Coop pulled his truck up to the entrance of the sports complex, Becky remembered back to the fireworks display four years ago. Things with Coop were just getting going back then and there was much she didn't know about him. She knew now that God had brought them together and was blessing them in so many ways. She smiled and whispered a prayer of thankfulness.

The parking lot was filling up already when they arrived. Sheriff Bert Bertell was directing traffic along with help from the Atkins police force.

"Seems more crowded than usual," Becky said to Coop. "We may not get our favorite seats."

Coop patted her hand and said, "I'll always remember how special this day is. It doesn't really matter where we sit. I'll think of our date here just a few years ago."

Becky smiled back and sighed. She remembered too. "It was special," she said. "I'll never forget it."

As they walked across the parking lot and headed for the bleachers, they were jostled around by the crowd. Coop led the way carrying Nicholas while Becky held tightly to Jenny's

223

hand. Elizabeth and Marla Jean joined elbows and walked together for stability.

Up ahead, the Martin's walked as a group with one addition. Becky smiled to see that Kendy Barkdale was walking with them, holding hands with both of Hannah's grandmas. 'That's so sweet,' thought Becky. 'Those ladies have adopted Kendy as a granddaughter!'

Kendy's parents walked together at a distance, separated by the press of the crowd. Becky noted that they were also holding hands. She smiled, realizing that Tabitha and Tom seemed much more relaxed and happier than when she had first met them. Tabitha's new job and plans for furthering her education had made her a new person. Much more self confident. Tom was less stressed, thanks to the added income from her paycheck.

But the changes had to be most related to their newfound freedom in Christ. Since they had acknowledged Jesus as their Lord and Savior, a new peace had come over them. Yes, the Christian walk was new for them and they were only beginning to experience the goodness of God. But they were diving deep into the Word and learning to trust in God's plan. Coop had told her that Tom, always a little more hesitant, was even beginning to participate in the men's group. Becky could see Tabitha growing spiritually almost week by week. She was asking great questions in ladies group, sharing from her heart, even starting to memorize some scriptures. Becky smiled as she remembered Jenny going over the twenty-third Psalm with both Tabitha and Kendy. She was so thankful for the missionary heart of her daughter.

Becky gave a sigh and prayed to Jesus in her mind. 'Thank you Jesus, for your Word, for Jenny's joyful sharing of the gospel, for Tabitha and Tom's open hearts. And thank you for loving us all so much that you would die for our sins.'

Becky's attention was drawn to a couple climbing the bleachers and looking for seats. Melissa and Dave had been together a lot lately. Working on the food pantry project, serving together on committees at church, and now here to watch fireworks.

'God has certainly worked a miracle in Melissa's life,' Becky thought once again. Four years before, Melissa had been mixed up with some wild men, planning to blackmail Coop, and living a sinful life. And now, she had become a born-again Christian and was living a life that was serving God. Becky, indeed, dozens of people, had witnessed the radical change and gave all the glory to the Lord. 'Miracles still happen,' she thought, 'they are not just confined to Bible stories of old.'

Coop noticed Melissa and Dave too and waved to them as they found seats. He was surprised to see Dave slip his arm around Melissa's shoulders and whisper in her ear. Melissa threw her head back and laughed. They seemed very comfortable together.

'God, who would have thought a few years ago that she would have come this far?' he thought. 'Only you could work out a plan like this. I tried, you know. I planted some seeds, like you told me way back then. But now here she is, a changed soul. And planting some seeds of her own.'

Coop's eyes went to a group of men working frantically to check over the firework set-up. As darkness crept in, Craig Cashman left the group of workers and took his seat with a man and woman on the front row. Coop recognized them but couldn't recall their names. He had seen them before but wasn't sure where. Coop recalled that Melissa had spent a lot of time with Craig, had even brought him to church. He had become a regular attendee, whenever his truck driving job allowed him to be home on a Sunday. Craig had been saved a few months ago and was now driving the church bus and serving in other ways.

Coop smiled to himself. 'Ripple effect,' he thought. 'You never know how God is going to move through a situation. God will work his plan, even when his way doesn't seem to make sense at the time.'

Chapter 38

A STICKY MESS

Jenny tugged on her mother's hand and said, "Mommy, can me and Hannah and Kendy go up there and watch the band? That's what we did last year. Well, not Kendy, 'cuz she wasn't here. But can we? There's a man handing out flags for all the kids."

"Let's check with the other moms. But it will probably be alright, as long as you stay where we can see you." As they all gathered at the bleachers to find seats, the three girls were allowed to go together towards the sidelines of the football field to watch the band getting into formation. A man offered them flags which they took gladly and began waving back and forth.

The high school band marched to the center of the field and played several rousing patriotic songs. The little girls pranced and waved their flags to the music. The atmosphere was festive and celebratory. Winslow really knew how to throw a party on the Fourth of July. And this year it seemed to have attracted people from all around the county. The crowd was full of people Becky had never seen before.

The public announcement speakers crackled to life as a voice came over the loud speaker. Becky leaned forward to

227

look as the grand marshal was being introduced. She beamed as Doc Larson took the microphone. He was being recognized for his many years of service to the community. As the beloved local veterinarian, almost everyone in the county recognized him. Becky had worked in his office as his assistant and considered him to be a father figure. He had even given her away when she married Coop. Yes, Doc Larson held a special place in Becky's heart.

"Let's all stand as the colors are presented by Boy Scout Troop 925. When the flags are in place, please join in singing while the band plays and the Winslow High School choir leads the National Anthem."

The crowd stood at attention. Becky nudged Coop and pointed down to the three little girls. All three had placed their right hand over their heart and held their flag stoically at their left shoulder. Becky quickly dug her cell phone out of her pocket, zoomed in as much as she could, and took a picture of the girls. She hoped she'd be able to edit the picture and cut out most of the crowd surrounding the girls. She thought Nancy and Tabitha would love to have a copy of this picture. These girls had become great friends, practically inseparable peas in a pod. Where you found one, you would usually find all three. The Brownies! Just remembering their self-appointed group name made Becky smile.

As the band marched off the field, Doc Larson announced that the fireworks would begin when it got a little darker. The mob of people standing near the sidelines moved back towards the bleachers to take their seats. Some onlookers had thought to bring their own lawn chairs and were settling down near the ends of the bleachers, but because of the larger-than-usual crowd, many were left standing.

The Brownies made their way through the crowd toward their parents. At times they were practically invisible, crowded as they were between much taller adults. When Becky finally saw them merging through the press of people, she let out her breath in relief. She didn't realize she had not exhaled since she lost sight of the girls. Then Becky smiled at the group, happy to see that they were holding hands and keeping together.

Jenny asked if they could take a blanket and sit on the grass to watch the fireworks. After promising to stay within sight of their parents, the girls were off to find a good spot. Three sets of parents watched as the girls spread their blanket and took their seats. A vendor stopped at the blanket and offered cotton candy to each girl. All three girls glanced up into the stands to wait for permission to accept the treat. Becky nodded and smiled, so thankful once more for her daughter, who could be headstrong and energetic, but really was a good girl.

Hannah and Jenny chose pink cotton candy; Kendy picked blue. They settled down to concentrate on the soft sugary treat. Soon lips and fingers were colored and the girls were laughing and having a great time.

Twilight was being overtaken by total darkness when the three Brownies, still carrying their paper cones stuck with bits of cotton candy, came back to the bleachers once more. Jenny called up to her parents in a stage whisper, "We need to go to the bathroom, Mommy. And this stuff is making us all sticky." She raised her hand and wiggled her pink fingers.

Hannah and Kendy giggled and said, "Yeah, we're sticky!" They did a high-five and pretended to be stuck permanently together. "We need water to get us free!" All three girls broke out in contagious laughter. People sitting nearby in the bleachers smiled at the antics of the three cute brown-headed girls.

"Wait, stay right there," Becky said. Once again she snapped some pictures with her cell phone. They were going to have quite a collection of photos to remember this fun time.

Greg stood and fished his cell phone out of his pocket too. "Here, take this with you," he said as he turned on the flashlight and passed it over to Hannah. "It's getting dark."

Nancy looked over at him and said, "Thanks. Good idea. But you do realize that phone is going to be a sticky mess when she gives it back to you."

Greg shrugged his shoulders and laughed. "Guess so. But it'll be worth it, just to know they aren't wandering around in the pitch dark."

With Hannah leading the way, the girls joined the line of people waiting to get into the bathroom. Coop and Becky and the other parents watched as the girls stood together. Their attention was drawn to the first of the fireworks being set off over the football field. The girls, too, were watching looking up as pops and bangs filled the sky with exploding lights.

Standing in the shadows of a cluster of trees near the bathroom, two men were looking elsewhere. Not interested in the pretty light show in the sky, these men were watching three cute brown-haired little girls. The taller of the two stubbed out his cigarette in the dirt and jabbed the other with his elbow. "Do it," he growled. "I'll get the van."

Chapter 39

TAKEN

Kendy came out of the bathroom and stood in the dark looking for her friends. She thought they had exited the bathrooms before her, but now, outside in the dark, she couldn't see them. She glanced over to the blanket where they had been sitting just minutes before, but the girls were not there. 'They must still be inside the bathroom,' she thought. 'I'll just wait for them here.'

She stood looking up at the sky, where bright lights and pops of explosions momentarily lit up the darkness. She took another bite of her blue cotton candy and spied a trash can near a tree. She headed that direction to throw away her trash when a loud popping drew her eyes upwards once again. While she was standing there, gazing at the array of pretty colors, a man walked out of the trees and crept up behind her. He slapped his hand over her mouth and Kendy immediately smelled something unpleasant. There was something yucky on the cloth he used to cover her mouth and her nose. She tried to struggle and get free, but with every breath the horrible smell entered deeper into her lungs. She was powerless to fight back. Her body went limp.

The man scooped her up and, still covering her mouth, walked quickly to the waiting van.

Chapter 40

A BROWNIE IS MISSING

"She was with us, Mommy. Right behind us. We all went into the bathroom and when we came out, she was gone." Jenny was clearly upset.

"We thought she went back to the blanket alone, but she wasn't there either." Hannah added. "I had the flashlight on, and we went back to the bathroom to maybe wait for her. But she didn't come out, and she wasn't waiting for us, and we called her name but she didn't answer."

"That's when we saw her cotton candy in the dirt. It was blue. I know it was hers." There was a quiver in Jenny's voice.

Coop gave her a hug and said, "Don't worry, Honey, we'll find her."

Sheriff Bertell was talking with Kendy's parents. They were obviously upset.

"How could she just disappear? Somebody must have seen something." Tom Barkdale was pacing, eyes always roving the crowd near the bathroom.

"I've got my deputies questioning the people that were nearby. Don't worry. We'll get to the bottom of this. Do you have a recent picture of your daughter? It would help to identify her."

Tabitha shuddered. 'Identify her' made it sound like determining identity of a corpse. She knew that wasn't what the sheriff meant, but it's all she could think of at the time.

Nancy noticed the shudder and put her arm around the worried mother. She couldn't imagine what she was going through. Every parent's worse nightmare.

"Heavenly Father, please watch over your child Kendy. Keep her safe from harm. Wrap your arms around her and protect her. Keep her calm. Give her peace. And God, help us find her. Lead us to wherever she is. Show the sheriff the way. Help us all God."

Nancy didn't end the prayer with 'Amen.' This was a prayer that wouldn't end until Kendy was reunited with her family.

"Becky took some pictures tonight. She has them on her phone." Tabitha caught Becky's eye and motioned her to come over. "Can you get the pictures you took of the girls? The sheriff needs to see Kendy." Her voice caught when she mentioned her daughter's name.

Becky showed the pictures to Bert and he asked her to forward them to his number. Just then, Mark Feldman, the sheriff from Atkins, came up to the group. "We've questioned everyone in the vicinity of the bathrooms. Most everyone remembered seeing three girls standing in the line before the fireworks started. Nobody noticed them after that. One woman reported seeing two men leaning against trees nearby, but she didn't know them and didn't see them while I was questioning her. She did say one was smoking, and we gathered up a bunch of cigarette butts in the area. Might get a DNA hit. Also picked up the cotton candy cone that was probably Kendy's. We'll check it for DNA, might have fingerprints too." He looked with compassion at the missing girl's parents. "Don't worry, folks, we'll find her. We have several police forces on the case already."

Overhead, the fireworks continued. The grand finale sent explosions into the sky in rapid succession. Most of the crowd was watching the show, unaware of the drama unfolding near the bathrooms. With bangs and booms and ohhhs and ahhhs, the rest of the party-goers were celebrating the beautiful display of lights and colors.

Not so the group of parents, grandparents and children huddled together. Their focus was elsewhere. A few bystanders were aware of the movement of police amongst them. Their curiosity was aroused but they stood back to observe and not be in the way.

Pastor Green walked quickly up to the group. "I just heard. Tom, Tabitha, we're here for you. We have the prayer team already lifting this need up to heaven." He turned to Sheriff Bertell and asked, "Is there anything else we can do? I'm sure members of our congregation will want to help any way we can. Are you going to form a search party? I'll get the word out for volunteers."

"Yes, that would be great. I know it's late, but if we could get a group here at the sports complex, we'll turn on all the floodlights and we can cover this area pretty quickly. Let's get a group here ASAP. We'll use the bleachers as a staging area. Say, twenty minutes?"

"Sure! I'm on it!" Pastor Green already had his phone to his ear. Soon cars and trucks came streaming into the parking lot. Most of the fireworks crowd had left as soon as the show was over, but some stayed when they heard what had happened. A missing child was certainly cause for alarm.

Several people from the Methodist church gathered at the sidelines to pray. Dave Cole, Melissa Madison and Craig Cashman were the first to volunteer for the search party. Before long, the group grew and Craig took the lead. He made sure everyone had a flashlight, sturdy shoes, and water to stay hydrated. They gathered quietly and waited for the sheriff's instructions.

Families with young children wanted to get home, where they could tuck their little ones safely into their beds and pray for the safety of the missing girl. No one wanted to think about what might be happening to the child. Everyone hugged their own children a little longer and stood watching over them as they fell asleep.

Marla Jean took little Nicholas home, praying as she drove through the dark night. Her prayers centered on Tom and Tabitha. She prayed for their peace. For calm. For a reminder that God would stay with them through this difficult time. For assurance that God was also watching over their daughter.

Hannah and Jenny went to the Martin's home with Hannah's grandparents. Although the girls wanted to stay and help look for Kendy, the sheriff insisted that children were not allowed. Greg and Nancy, Coop and Becky, and of course Tom and Tabitha stayed behind to help with the search.

On the drive to her house, Elizabeth prayed too. Her prayers were for those searching for Kendy. "Be with them

Lord. Guide them and direct them. Help them find clues that will lead them to Kendy. Give Bert and his deputies eyes to see and wisdom to discern. Help them, Lord. Help them find that sweet little girl."

All over town, prayers were being said for the lost child. Cell phones chimed with updates. Several photos of Kendy were posted on the local neighborhood Facebook page. One picture in particular caught the eye of a woman who had been at the football field that night. The picture showed the three little girls, standing at attention with their flags raised. But in the background, the woman recognized two men who were pictured looking at the girls. She immediately got on the phone to Sheriff Feldman.

The search party was given directions and covered the area in a grid pattern, looking for any clue that might help them find the missing girl. As the group moved slowly across the park, Craig Cashman called out, "Found something," and the searchers stopped moving. Sheriff Bertell hurried over and looked at what Craig had found. He tagged it and put it into a bag.

"Move on," he called out, waving his arm for the group to proceed. The object that was found was an old tennis shoe, sole torn loose, a hole in the toe. Probably didn't have a thing to do with the missing child.

Sheriff Feldman hurried over to Bert with news. "Just got off the phone with the woman who saw the two men lingering near the bathroom." He scanned his notes. "Hey, Judith Hey is her name, from Atkins. She recognized the men in background of one of the pictures that went out in the news. She doesn't know who they are, but swears they are the same men that were smoking by the bathroom, just before the girl disappeared."

"Great – might be the break we need. Let's get their pictures enlarged and sent out. Somebody has to know who they are."

Before long, close-up pictures of the men were circulated in social media. They were listed as persons of interest. Newscasters broke into regularly scheduled programming to announce the Amber Alert and to post pictures of the two men. If anyone knew the identity of the men, or their whereabouts, they were urged to contact the police.

Sheriff Bertell called off the search. It was well past midnight. They had covered the sports complex and found nothing that might indicate what had happened to the child. Fortunately, they hadn't found her body either, which at least indicated that she hadn't been killed. Not here anyway.

He spoke calmly to the Barkdales. "We've done all we can do here tonight. You folks go home and try to get some sleep. We do have a few leads that we will be working on through the night. And I'll let you know the minute we have some solid information to share with you."

"I can't," Tabitha cried. "I can't go home without Kendy." She buried her head into Tom's shoulder and sobbed. He threw his arms around her to hold her up. She was about to collapse. Becky, Coop, Greg and Nancy circled around their grieving, frightened friends.

"Father God, draw near to us now," Coop prayed. "Come over Tom and Tabitha; wash them with your peace. Assure them of your love. Comfort them. This is hard, God. We're all afraid. We are worried. Your word says we should pray and then give thanks. That doesn't seem like something we can do right now. Show us Lord. Show us how to praise you, even in this hard time."

Greg joined in, "We will praise you, Jesus. You are worthy of our praise. You are with us. You are with Kendy. Comfort her, Lord. Let her feel your presence. Take away her fear. Draw near to her and keep her safe."

"Jesus, help us. Help us find Kendy. We love her so much," Tabitha prayed. "And you love her too. Tell her. Tell her not to be afraid. Tell her we will find her."

Tom surprised everyone by praying too. "God, I believe in you, and I believe you love my little girl." A lump rose in Tom's throat and he could barely talk. "Send some angels to protect her, God. Please don't let anything happen to our sweet girl. Show us the way to find her. Please bring her back to us."

Nancy's prayer was one of praise. "We thank you, Lord, for Kendy's salvation and we know how much you love her. You love her parents too, and you are working all things out to our good. We believe that, and we trust you, and thank you for all your faithfulness and protection. We know you will be with Kendy tonight. Thank you."

"Jesus," Becky began. "Oh Jesus, draw near to your child Kendy and her parents Tabitha and Tom. Jesus, touch them with a sense of your presence. Let them know you are with them. They are not alone in this. And God, be with the sheriff and all his helpers. Give them wisdom and guide them as they search for Kendy. Speak to anyone who might be able to help with the search. If anyone knows something, or saw something, nudge them to come forward."

The six parents stood huddled close together for a few minutes, feeling the comfort of each other and the love they shared for the Lord. There were tears, yes, but the feeling of panic and dread had lifted. Somehow they knew that everything was going to be okay. And no matter what, God would see them through.

Sheriff Bertell stood nearby, watching and listening. He didn't particularly believe that these prayers were going to make any difference, but he was impressed by the sincerity he witnessed, and the sense of calm that settled over the group. They were strong people, to be able to look at this disaster and still have hope. To be able to be thankful through all this, that was sure an unnatural reaction. He wondered where that kind of strength came from.

Chapter 41

IN THE DARK OF THE NIGHT

Frank James maneuvered his van down the barely visible path that had once been a driveway. Thick underbrush rubbed the side of the van. He found a clearing near an old cabin and parked. He was mad, really mad, and he rubbed his neck with the palm of his hand. Things were not working out like he had planned, and it was all Howard's fault.

"You're an idiot, Howard. A dang-blasted idiot. You had one simple job." Frank slammed the door of the van and turned on his buddy. "I ought to just shoot you for this. Stupid idiot." He stomped up the steps of the cabin. The boards on the steps were dilapidated and broken and he had to choose his foot placement carefully, which was hard to do in the dark. His foot went down in a hole and he swore loudly as he fell.

"I said I'm sorry," Howard mumbled again while he bent to help Frank up.

Frank jerked away and turned to face Howard. His face was red and his eyes glared as he stood staring at his younger partner. "You are sorry, all right. A sorry excuse for a man. A bumbling idiot, that's what you are. You made a mess of everything."

"I said I was sorry. What more do you want from me?" Howard hung his head. "It was dark. They all look alike. I thought I got the right one."

"One simple job." He pushed open the cabin door, went inside and lit a lantern. "Did you at least tie her up tight?"

"I did. Hands and feet, just like you said."

Frank roamed around the cabin and opened a dust covered chest he found in the corner. "Here. Put this blanket over her. And see if she wants some water." He turned to Howard and threw an old blanket at him.

"What are we gonna do with her? We're not gonna hurt her, are we? That would just make it worse."

"Just shut up. I need to think. This changes everything. Get out there and keep an eye on her. She'll be waking up. Wear your ski mask. Don't want her to see what we look like."

"Okay." Howard fished a dirty black ski mask out of his back pocket. He pulled it over his face and headed to the door. Hand on the knob, he turned back to Frank. "I'm really sorry."

"Shut up and get out of my sight," Frank yelled at him. "Get out!"

In the van, Kendy Barkdale was just coming to. She lay on the floor of the van in a fetal position. Her legs were bound together at the ankles with twine. Her hands were also secured with twine. Her wrists were already reddened from chaffing. Kendy tried to wiggle her hands and the twine rubbed a raw spot. She moaned in pain as tiny drops of blood spotted her wrist. Something had been stuffed in her mouth and an old bandana was tied across her face. Kendy couldn't talk or call out. There was a bad taste in her throat. Her face was pressed into the floor of the van. She could smell dirt and felt pebbles and sticks against her cheek.

Kendy groaned and rolled her head around, trying to figure out where she was. It was dark and smelly, that's all she knew for sure. Her eyes adjusted slightly to the darkness and she could see to the front of the van. A steering wheel, two seats, a cooler on the floor. Dangling from the rearview mirror was a green Christmas tree air freshener. It wasn't helping.

Howard opened the door and stood silhouetted in the opening. He looked at her carefully, or as carefully as he could in the dark. 'Oh great,' he thought. 'She's starting to wake up. At least she isn't dead. Pretty little thing like her, wouldn't want her to be hurt.' He moved into the van.

Kendy's eyes widened in fear. She struggled to sit upright and pull her feet in, to get out of his reach. His figure was dark and menacing in the blackness of the night. He sat on the floor near her but not touching. He just looked at her. Looked and looked.

After a minute, he spoke. His voice was a bit distorted because the mask covered part of his mouth. "Don't be scared, little girl. I won't hurt you. Here." He threw the blanket over her. "In case you get cold out here tonight." He stroked her hair gently with his hand. "We're not going to hurt you," he repeated.

Kendy ducked away from his touch. She tried to talk but her mouth was dry. The cloth of the bandana was choking her. She manipulated her chin, trying to loosen the binding. "I wanna go home," she mumbled as best she could.

"Here, you want some water?" Howard asked. He got a bottle out of the cooler and turned the cap. "I'll take your gag out, but no sense yelling. There's nobody out there that could hear you anyway."

He held the water bottle up to her lips and tipped it slightly. Kendy took a big gulp, again and again, trying to wash the terrible taste out of her mouth. Finally her tongue felt moistened and she tried to talk again. "I want to go home," she said again. "Please, take me home."

Howard capped the bottle and put it back in the cooler. "I don't think we can do that," he said. "That's up to Frank." Instantly he slapped his hand over his mouth. Frank had warned him about not using names. 'Oh man, I blew it again,' he thought. Quickly he added, "Fred. I mean Fred. Not Frank, Fred."

Kendy bit her lower lip, trying hard not to cry. Her eyes filled with tears anyway.

"I have to put this back in your mouth," Howard said, bringing the gag closer to her face. Kendy tried to pull away but he grabbed her chin. "I have to. You have to keep quiet. At least till we figure out what we're gonna do with you."

The tears fell. Howard wiped them off her cheek with his thumb and Kendy winced. "Don't cry. Just lie down and go to sleep." He tucked the blanket up over her shoulders and left, locking the doors behind him.

Kendy closed her eyes tightly and took a deep breath through her nose. The gag seemed a little looser than last time, and at least she could swallow better. She tried to think. How did she even get here? She couldn't remember. She was watching fireworks. Then she was waking up in this stinky van. Somebody was smoking. She didn't like the smell of cigarettes.

She could smell it in the van even now, even when the man wasn't here.

Man. No, there were two men. Did they both smoke? She didn't know. One was Frank or Fred, she was pretty sure of that.

She tried to look out of the windows, but it was dark. Really dark. No moon, just a few stars. And trees. Everywhere she looked she could see the shadowy shape of trees. There was a cabin, too, but she could only see the roof and chimney from her position lying on the van floor.

Maybe this was all a bad dream. Maybe she would wake up in her own bed at home.

Home. Mommy and Daddy. The tears fell. And she let them. She missed her parents. She wondered if she would see them again. She wondered if they were looking for her. Did they know she was gone? Was anybody looking for her?

Kendy's shoulders shook. She wanted to take a deep breath and calm down, but that terrible taste was in the back of her throat again. She wanted to spit it out, but the bandana was preventing it. She cried until she couldn't any more.

'I have to be brave,' she thought. 'I have to be calm.' Suddenly a scripture verse popped into her head. It was the verse she was learning with Mommy. Jenny was teaching them. The part about walking in the shadow of death. "I will fear no evil," she mumbled through the bandana.

She closed her eyes and pictured sitting on Mommy's lap, saying the verses over and over. '"I will fear no evil." 'These guys are evil. But I won't be afraid.' Many thoughts went through Kendy's mind. God was calming her, and she didn't realize it. All she knew was that she was starting to relax a little.

She remembered another verse, one she had learned at Wednesday night kid's club. Joshua 1:9 "Be strong and of good courage. Do not be afraid, nor be dismayed, for the Lord your God is with you wherever you go."

Kendy began to pray. 'Jesus, I know you love me, and I love you too. I know you are with me, God. I learned that you will never leave me. So you are here. And you'll keep me safe. Help me not be afraid. Help me be brave. And God, help somebody to find me. I want to go home. But I will trust you and not worry. Tell Mommy and Daddy not to worry, too."

Exhausted, she drifted off to sleep. She dreamed there was an angel sitting on top of the van and another standing guard by the door. Despite the gag and bandana, Kendy smiled in her sleep.

Chapter 42

NIGHT TERRORS

Somewhere in the middle of the night, Kendy woke up. At first she was confused, not remembering where she was or why. It was so dark! It took awhile for her eyes to adjust to the blackness. Outside the van, she heard noises. Someone was walking, stumbling a bit as he went. He had a flashlight, Kendy knew, because every once in a while she'd catch a glimpse of a wavering light roaming through the darkness.

The man, yes, it was a man, the big one that wasn't very nice, and he was talking to himself. His words were slurred and Kendy couldn't quite understand what he was saying. It sounded like he was walking towards the woods. His voice faded out as he walked further away. Before long he came back, singing at the top of his voice. This time Kendy understood. "Lions and tigers and bears, oh my!" he said over and over.

The man approached the van and leaned against it, chanting even louder than before. "Lions and tigers and bears, oh my! You hear that, little girl? They're going to get you! The lions and tigers and bears are hungry tonight." He began to rock the van, lifting up the back end by the bumper, then letting it drop. He tried to growl like a bear to scare her more, but it came out more like a gargling sound. He coughed and cleared his throat.

With every drop of the van, Kendy was jolted and tossed around. With her feet and hands tied, there was no way to catch herself. "They're coming to get you, little girl! Oh, maybe I need to come in there and keep you safe. I can protect you. I won't let those wild animals get you." He stumbled towards the van door. "Don't you worry, honey. I'll take good care of you." He gave a guttural laugh and pulled on the handle. The door was locked.

He cursed and fumbled in his pants pocket for the keys. Not finding them, he cursed some more. Kendy pushed her shoulders up as far as she could, trying to cover her ears. She didn't like this yelling, or the tone of his voice. He was scaring her.

Suddenly a loud howling sound was heard from deep in the woods. The man by the van stopped dead in his tracks, listening as one, two, no, at least three animals began to howl. "What the…?" he whispered in terror. The howling was definitely getting closer. "Wolves!" The man turned on his heel and ran for the cabin. Stepping on the broken porch floor boards, he fell face first and cursed some more. In a panic he scrambled to his feet and hurried inside, slamming the door behind him.

Kendy sat very quiet in the van. Before long, the sound of wolves was gone. Kendy exhaled slowly, surprised to find that she had been holding her breath. She started to relax and smile. The bad man was gone, the wolves were gone, and nobody hurt her. She giggled a little and thought 'I gotta tell

Jenny and Hannah about this! They're not going to believe me when I say the wolves protected me from the bad man!'

Chapter 43

MEDIA CIRCUS PAYOFF

Sheriff Bertell mulled over the DNA reports on the cigarette butts they had found. Most showed no match to anyone in the system. One was interesting though. It connected to DNA found months ago at the scene of another crime. Just a simple gas station robbery in another county. The suspect hadn't been identified and the case had gone cold. The only other useful information was that the thief left in a white van, driven by an unidentified person. No license plate, no video surveillance, no eye witness except the station clerk, who only saw one man in a dark ski mask.

Apparently, the thief, or thieves, had moved on from robbery to child abduction. And child abduction usually meant kidnapping, and kidnapping usually led to a ransom demand.

Bert had already asked Sheriff Feldman to get a trace set up on the Barkdale's phone. If they got a call for ransom money, there would be a way to find out who had made the call and where it came from. If there was time. Sheriff Feldman had walked the Barkdales through the process. He left one of his deputies there to monitor the phone calls. Tom and Tabitha stood by, waiting and hoping and wondering how they would ever come up with ransom money. They barely had enough to pay their bills month to month. How on earth would they come up with a ransom?

Greg Martin was with the Barkdales too. He was a strong shoulder to lean on. His experience as a lawyer gave him a take-charge demeanor. He brought an attitude of calm to the situation. It was good to have a friend to lean on. Tom especially appreciated his presence with them during this waiting time.

Bert glanced out his office window, his attention drawn to the news van that had just pulled up in front. He recognized Stephanie Sanders, news anchor from channel eight, as she got out of the van, followed by her cameraman.

'Here we go,' he thought. 'Let the media circus begin.'

Miss Sanders approached with a big smile. "Thanks for agreeing to meet with me, Sheriff. This is breaking news, and everyone wants the latest information. Channel eight is dedicated to helping the communities we serve. Together, we might be able to help you solve this crime."

"We appreciate that, Miss Sanders. We want to find this little girl, and the sooner the better."

With a nod from the cameraman, Miss Sanders took her microphone and began the interview. "I'm standing here in the office of Sheriff Bert Bertell of Winslow, a small farming town in southern Kansas. Last night, during the community's Fourth of July celebration, the unthinkable happened. Eight-year-old Kendy Barkdale was abducted. Sheriff, what can you tell us about the investigation so far?"

She put the microphone in front of Bert and he looked into the camera. He'd done television interviews before and, although not especially fond of the limelight, he could handle himself professionally. If it would help to solve this case, he'd do whatever was necessary.

"We are following up on a few leads, but at this time we have nothing solid to go on. Kendy has been missing for about twelve hours now. As you know, in most of these cases, time is critical. We want to find her as soon as possible."

"Of course. I understand that the whole community has assisted in the search. Has this type of criminal activity ever happened in Winslow before?"

"Winslow is a small quiet community. We've had some petty crimes, but never anything like this. Never a child abduction. This is different."

"We reported earlier that you are looking for two men. Can you tell me any more about them?" Stephanie was pressing for details.

"The two men you're referring to are persons of interest. They were seen in the vicinity of the abduction. We need to find them and possibly get more information. They may have observed suspicious activity."

"Thank you, Sheriff Bertell," the reporter said. She turned back to face the cameraman. "If you have any information about these two men, contact the Winslow police department at the number on your screen. Your information could help to bring Kendy Barkdale home. This is Stephanie Sanders, KLJA television news."

As the cameraman packed equipment into the van, Stephanie shook the Sheriff's hand and said, "Good luck, Sheriff. We're all hoping for a happy outcome." She left just as the Sheriff's phone started ringing.

"Sheriff's office," he answered.

The man's voice on the phone was hesitant. "Um, Sheriff, this is JJ, Jonathan James, I mean. I'm calling about them pictures you're showin' on tv. The men that might know about that missing kid."

"Thanks for calling," replied the Sheriff. "You know the men?"

"Yeah, I know one all right. It's my son Frank. I don't know the other guy. But it's Frank for sure. The big one.

"Give me your address and I'll be right over to talk with you."

Chapter 44

IDIOT

Howard untied Kendy's ankles and wrists. "No running away, ya hear? And no yelling." He removed the gag stuffed in her mouth.

"Thank you," Kendy answered. "Can I go to the bathroom?"

"We don't have a bathroom but you can go to the outhouse. This way."

Howard led Kendy through some trees to a small wooden structure.

"What's an outhouse?" Kendy asked.

Howard laughed and said, "I think you can figure it out." He held the door open for her and Kendy stepped in. She was overwhelmed by a smell of rot and decay. Disgusted, she covered her mouth and nose with her arm.

It was a small dark place, barely big enough to turn around in. A little bench lined the wall opposite the door. There was a circular hole in the seat and Kendy knew what to do.

When she came out she asked, "Can I wash my hands?"

"Back at the cabin. We have water."

"Soap?"

"No soap. But we got food. Let's go."

A little morning sun was filtering into the cabin through boarded windows. It wasn't completely dark inside. Kendy was set on a stool and pushed up to the table. Howard tied her legs to the front legs of the stool and said, "There. You ain't goin' nowhere." He put a bowl of dry cereal in front of Kendy and said, "No milk. But at least you can eat something."

Kendy was happy for the food and took a second to bow her head and thank God for her meal. From a dark corner, the other man scowled gruffly. He let out a "Pfft" and shuffled outside. "Don't let her out of your sight," he shouted as the door slammed behind him.

Kendy ate her dry cereal, stale though it was. She was glad to have her wrists free, and that terrible gag out of her mouth. She looked around the little cabin. It was sparsely furnished with a mattress on the floor, a rickety looking couch and one wooden chair. The table she sat at was wooden and wobbly, with barely enough room for two people to eat at once. There were only three windows, each boarded up to keep out animals. Someone had hung curtains, but they were moth-eaten and dirty from years of hanging in the seldom used cabin. A stone fireplace was littered with ash from a fire long ago. It smelled like burnt wood, cigarettes and dust.

Kendy took it all in and wondered where in the world this place was. And how would anyone find her? She closed her eyes and prayed to herself, 'Help me Jesus. Send those angels back to be with me.'

The big man came back, 'What is his name?' Kendy wondered. 'Fred? Frank?'

He walked to the other man and said, "Get her tied back up in the van. We have to talk. Privately."

Howard freed her feet and pushed her towards the door. Kendy stopped and looked at the bigger man. His face mask was brown and had some football team on it. For the first time Kendy noticed that he had tattoos on his arms. It was too dark to tell what, exactly, but one arm was covered. "Thank you for the breakfast," she said. And the man just growled.

Back in the van, Kendy was allowed to drink some water before her wrists were retied. Then her feet were secured and she was left alone. For some reason, the man didn't gag her. Kendy was thankful for that. She also knew better than to scream for help. It would be pointless; there wasn't any help in these woods.

Inside, Frank was pacing. He took off his ski mask and Howard did the same. "I've been thinking about this all night," he said. "Thanks to the mess you've gotten us into, we have to change all our plans."

"I said I'm sorry."

"Shut up and listen. You got the wrong kid. You're sorry. You're an idiot. We know all that."

He sat at the table and continued. "We can't ask for ransom money, 'cuz her parents ain't got no money. IF you had gotten the Martin girl, we could be counting our money right now and leaving the country. That big-shot lawyer and his fancy house and boat and swimming pool – he'd have plenty of money to buy his kid back. But no, you got the kid from the poorest family. Idiot."

"So, what are we going to do with her?" Howard asked.

"We're going to dump her somewhere and get out of here fast. We'll have to come up with another way to make some money later. But for now, we have to cut our losses. As long as they don't find us, we'll be fine. We have to lie low for awhile, split up so they can't track us both together. We'll leave tonight when it's dark. I'll drive you a couple of counties away and then you're on your own."

"Gonna leave the girl here? Or take her with us?"

Frank slammed his hand down on the table. "Are you kidding me? Now why would we take her along? Her picture's probably been plastered all over the place by now. Just what we need, to be seen with the kid. Idiot."

Howard hung his head. He wanted to ask Frank if 'idiot' was his favorite word but thought better of it. Wouldn't do to have Frank madder than he already was.

"We'll take her down to the boat dock. Tie her up in the fishing shack down there. Take some water along, and some of the stuff we left in the van. We don't want her starving before they find her."

"What if nobody finds her? What if she dies out there?"

"Then we got real problems. But we can't exactly call the cops and tell them where she is, now can we? Idiot."

'Yup, it's his favorite word,' Howard thought with a smile. He turned his back on Frank so the smirk couldn't be seen. "There's bears out in these woods. Maybe a bear will eat her. Then it wouldn't be like we killed her or anything."

"For god's sakes, Howard, just shut up! You're making me crazy." Frank lit a cigarette and took a deep drag. He blew the smoke out towards the ceiling thinking, 'The sooner I get rid of this idiot, the better.'

Chapter 45

THE FIRST REAL LEAD

Sheriff Bertell parked his cruiser in front of the house, checking the address to be sure. It was a modest one-story ranch with an attached garage. An outbuilding stood off to the side, with the door hanging off a broken hinge. An old John Deere lawn tractor stood inside, with a flat tire. The grass in the yard didn't need mowing yet, but that tractor wouldn't do the trick, in that condition.

Over the front door of the house was a sign that said 'James'. This was the right house.

Bert pushed the doorbell but heard nothing, so he knocked several times. He was about to give up when he heard a shuffling noise coming from inside. The curtain at the front window was pushed aside and a bald head was visible. The curtain fell back into place and the door was opened.

"Good morning Sheriff," said Jonathan James. "Come on in."

"Mr. James, thank you for calling me about the identification of one of the men we're looking for. So you say you think it's your son?" asked the sheriff.

"Don't think. Know. See here." JJ went to a drawer in an end table and took out a photo. "This is the last picture we have of our son. You can see it's the same man."

"This picture is pretty old. But yes, I do see the resemblance." He gave the photo back to Mr. James. "Does your son live here with you?"

"Oh, no, Frank doesn't live here anymore. Haven't seen him for years. Seeing his picture on TV was a big shock. He hasn't been in touch with us for , geeze, maybe ten years. Just when he wanted money." JJ looked over his shoulder as his wife Bev came in from the kitchen. She was drying her hands on a dishtowel and looked worried.

"Do you think he's involved in the child abduction last night?" Bev nervously twisted the towel around her hand. She bit her lip and looked expectantly at the sheriff.

"We're looking for him and another man because we think they might have some information about the abduction. Not necessarily that they are responsible." Bert went on, "Do you know where he might be?"

"Like JJ says, he hasn't been here for years. We don't know where he lives, or where he works or anything." She looked at JJ for confirmation. He nodded and she went on, "He left and we haven't seen him or heard anything from him. Until we saw his picture on TV this morning, we didn't even know if he was alive or not." It was clear that she was about to get emotional.

"Do you know the other man we're looking for?"

JJ answered, "Well, sorry, but we can't help you with that Sheriff. Don't know that guy, don't know where Frank is, haven't seen him for years. Like we said, we didn't even know if he was still breathin'. Seeing him on TV this morning was a big surprise – first we've seen of him in, like I said, maybe ten years. But if you find him, you tell him I'd like to give him a piece of my mind. What he's put us through, and his mother's been so worried over him. Ungrateful rotten kid."

"Let me ask you this. Is there anywhere you can think of that Frank might go to hide? A place that he's familiar with, maybe has been to before. A place he might think would be safe."

"That's starting to sound like you think he's guilty of this. Well, who knows – he's been in trouble before." JJ was deep in thought. "Only place I can think of is our old family hunting cabin. It's been in our family for years and all us usta' to go hunting and fishing at Lake Carson. Hasn't been anybody up there for years, far as I know. Not much of a place, but he might go there to stay out of sight for awhile."

"Thanks for your help, Mr. James. I appreciate it. If you do hear from him, please let me know. Here's my card. Call anytime."

As soon as the door was closed, Bev fell apart.

"Oh my goodness, what do you suppose Frank has gotten into now? What else can go wrong? First you nearly die with kidney cancer, and now this with Frank. I don't know how much more I can take. I need to go lie down. I feel faint."

JJ shrugged it off. "That boy's been nothing but trouble. All his life he's been a mess. Who knows what he's done! He just better not come a'runnin to us for help. He walked away from us a long time ago. And he better think twice before asking us to bail him out of whatever trouble he's in. Serves him right for walking out on us."

Bev sat on the couch and moaned, "Oh, I don't feel good. I can't breath. This is just terrible. Our boy's in trouble, I just know it." She picked up the newspaper from the coffee table and fanned herself. "I can't take any more troubles. I just can't."

"Does make you wonder though, doesn't it? Where's he been? What's he been doing?" JJ picked up the sheriff's card and turned it over in his hands, looking at it mindlessly. "Where is he now? I can't believe he'd be involved in this kidnapping thing. Guess it's possible. We really don't know him any more. I wonder if we'll ever find out what he's been up to."

The sheriff went to his office and made several quick phone calls. Officers from three jurisdictions joined into the search. Citizens of Winslow were also allowed to help with the hunt. Soon a parade of cars and trucks was headed toward Lake Carson. It would be a two-hour drive, and no one could predict what they would find once they got there. Maybe nothing. Maybe a frightened but safe little girl. That's what everyone was hoping for. Sheriff Bertell was realistic. He was aware that the outcome might not be as positive as everyone wanted.

All over town, groups were meeting to pray for the rescue of Kendy Barkdale. In churches, in the diner, at the post office, wherever people gathered, several could be found with heads bowed. Tom and Tabitha had been told to stay near the phone, so they were at their apartment. Nancy and Becky sat with them, waiting. Waiting for a call from the kidnappers demanding ransom. Waiting for a call from the sheriff with good news. Please God let it be good news.

Coop drove his truck with Greg Martin in the passenger seat. Behind them sat Jenny and Holly the collie. Holly was laying on the seat with her head on one of Kendy's tee shirts. Tabitha had given it to Jenny earlier that afternoon. Coop knew that the sheriff wouldn't be pleased about having Jenny in the search group, but she had begged him to allow her to go, and bring Holly. "Holly has a great nose," she said. "She knows how to sniff out people. She can help." Coop had agreed but told her she would have to stay in the truck if the sheriff told her to.

Chapter 46

BREAKTHROUGH PRAYER

At the Barkdale's apartment, Nancy and Becky were in the kitchen with Tabitha. It was crowded with the three of them working together in the small space. Tabitha had decided that she needed to do something to take her mind off the situation, so she was making rice krispies bars. "When Kendy gets home, she'll want a snack," she had explained. "I was thinking I'd make brownies, but then I remembered we used all the cocoa powder for Kendy's contribution to the picnic competition." She paused for a second before going on, "Was that picnic just yesterday? It seems like it was forever ago."

Nancy hugged her and said, "All time is in God's hand. Psalms 31:15. Yesterday, today and tomorrow, God's word never changes. And God's love for his children is eternal."

Tabitha smiled and got marshmallows out of the pantry. The moms got to work on the snack. Tom and the deputy were talking quietly in the living room.

Worship music was playing on Becky's Pandora app and the atmosphere in the kitchen was one of calm. Their worries were covered with a peace that would have been hard for an

265

outsider to understand. 'A peace that passes all understanding' Becky thought.

Becky thought back to Tom's prayer earlier in the afternoon. As soon as the search party had headed for the cabin, Tom had fallen on his knees in the living room. He knelt before the couch as before an altar in church. Tabitha joined him there, as did Becky and Nancy. The police deputy, sitting across the room, watched and listened as Tom poured out his heart to the Lord. Becky was surprised at the passion and spirit with which he prayed. She had only heard him pray out-loud once before, last night. His prayer now was completely different. Not tentative, halting or uncomfortable. It was a new side of Tom that was being revealed to her. She could sense that he was filled with the Holy Spirit as he prayed.

It was a prayer from the heart, raw and genuine. "Oh Jesus, please help us. That's all I know to say. But somewhere in the Bible it says that you know the desires of my heart. You pray when we don't even know the words to say. You know what we need. So I'm asking you now, Jesus, that you watch over Kendy. Our sweet Kendy. Send an army of angels to keep her from harm. Keep her safe. Send her help. May whoever took her show mercy and kindness. May they not hurt her or scare her. And oh God, help the people looking for her. Send an angel to lead the way to wherever she is. Help us God. Help all of us. But especially right now, just keep our little girl safe." He paused and took a deep breath. "And thank you, God, for being with us. For all the helpers, for all the people praying, for the comfort you are giving us. We trust you. I trust you to work all this out to our good. That's what the Bible says and I want to trust you to be true to that promise."

He didn't say amen. The room continued in an atmosphere of prayer as the women whispered prayers of their own. Part of Becky's prayer included praise. Tom's conversion, though recent, had lit a fire in his heart. He was learning the importance of prayer and trust.

'Sometimes,' she thought, 'it takes a tragedy to awaken a need for Christ in a person. This tragedy, frightening as it is, has helped Tom to feel the power of prayer.' After an extended time of quiet, Tabitha hugged Tom and stood up. She walked past the deputy as she went into the bathroom to wash her face. He smiled at her compassionately. Becky and Nancy got up too, leaving Tom on his knees where he stayed for many more minutes

When the rice krispie treats were pressed into the pan, cooled and cut in squares, Tabitha poured coffee for everyone and they all sat at the table. It seemed like time was crawling as they tried to make small talk to keep their minds off the silent phone. Sheriff Bertell had told them that a ransom call was probably not going to happen. It would have come by now, he said. But just in case, they should stay near the phone.

"The sheriff really knows how to handle emergencies, doesn't he?" Becky said. "He seems like such a quiet, behind the scenes guy, but when he's needed, he can take charge and get things done."

The deputy spoke up, "Winslow has been a quiet town, partly because of Bert's no-nonsense approach. He let's people know what behavior is expected, and he knows when to take action. He's highly respected in the county. Could have his pick of towns to work in, but he likes it here."

"We're lucky to have him," Becky said. "He sure helped when Coop went through that trouble a few years ago. That whole mystery was solved quickly."

Nancy agreed. "I trust in God, and I trust in the people he has put in place to bring this issue to a close too."

Everyone was startled when a knock came to the door. The deputy stood beside the door while Tom looked through the peep hole to see who was there. He backed up and said, "It's some ladies from church. Can I let them in?"

The deputy nodded and Tom opened the door. Two women from the Wednesday night ladies group came in bringing boxes of food. "We figured you wouldn't feel like cooking," Harriet said to Tabitha. "So some of us decided to make you supper." She took a casserole dish from the box and said, "Rose made some pulled pork. Ellen chipped in some rolls."

Vicky reached into her box and said, "Andrea made coleslaw and I brought my famous strawberry poke cake. Fresh strawberries on the top and everything."

Tabitha hugged them both and smiled. "Thank you so very much. You're right, I hadn't even thought about food. This smells delicious."

Nancy smiled her appreciation to the ladies from her group. "God's people, blessing others in their time of need," she said out loud.

"Have you heard anything yet?" asked Harriet. "It's getting dark."

The deputy spoke up. "They should be about to the lake. Then the real search begins. I'm sure Sheriff Bertell will call as soon as there's any news."

Chapter 47

ON THE MOVE

The hours passed and darkness crept into the woods. Howard and Frank put their masks on and Howard took Kendy out of the van and brought her back into the cabin. He had made a bologna sandwich for her and put it on the table with a bag of chips. "Eat up!" he said. "It might be the last real food you get for awhile."

Again Kendy prayed before she took a bite of her sandwich. Again Frank shook his head in disgust.

When it was fully dark, Frank led the way through the woods, headed to the lake. Kendy stumbled and nearly fell a couple of times. It was hard to see where she was going. The big man held a lantern, but he was up ahead and the light didn't fall where she was walking. The other man, she didn't know his name, walked close to her and caught her when she tripped.

"Thank you for helping me," Kendy said. "God sent you to help me. I know God is with me right now."

Howard gave her a look of disbelief. How could this little girl be so calm? Since the tears last night, she had seemed much more at peace. It was like she wasn't afraid of anything now. What changed her?

Kendy saw the outhouse but they kept on walking past. She wondered how much longer she would have to walk. She was getting tired.

They walked on further into the dark woods and suddenly Howard's toe got caught on an exposed tree root. He grabbed at a branch to keep from falling but it didn't hold. The branch broke and he fell to the ground, screeching in pain. "Frank, stop," he yelled. "Wait a minute, will ya?"

Frank stopped and came back to see what had happened. He walked up to Howard and smacked him across the face with his bare hand. "I said no names, you idiot."

Howard ducked, expecting another blow. "Sorry boss. I won't do it again." He pulled up his pant leg and looked at his ankle. It was already starting to swell. He rubbed it and winced. "Tripped on something. I think I sprained my ankle. Cut up my hands too."

"Oh, look, your arm is bleeding," Kendy said with concern.

There was a gash on Howard's upper right arm and blood was trickling past his elbow. Frank reached into his back pocket and took out the gag and bandana that had been used to keep the girl quiet. With the wadded up gag, he dabbed at the cut and soaked up the blood. Then he used the bandana to tie around Howard's cut. The gag fell unnoticed into the dirt.

"We can stop here a bit," Frank said. "But not long." He took his pack of cigarettes out of his shirt pocket and offered one to Howard. They all sat leaning against tree trunks, resting.

Kendy was thankful for the chance to catch her breath. She leaned her back against a tree and closed her eyes. Then she had an idea. She looked up at the men to make sure they weren't watching her. Nonchalantly, she picked up a stick off the ground and began digging in the dirt. She carved K E N D Y and then broke little sticks to line the letters. She was working on the letter D when the men prepared to move on. She stood and walked over to Howard. Her name was not finished, but she didn't want the men to see it.

Howard found a fallen tree branch to use as a walking stick and hobbled as quickly as he could. Frank wasn't happy, but they had to slow the pace.

Before long the trees cleared and they crossed an open meadow. They were walking downhill now, and Kendy saw the lake ahead. A sliver of moonlight reflected on the water and as they got closer, Kendy could see a small building next to the dock. The big man opened the door and motioned for her to go in. As she walked through the doorway, an overpowering smell of fish washed over her. "Yuck, it stinks in here," she said.

"You'll get used to it," said the big man. "Now sit down."

She looked around but saw no chair, just a wooden table against the wall. Something slimy was on the table. It seemed to be the source of the smell.

"On the floor. There. By the cleaning table." He had brought along a rope and used it now to tie Kendy to the table. Wrapping the rope around her waist several times, he secured it tightly and said, "There. You're not going anywhere." He tied her feet with twine. "Now your hands," he demanded.

"Wait, if you tie her hands behind her back, how can she eat? You better let her have them in front. I'll do it." Howard took the twine and tied Kendy's wrists. He left it a little loose and Kendy looked up at him appreciatively.

Frank didn't notice. He threw the old blanket over Kendy's feet, placed a few bottles of water within her reach, and kicked a box of granola bars in her direction. "Have fun kid," he laughed. "Let's get out of here," he said to Howard. "We need to hit the road."

"Thank you for not hurting me," Kendy said as they left. "God kept me safe, just like he said he would. He never left me. His angels will keep me safe."

The men stopped at the door and stood looking at each other with a puzzled expression on their faces. Then Frank led the way through the trees and an eerie stillness fell over the fishing shed.

Kendy's eyes adjusted to the dark. She listened to the sounds of the night. Water lapped on the shore of the lake. Owls hooted back and forth in the trees. Frogs were croaking and insects buzzed. She could see the flashing lights of a lightening bug that had gotten trapped with her in the shed. A breeze was stirring the treetops. Kendy pulled the blanket up to her shoulders as best she could with hands bound together.

She began to sing all the songs she could remember from kids club and Sunday school. She even sang "Away in the Manger" that she had learned for the Christmas program. That made her think of her mommy and daddy. She missed them. She wondered what they were doing. She hoped they were looking for her. 'Of course they are looking for me,' she chided herself. 'They love me and they will keep looking for me until they find me.'

Suddenly Kendy remembered a story Jenny's mother had told her. The story about the lady that lost her coin and looked everywhere for it. She kept looking and didn't stop until she found it. "I know Mommy and Daddy love me more than that lady loved her coin. They will look and look until they find me. I know it. And then when I'm safely home, we can celebrate like the lady did when she found the coin."

She leaned against the table leg and tried to get comfortable. As she drifted off to sleep, she imagined there was an angel standing outside the door and another inside the shed. She said to herself, 'Thank you for being with me, God. I'm not scared because you are with me. Angels will help Mommy and Daddy. They will find me.'

Chapter 48

SEARCH PARTY

Sheriff Bertell had a global earth map that showed the location of all of the cabins and structures around Lake Carson. One by one, the police approached each cabin. The citizen search members were told to wait until the area was declared safe. Then they could begin combing the property. They had explored around three cabins, finding nothing, by the time darkness fully enveloped the lake. Flashlights came on and the search continued.

Coop and Greg didn't want to give up, but wondered how thorough of a search they could do with just flashlights. It seemed like they would surely miss something. Coop prayed out loud as he parked the truck and waited for the sheriff's signal to move in. "Oh Lord, open our eyes. Help us to see. Break through the darkness and give us clear vision. Be our light in the darkness."

From the back seat, Jenny said, "Daddy, Holly can see good in the dark. Remember when she saw the fox in the woods? We couldn't see it, but she did. She has good eyes."

"Good eyes and a good nose. That might come in handy tonight." Greg reached around and patted Holly's head. "You'll help us, won't you girl?"

"She loves Kendy. She'll help." Jenny put her arms around Holly's neck and nuzzled her fur. "We have to find Kendy," she said to the dog. "I know you can do it. Just like when we play hide and seek."

Holly tilted her head and looked at Jenny with an almost human like expression of understanding. Jenny hugged her again.

Sheriff Bertell and the other police officers stood huddled near the cabin, studying the ground. They could see evidence that a vehicle had been parked in this area recently. The grass was pressed down and tire tracks were visible in the dirt. Cigarette butts littered the area. One of the officers gathered them up and bagged them as evidence. Another officer photographed the tire tracks.

Slowly Sheriff Bertell and Sheriff Feldman approached the cabin. There seemed to be no one inside, but they were taking no chances. When they determined that the cabin was empty, they allowed the other searchers to get out of their vehicles.

As soon as Greg and Coop and Jenny and Holly neared the place where the van had been parked, Holly began to whine. She sniffed on the ground and then began to pull towards the cabin. The sheriff noted Holly's reaction and nodded to Coop. "Let her off the leash," he said.

Coop knelt down and unclipped Holly's leash. Jenny knelt beside the collie and said, "Smell Kendy's shirt? You know Kendy. Go get Kendy. Go find her, girl." she said. Holly bounded up the steps of the cabin and ran through the door. She sniffed all around the table where Kendy had been sitting. Then she turned and left the cabin, following an overgrown trail through the woods. The sheriff followed close behind and Coop and Jenny came next. They had to walk quickly to keep up with the dog.

When the outhouse came into view, Holly took off. She circled the building and pawed at the door. "Kendy, can you hear us? Kendy, are you there?" the sheriff called as he ran up to the little building. But when the door was opened and flashlights shone inside, everyone groaned. They thought for sure they had found her. But Holly had moved on.

The trail was pitch black and Jenny was having a hard time keeping up. Coop hoisted her up onto his back and she wrapped her arms around his neck and held on tightly. He gripped her legs and walked as fast as he could safely. Greg was beside him, holding two flashlights.

Up ahead, Holly had her nose to the ground. One of the deputies called to the Sheriff, "Got something here." Wearing latex gloves, Sheriff Bertell stooped and picked up the discarded gag. "Looks like blood," he said and a hush came over the group. "Not much though," he added with reassurance. He put the gag in an evidence bag. Looking around, he found two cigarette butts and bagged them also. Holly was pawing at the ground by the tree that Kendy had leaned against.

Coop slid Jenny off his back and she went over to talk with Holly. "You're doing great, Holly. You are leading us to Kendy, aren't you? Such a good girl."

"Did you find something?" Coop asked, walking over with a flashlight. He shined the light around the tree and found the place where Kendy had scratched in the dirt. He saw the broken sticks spelling out K E N. "Sheriff, over here," he called.

"She was here," Sheriff Bertell said. He asked that a photo be taken of Kendy's handiwork. "Smart girl."

The group moved on. Holly led the way through the meadow. She began barking as they approached the fishing shed.

Inside, Kendy was awakened by the sounds of people calling out her name. She heard a dog barking and scratching at the door. She wasn't afraid; it was a familiar bark. "I'm here Holly! You found me!"

Chapter 49

THE LONG-AWAITED PHONE CALL

Tom was awake, though his eyes were closed in prayer. It was late, getting close to midnight. Kendy had been missing for more than twenty-four hours. Tabitha paced around the room quietly. The other women sat dozing in their chairs, stirring from time to time to get into more comfortable positions. The deputy sat at the table with his head propped up on his hand. He was struggling to stay awake. It had been a long day. He was due to be relieved at midnight, but the clock was moving slowly.

Everyone came awake abruptly when the phone began to ring. Tom sat frozen, wondering what to do, fearing what he might hear. The deputy nodded and Tom answered. He was silent for a minute while he held his breath and listened to the voice on the other end of the line. Then he sat down onto the couch and let out his breath in a long sigh. "Oh, thank God!" he exclaimed, He reached for Tabitha's hand and smiled broadly up at her. "She's alright. They found her. She's okay!"

A loud cheer broke out in the apartment. Hugging and crying and laughing broke the silence of the moment before. Tom waved his arm and got them to quiet down. He listened to the phone a minute and then motioned for Tabitha to come near.

Tom held the phone out to his wife. "Your daughter would like to speak to you!" he said.

Through tears of joy, Tabitha said, "Oh Sweetie, I'm so glad you are coming home. I missed you so much. Are you okay?"

"I'm hungry," Kendy replied. "I only got some cereal and a sandwich and some water."

"But you're okay? You're not hurt?"

"No, I'm not hurt. The angels kept me safe."

"Angels?" Tabitha asked.

"Yeah, there were two big angels. And a bad man that was kinda nice. And Holly! Holly found me!"

"Holly found you? That's wonderful! Oh, I can't wait to see you and hug you and kiss you!"

"I love you, Mommy. The sheriff wants to talk to you again."

"Okay Sweetie. See you soon."

Sheriff Bertell came on the line and said, "She's really fine. A little dirty and a lot hungry. We have a paramedic here and she checked her over real good. No physical harm at all, except for a little chaffing around her wrists and ankles where she was tied. But she's fine. And emotionally, well, she's amazing. Doesn't act like she's been through a trauma at all. She's calm, singing, loving on the dog. That's a pretty remarkable little girl you have."

"Thank you for finding her, Sheriff. We are so grateful."

"You're welcome, ma'am. But really, it was the Smith's dog who found her." He chuckled a bit and went on, "We've got people here who have brought some food along, so she'll be getting cleaned up and get something to eat. We should be dropping her off at your apartment in a couple of hours. In the meantime, I do want to ask her some questions about what happened. Usually we do that with a parent in the room. But I'd like your permission to talk with her right away. It's best not to wait, so it's all fresh in her mind. Would it be alright if we asked another adult to observe in your place?

Tabitha and Tom talked it over and agreed. They requested that Coop Smith be with Kendy when the sheriff talked with her.

The deputy gathered up his phone tracing equipment and left the apartment. Two hours later, the best reunion possible took place at the Barkdale's apartment. The celebration was short lived, however, because everyone was tired. The past thirty-six hours had been a whirlwind of emotions. They all needed sleep.

Before long, Tabitha and Tom stood in the doorway of Kendy's bedroom, watching her sleep peacefully in her own bed. Tabitha didn't want to take her eyes off her beautiful baby girl. She was so relieved to have her daughter home where she belonged. Tom pulled her gently down the hall to their own bedroom. They sat together on the bed, wrapped in each other's arms and crying tears of relief. They thanked God for protecting Kendy, for keeping her calm and safe, for bringing her home. They had a lot to be thankful for.

"I want to hear more about these angels," Tom said.

Chapter 50

HOME SWEET HOME

Driving to the farm, Coop couldn't stop talking. "She is an amazing little girl! I always thought she was shy and quiet, nothing like Jenny and Hannah, but tonight she was animated and talkative. Went on and on about the angels who protected her last night. She was tied up, she said, and laying on the floor of a van. But there were two big angels with her. They stood outside the van, protecting her she said. And after she saw them, she stopped crying and went to sleep. And she wasn't scared because she knew God was with her, and the angels would keep her safe."

"That's wonderful!" Becky exclaimed. She looked into the back seat at Jenny who was sound asleep. Her head was lying on Holly, who was resting but not asleep. "Tom prayed and asked God to send angels to protect her."

"Tom prayed? That's wonderful too!"

"He did! And it was like he was filled with the Holy Spirit! He prayed on and on, all from the heart. It gave me goosebumps!"

"I loved watching him when we came to the apartment. He barely let Kendy out of his arms. But when he finally let

Tabitha have a turn, he got a hold of Holly and gave her the biggest hug possible. He called Holly an angel too."

"Lots of angels on duty tonight!" Becky laughed.

"A funny thing is, Kendy asked me if angels could howl like wolves!"

"Now, where in the world did that question come from? And how did you answer her?"

"It took a while to get it out of her, but the best I could figure out is that one of the men was going to hurt her, but he heard wolves howling and got scared and went away. So Kendy was thinking that the wolves were angels."

Becky thought a moment, then said, "Well, I guess it's totally possible. One way or another, God protected Kendy tonight. If the wolves helped, then I suppose they were being angels. So I guess angels can howl like wolves if they want to!"

"It will be so good to get home. I can't believe I'm still awake. I guess I'm running on adrenalin and hot coffee."

"Jenny's exhausted," Becky said, yawning. "It's been a really long day for her too. For all of us. So the sheriff didn't mind having her along?"

"No, not really. She didn't slow us down a bit, and Holly was so well behaved. Jenny has done a great job with her."

"She has. And Holly is such a good girl."

The truck pulled into the driveway. The old farmhouse was dark except for a porch light. Coop thought how odd it was to see his old house sitting so dark and silent. Always a place of warmth and activity while he was growing up, the farmhouse had become quiet and empty since the changes of the last few years. His brother Michael had moved away and gotten married. His dad had passed away. Now Dana was off to foreign adventures. And Coop and Becky had their own new house in which to bring up their family. His mom really had the big old house to herself. 'I wonder how she's doing, with all the changes,' Coop thought.

Several lights were on at the new house. Coop's thoughts were brought back to the present when Becky said, "I hope your mom did okay with Nicholas. It was a long day for her too, I'm sure."

They found Marla Jean asleep on the couch, one year old Nicholas cradled in her arms. Becky lifted Nicholas gently and spoke softly, "We're home, Marla Jean. I'll put the baby to bed."

Marla Jean stretched a little and asked, "So, is everything okay? How's Kendy? You found her?"

Coop answered, "She's fine. She's home where she belongs."

"Holly played hide and seek and found Kendy," Jenny answered sleepily. "I'm tired. I'm going to bed. Let's go, Holly." The collie followed Jenny down the hall and took her customary position on the floor beside Jenny's bed. Jenny kicked off her shoes and fell onto the bed, asleep almost before her head hit the pillow.

"So what happens now?" Marla Jean asked Coop. "Did they catch the men?"

"No, nobody was there when we found Kendy. The sheriff found a lot of evidence and they will keep on looking for the men. But for now, the important thing is that Kendy is home and unharmed."

"Does Pastor Green know?" Marla Jean asked as she put on her sweater. "There have been so many people praying."

"Greg Martin called him as soon as we found Kendy. I'm sure there's been a lot of rejoicing all over town, praising God for answered prayers. What a night." He raised his arms over his head and stretched the kinks out of his back. "Well, Mom, thanks for all your help tonight. We really appreciate it. I've got to get to bed."

"Goodnight, Cooper. I'm glad everything turned out so well."

He gave his mother a hug and she walked slowly across the yard to the big house. He watched out the window until lights were turned on inside, then he headed down the hall to his bedroom. Becky was there, already dressed in her nightgown. She was in the bathroom brushing her hair. He put his hands on her shoulders and leaned against her. "It's good to be home. To be all together," he said, nuzzling her neck. "I love the family God has given me."

Becky turned and wrapped her arms around him. "I love our family too. And I love how God answered our prayers and brought Kendy home safely. I also love how this difficult circumstance seems to have brought Tom closer to Jesus. I think he really understands the power of prayer now. I mean, he was just on fire when he prayed. You should have heard it."

"The Lord works in mysterious ways," Coop said while stifling a yawn. "I need sleep. You coming to bed?"

"In a minute." She walked quietly to Jenny's room and stood beside her bed. As she gazed upon her sleeping daughter, Becky prayed, "Thank you Lord, for this girl. Thank you for her heart, her love for her friends, and her trust in you." Holly lifted her head off the floor at the sound of Becky's voice. "And thank you for Holly," she smiled. "Such a good girl!" Holly put her head back down with a sigh. "You are a good good father, Lord. You protected Kendy. You calmed her parents. You listened to Tom's heart cries. You answered his prayers. You sent angels to minister to us all. I praise you Lord, You are worthy of our praise. Amen."

Coop was hugging his pillow and sleeping soundly when she returned to the bedroom. She kissed him softly on the forehead and climbed into bed beside him. He repositioned himself and drew her close. "I love you," he mumbled in his sleep. Becky settled in comfortably beside him and slept peacefully.

Chapter 51

IN THE NEWS

Stephanie Sanders and her camera man were set up and ready to broadcast on the sidewalk in front of the sheriff's office. Sheriff Bertell and Sheriff Feldman were in position. The Barkdales were there, of course. Jenny walked up with Holly on a leash and Kendy hurried over to give the dog a hug. The camera was rolling and caught the interaction.

The reporter smoothed her hair and stood up tall. "Eight-year-old Kendy Barkdale was found unharmed late last night. She has been reunited with her parents and they are all here with us today." She turned to Tom and Tabitha and asked, "How does it feel to have your daughter back home?"

Tabitha spoke up, "It's wonderful. We were so worried, but she's home now. We want to thank everyone who helped search for her. And thanks to so many people who were praying for her safety. God answered our prayers!"

Stephanie held the microphone toward Tom and said, "I understand there was no demand for ransom money. Do you have any idea about why the men would have taken your daughter?"

"No, I really don't. But they didn't hurt her, that's all that really matters. And that she's home. That's the most important thing."

Stephanie turned toward Sheriff Bertell. He took a step forward as she asked, "What can you tell us about the search for the kidnappers, Sheriff?"

"It's an ongoing investigation, so I can't give you much information. We do have some leads and will be following up in the days ahead. When we catch the men, and I have all confidence that we will, our questions will be answered. This was a joint effort with the Atkins police department, Sheriff Feldman and our entire community. Everyone played a part. I'm proud to live and serve in this wonderful town, where our neighbors are all like family. Last night the family pulled together, got to work and found Kendy and we have a happy ending." He looked directly into the camera and added, "Thank you, everyone, for all of your help."

"I understand that the real hero of the hour was Kendy's four footed friend. This is Holly the collie. She belongs to the Smith family and was trained by Kendy's friend Jenny Smith." She moved the microphone over to Kendy and said, "Tell me what happened, Kendy. Did Holly really find you?"

"Yes, she did. I was sleeping and the angels were with me and then I heard barking and I knew Holly was coming to get me. It's like Holly is an angel too! But she had practice because Jenny and Hannah and I played hide and seek with her. She looked and looked until she found me. Just like the lady in the Bible."

Stephanie looked a little puzzled and moved to Tom for an explanation. He smiled sheepishly and said, "There's a parable in the Bible. Kendy told me about it. A lady lost a coin and didn't stop looking for it until she found it. When Kendy remembered that story, she knew that we were all looking for her and wouldn't stop until we found her. And she was right!" He gave Kendy a hug and Stephanie wrapped up her report.

The cameraman took some still pictures of Kendy and Holly, with Jenny and Hannah standing behind them. "Be sure to tell everybody we are The Brownies," Jenny said.

"The Brownies?" Stephanie asked.

"Yeah! Because we all have brown hair! We're The Brownies!"

"Oh, yes, I see that!" Stephanie replied. "I'll be sure to mention it! Thanks for your time, folks. This should be on the news at noon and six. Channel eight." And she was off.

"We're going to be on television?" Hannah asked. "Cool! We'll be famous!"

"Holly is the real famous one. She saved the day," Kendy gave the dog another big hug and Holly licked her face. Amidst giggles, Kendy turned to her dad and said, "See, I told you we should get a dog!"

"If every dog was as smart as Holly, we'd have to give it some serious thought." Tom turned to his wife and tilted his head with eyebrows lifted as if to say, 'What do you think, Mommy?'

"Becky tells me that collies are all super-smart. But in our apartment, it just wouldn't be fair to the dog." She turned to address her daughter. "And like I've told you before, a dog is lots of work. Brushing and training and walking and feeding."

"I know, Mommy. And loving. Lots of loving." Holly nuzzled into Kendy's neck and began to lick her ear. Kendy's giggles turned to hoots of joy.

"We'll talk about it," Tom said and Tabitha nodded.

292

Chapter 52

GOOD REASONS TO CELEBRATE

Church that weekend was one big celebration! Between the joy of Kendy's rescue and the memory of the recently announced safety of Dana and the mission team, there was much reason to praise God and rejoice in his goodness.

During the adult Sunday school class, Coop and Greg decided to open up the discussion to anyone who wanted to give a testimony. "There are lots of examples of God's goodness and provision all around us," Greg said, "and we don't always take time to share the amazing things God is doing in our lives every day."

One woman shared that she had lost her wallet in the grocery store parking lot and she didn't realize it until she went to pay for her groceries. She had been ready to walk out of the store without any purchase but the man in line behind her offered to pay for her things and wouldn't take no for an answer. When she got home, the store called to tell her that her wallet had been turned in at the customer service desk. When she went back to get the wallet, she learned that a teenager had found it and returned it to the store. He hadn't taken any money or credit cards. "I want to thank God for good people, for honest people, and for his provision, even in difficult circumstances."

A man talked about a dead battery on his car. After trying and trying to start the car, he finally decided to pray. To his great surprise, the car started with the next attempt. He said he had learned from that to pray first instead of as a last resort or an act of desperation.

A young mother told of her son's baseball glove. It was left behind after practice one day and they never expected to see it again. But when they went back to the park to look for it, there is was, lying on the player's bench. Her son told her that he had been praying that they would find it, and they did. It was a great lesson in faith building for her son, and she admitted that it was eye-opening to her as well. She learned that God cares about every little thing. Anything that is important to us is important to him.

There were others who talked about health issues and financial issues. God was moving among the people in the class. It was wonderful to hear how he was caring for his children.

Tom cleared his throat nervously and stood up. "You know I'm pretty new at this. I only came to Christ a few months ago. So I didn't know about praying or reading the Bible, and I still feel like I'm way behind all the rest of you. But in the last few days, I've seen and felt the hand of God working, and it is real, let me tell you!"

A chorus of "Amen" and "Yes Lord" broke out around the room.

"I can't begin to describe how it felt to have others praying for me and Tabitha and Kendy. The peace that came over us, even while Kendy was missing, was absolutely from God. I can't imagine going through the horror of those hours without knowing that God was there, holding our hands, holding our daughter."

He paused and looked at Tabitha. "Tabs and I agree that, as horrible as this experience has been, it has also been good for us. We feel closer to God, even closer to each other, because we've been through this. And it's given us something to always remember. If hard things come along in the future, like they surely will, we have this experience to look back on. We'll be able to say, 'Remember how God helped us then?' And we'll know, without a doubt, that God can help us again."

Again amens could be heard throughout the room. Becky had tears in her eyes as she remembered times in the past when God had helped her. Through self-condemnation, insecurities, and near depression, God had somehow always sent the right people to encourage her or share scripture that put her back on track.

The class closed with everyone standing, holding hands and singing,

> *To God be the glory great things he has done*
> *So loved he the world that he gave us his son*
> *Who yielded his life an atonement for sin,*
> *And opened the life gate that all may go in.*
> *Praise the Lord, Praise the Lord*
> *Let the earth hear his voice*
> *Praise the Lord, Praise the Lord*
> *Let the people rejoice*
> *Oh come to the Father, through Jesus the Son,*
> *And give him the glory great things he has done.*

Chapter 53

THANK YOU TREATS

Bert was in his office, finalizing some paperwork. An alert had gone out and law enforcement officers state-wide were on the lookout for the two men. Kendy had identified them from pictures, even though she had only seen their faces with masks on. She described the tattoos on one arm, she told about the white van but hadn't seen the license plate, and she talked about their names. She said one was Frank or Fred but she thought it was probably Frank. She said that man was mean, but the other one was nicer to her. She had heard the mean man say the other one's name but only once. Howard. That man had a cut on his arm. Both of them smoked. That was about all she could tell them about her captors.

It wasn't much to go on. But Bert was determined to get to the bottom this, no matter how long it took.

He looked up from his desk as someone came in the door. Kendy Barkdale came in carrying a box. "Well, hello, young lady. How are you doing today?"

"I'm good," she answered. "I brought you something." Tabitha came into the office behind Kendy and shut the door.

Kendy handed a home-made card to the sheriff. He looked at the front of the card and read, "Thank you Sheriff Bertell." Kendy had drawn a picture of the sheriff, complete with blue uniform, cap and a shiny badge. Inside the card she wrote "I'm glad you found me. Jesus loves you and so do I." There was a heart with Kendy's name written in it.

"Well, this is really something," the sheriff said. "Nobody's ever given me a thank you card before! I appreciate it!"

"There's more," Kendy added. "Mommy and I made you something. Here, open this." She pushed the box toward him and he put it on the desk.

With his letter opener, he cut open the box. Inside, wrapped in tin foil, he found a plateful of rice krispie treats.

"You made these for me?" he asked.

"We did," said Kendy. "Mommy had some for me when you took me home and I was thinking you should have some too. But we ate them all, so after church yesterday, we made some more for you. To say thanks."

"That was mighty kind of you. I haven't had rice krispie treats in a long, long time. I bet they taste great!" He smiled at the little girl and thought how fortunate it was that no harm had come to her.

"It's the least we could do for you, Sheriff. I just can't thank you enough for finding Kendy so quickly." Tabitha walked close to him. "Is it okay to give you a hug?"

"Well, sure, I think that's a fine idea!" He stood up and they hugged.

"You saved our little girl's life," Tabitha said as the parted. "I was praying so hard that God would help you find her. And he did."

"Well, the dog had a lot to do with it too!" Bert laughed. "But thank you for your prayers. I saw how so many people were praying for Kendy, and I guess it's nice that you were praying for me too."

"Before we moved to Winslow, I didn't go to church or pray or know much about God. But recently, I've learned about the power of prayer. I've learned that God is always with us and loves us all so very much." Tabitha had a new boldness. Talking about her Savior was easier now. She had experienced first hand the comfort that God gives in times of trouble. She had a willingness, even a desire, to tell others.

Kendy added, "I was thinking about Jesus while the bad guys had me. I remembered some verses and some songs and that helped me feel like Jesus was with me. And I knew the angels were keeping me safe."

Tabitha put her arm around Kendy and said, "And Jesus will never leave you. He's always with you, in your heart and in your mind and in your soul." She looked back at the sheriff. "We'll leave you now, Sheriff Bertell. But always remember how grateful we are. We can never thank you enough."

When they left, Bert ate a rice krispie treat and thought about what they had said. He looked at the card Kendy had given him. "Jesus loves you and so do I." There was something so simple about that statement, but it made him smile.

Chapter 54

BEST PART

Jenny was in bed, waiting for her parents to come in to have nighttime prayers with her. She had the Bible story book ready to the next chapter, the story of the poor widow who gave everything she had to the church. It was Daddy's turn to read the story, and Jenny loved to hear him read. Even though she could read the stories for herself, Jenny treasured these times together. And Daddy always had a good way of explaining the stories so they were easy to understand.

It seemed to be taking Mommy and Daddy an extra long time to get Nicholas in bed tonight. Since he had learned to walk, he seemed to be moving all the time.

Holly came into the bedroom and jumped up on Jenny's bed. She pawed at the blanket and made circles before lying down. Jenny rubbed the collie's head and looked around her room. Her eyes rested on the hand pictures she had made weeks before. The words S A V E D and S A F E brought a smile to her face. She thought about her friends and was once again thankful that Kendy was alright. She liked knowing that all of the Brownies would be in heaven together forever. Safe in heaven forever.

She was glad that Aunt Dana was safe too. She had been able to send Daddy an email that told of some of the things the team was doing in Nicaragua. She talked about the floods and the mess left behind. She talked about the big clean-up job and how one day Tucker's boot got stuck in the mud and then he fell and got all dirty. It was a funny story, but Jenny was smart enough to know Dana was telling them this funny story so they wouldn't think about the hard things she was doing. Grammy figured it out too.

Jenny didn't want Grammy to worry, so she thought they should pray about that tonight, after story time. If Mommy and Daddy ever got here anyway.

Eventually, they came in, holding hands. Bedtime was one of their favorite times of the day. And now, after the rollercoaster of emotions they had been on, they were especially glad for family time. Just to be all together, under one roof, safe for the night – that was good for the heart.

Jenny was getting sleepy but brightened up when Coop started reading about the poor woman who didn't have much to give but gave all she had. When the story was over, Jenny asked, "Was that the same woman that lost her coin and looked everywhere till she found it?"

Becky answered, "Well, Sweetie, we don't really know the answer to that. I guess it might have been, but there were a lot of really poor women back then. Besides, the parable of the lost coin was just a story Jesus was telling. He wasn't really talking about one particular woman."

"Oh, okay. That makes sense. But I was thinking about all the lost things we've talked about lately. Lost coins and lost sheep and lost Kendy, and we could say lost Aunt Dana because we didn't know where she was. But all the lost things got found. So it's a happy ending."

"True," said Coop. "But don't forget the most important thing that was lost and then found."

"Kendy! I said her already!" Jenny suddenly sat up straight in bed. "Oh, that's not what you mean. You're talking about our souls. Like in my hand pictures!"

"You're right, Jenny. Once we give our lives to Jesus, our souls are saved. And that's the most important kind of saving." Becky looked at Coop and he nodded.

"Then we are promised the safety of heaven. Salvation from sin leads us to an eternity in heaven, where our souls will be saved from the punishment Jesus took in our place."

"And our names are written in God's big book. We are marked safe, like Aunt Dana was."

"That's right, Honey, marked safe. Now let's do our' Best Part' and get to bed. Who wants to go first?" Becky asked with a stifled yawn. "It's getting late."

"I'll go first," Coop replied. "My best part of today is that we are all here together. My beautiful, hard-working and kind wife and my walking little boy and my wise daughter. I love you all and I'm so blessed to have this great family."

"My best part," said Becky, "is watching Jenny ask good questions and show good understanding. And she has a heart full of love for the souls of others."

"Hmmm," thought Jenny, "I don't know what to choose today." She was looking around her room, trying to think of what to say. Finally she knew. "My best part is just knowing that all of us, the Martins and the Barkdales and us, we're all saved and safe. Other things have been good today, but that's the best. I will go to sleep easy tonight because I know about the big book in heaven with my name and everybody else's written down. All of us marked safe."

Enjoy this excerpt from Heaven's Waiting Room, due out in the spring of 2024.

She awoke suddenly with a jolt. It took a bit for her eyes to adjust to the darkness and her memory regain perspective. Where was she and why did she wake so suddenly? What was the noise in the hallway? She glanced at the clock on the bedside table. The large numbers glowed an iridescent blue – 2:18. Why on earth was she awake?

She rolled onto her back and stared at the ceiling. Heavy footsteps and muffled voices from the hallway added to the confused fog in her brain. Slowly she became aware of a flashing light coming from the parking lot. Red pulses of light shown through the curtains at her bedroom window.

An ambulance.

She sat up slowly, curious but cautious. Should she go to the door to see? That might be inappropriate. She didn't want to be known as a busy-body. But curiosity got the best of her and she stood. Reaching for her walker, she made her way slowly to the apartment door. She opened the door just a crack, just enough to see that the paramedics had gone into the apartment down the hall. Rachel's apartment.

She closed the door and went to sit at her little kitchen table. She immediately bowed her head and prayed for her new friend. "God," she said out loud, "please come and be with Rachel. Let her know you are there. She is not alone. Help the medics to know how to care for her. Touch her, Lord, and give her peace. If it be your will, bring her back to full health. Restore her body. But mostly God, just surround her with your love and comfort. Help

her not be afraid."

Sounds from the hall pulled her back to the door. She looked through the peep hole in time to see a stretcher being rolled quickly towards the elevator. Rachel lay there, with a blanket covering her frail body and an oxygen mask over her face. A security guard walked along at her side, holding her hand.

Then they were gone.

Elizabeth went back to her bed and lay down. Soon the flashing lights from the ambulance moved out to the exit and onto the highway. Only then did the sirens start wailing. The sound went east, toward the hospital.

She couldn't sleep. Prayers continued for Rachel. Prayers for healing and prayers of gratitude. Just last week they had shared their testimonies. Elizabeth knew that Rachel was a child of God. Heaven was in her future, whether it be tonight or some future day.

What was it Robert and Alice Appleton had called this place? Heaven's waiting room. Indeed. We're living here, but waiting for heaven. Just waiting.

Elizabeth shook her head to clear her thinking. 'I'm ready for heaven, too, Lord, but as long as you give me breath,

I want to live well. I want to tell others about you and your plan of salvation. I want to be a good and faithful servant. Help me Lord, to honor you with all the days I have left.'

A picture of Bert Bertell drifted into her mind's eye. With a smile on her face, Elizabeth slept.

9 7 9 8 9 8 8 1 4 7 1 9 0